PRAISE FOR 7

"*The Lost Son* is an unflinching ... .ow one woman, and her two sons, reinvent themselves against a backdrop of violence and violation. Julia is unstoppable as she grapples with her present and her past. The search for her long-lost son, and the fallout resulting from his recovery, produce (to use Julia's words) a study in "all the ways love and family can go wrong." And yet, Julia triumphs. I loved this book."

— Benjamin Ludwig, author of *Ginny Moon*

"There's a lived-through quality in every detail, an exquisite perfection of tone and emotion, an underlying sense that Stephanie Vanderslice has lavished a lifetime's worth of love and care in order to honor the people and the story of this novel. *The Lost Son* feels like much more than a novel, to say the truth; it is a piece of someone's heart."

— William Lychack, author of *Cargill Falls*

"*The Lost Son* begins with such a heart-stopping act of betrayal, it's almost impossible to imagine a way forward for Julia Kruse, a grieving immigrant mother left to raise her son with an unsympathetic sister. As the story moves between gorgeously rendered 1920s New York and WWII Germany, we watch her son grow up lovingly determined to right the wrong his mother endured, and we mourn as Julia pushes away the life-affirming love affair that comes to her in grief—a love that might just change everything. With language, longing, and passion reminiscent of Elena Ferrante's *My Brilliant Friend*, Vanderslice's novel honors the kinds of people who make terrible things better. It is a story, too, that shows us how the end of longing can mean risking everything all over again."

— Diane Zinna, author of *The All-Night Sun*

The Lost Son

Stephanie Vanderslice

Regal House Publishing

Published by
Regal House Publishing, LLC
Raleigh, NC 27587
All rights reserved

ISBN -13 (paperback): 9781646032150
ISBN -13 (epub): 9781646032167
Library of Congress Control Number: 2021935998

All efforts were made to determine the copyright holders and obtain their permissions in any circumstance where copyrighted material was used. The publisher apologizes if any errors were made during this process, or if any omissions occurred. If noted, please contact the publisher and all efforts will be made to incorporate permissions in future editions.

Interior design by Lafayette & Greene
Cover design © by C.B. Royal

Regal House Publishing, LLC
https://regalhousepublishing.com

The following is a work of fiction created by the author. All names, individuals, characters, places, items, brands, events, etc. were either the product of the author or were used fictitiously. Any name, place, event, person, brand, or item, current or past, is entirely coincidental.

Printed in the United States of America

For Jacob and Julia and for John, always

PART I

NEW YORK, NY

March 1945

Julia shivered in the thin cotton gown, the vinyl edges of the examination table cold against her thighs. Her usual doctor's office was cozy and warm; her usual doctor's office took the state of dress of the patients into account. Regardless of what this doctor told her, Julia did not think she would be coming back.

She continued reading the magazine she'd brought from the waiting room, *Medical Hygiene for All*. In the advice column, a woman whose husband had been killed in the South Pacific wanted to know what she should do with certain longings that she could no longer fulfill.

Find hobbies to occupy your time, the doctor in the magazine counseled. Needlework. Volunteer work. Certainly, any number of organizations on the home front could use her help these days. Stay away from dance halls, from USO parties, most of all from other women's husbands, to whom she was now, whether she intended it or not, a threat.

It was, Julia thought, a typically American answer. Americans with their strange ideas about sex, as if it were some unnatural force to be denied, tamped down, regarded at arm's length like a soiled diaper. Occasionally, the girls she worked with at the bakery giggled, their faces flushed, over the subject, but only when one of them was getting married and the other married women felt obliged to prepare her.

Julia knew from the way her father had spoken of her own mother, from the gentle attentions he lavished on his two daughters, the mugs of cocoa and homemade *brötchen* set out every morning, the hair tenderly brushed and braided, that her parent's marriage bed had been more than something to be endured.

"Your mother used to let me brush her hair," Papa would

tell her as he tied the wide white ribbons that all the girls wore to the ends of her braids. "That's why I do it so well. You have beautiful hair, Julia. Just like she did. You must never cut it." This last in response to the photograph her sister, Lena, had sent from England in her student nurse's uniform, her dark blonde hair bobbed to her chin.

And so Julia *was* vain about her hair. The color of walnut shells, even braided it almost reached her waist, though she kept it coiled and pinned at the back of her head when she grew older. It was this vanity, so many years ago, that Robert had appealed to when he persuaded her to let it down, again and again, before their wedding night. Vanity and the promise of the way his lips at the nape of her neck could raise even the finest hair along her tailbone.

Needlework. Community work.

Julia was not a widow, of course, not officially—though oh how many times had she wished it so after Robert was gone. And there had been no energies to redirect at first, nothing left beyond what she had to summon in the beginning to get out of bed each morning. But for the regularity with which her cycle always arrived, there were times when she thought that her change of life had already come and gone.

Then, when she had long since retired the memories of a hand gently cupping her breast, there was Paul.

The door opened. Even though she had been waiting for him, Julia startled as Dr. Coleman stood before her.

"We have the results, Mrs. Shaefer." The doctor rolled forward on his feet as if certain he was the bearer of good news. "You are not expecting."

Even as he stood in the doorway of her examination room, it took Julia a moment to realize that the doctor was addressing her. She had selected "Schaefer" from the Queens phone book. She liked the sound of it; it was a name she would have chosen if she could.

"Are you certain? Then why—" He was younger than she was, this Dr. Coleman, Julia was almost sure of it, with curly black hair and strangely pointed ears that made him look more like a character from a children's play than a medical doctor. Dr. Crawford, her family doctor for years and a friend of her sister's, made for a much more convincing physician, with his salt and pepper hair and thick, dark-rimmed glasses.

"You're getting older, Mrs. Schaefer. As the body prepares itself for its next phase, the monthly cycle can become…irregular."

Julia did not understand. She was only forty. "Does this mean," she paused, trying to remember his exact words, "that this new phase will come soon?"

"Not necessarily. It can take many years." He leaned hard on the doorknob with his left hand, his right hand still in the pocket of his white coat. "When did it happen to your mother?"

Julia paused. "She died when I was born."

"Oh. I'm sorry. Do you have any sisters? Older sisters?"

"One, yes." Lena was forty-eight but until she'd left for California that fall to nurse soldiers at Stockton, Julia still noticed the occasional faded russet stain on her underclothes when she folded their laundry.

"You might ask her, then," he suggested. "Come back if your cycle doesn't return in another month or two. But I'm fairly certain it will."

And then he was gone and she was alone again in the room. Julia had expected to feel some relief but realized, as she fumbled for her clothes, that she'd grown used to the idea of life fluttering inside her again. Pregnancy had always suited her, so much so that years later she still dreamed about it from time to time, and in her dreams the churning of elbows and feet in her belly felt as real as it ever had.

On the long ride from Delancey to Myrtle Avenue, where she would change trains, couples got on and off at every stop, pairs of uniformed schoolgirls, arm-in-arm, an elderly couple who sat across from her, staring ahead in companionable silence, a young mother struggling with packages and a wispy-looking boy clutching her sleeve. Of course, she had told no one what she suspected. Not until she knew for sure. That was precisely why she'd chosen a doctor in Manhattan, so the news would be hers and hers alone, until she was ready. While she waited for the appointment, she considered what she would do next and savored having this secret baby all to herself.

STUTTGART, GERMANY

March 1910

"Lena misses our old house in Munich," Julia remembered informing her father one morning. She must have been quite young; Lena was already downstairs at her lessons with Mrs. Stephens, the governess. Julia would be spending the morning in the nursery with the youngest Kruse daughter, Marie Therese. It would be another year before they could join the older two children, Henriette and Robert, in their lessons. "She said that Mama used to take her to Meier's every fall and spring to have new dresses made.

"Nanny Keppler takes you and Lena to get lovely dresses at Westervelt's," Papa said.

"I want to see where you lived with Mama," Julia told him. "Besides, it would make Lena happy."

"If that is what it would take to make Lena happy, I would do it." He turned her to face him, holding the end of one long, unfinished plait in the air behind her to keep it from unraveling. "But Lena has decided, I think, that she wants to be unhappy."

"Was she happy before Mama died?"

Here her father paused, gently turning her forward again to finish her braid. "Lena was…content. I would not say she was a happy child. Not like you were, anyway. You, you were a curiously happy baby, given the circumstances. Lena was quiet and intent. She liked to be watching, all the time watching."

"I never cried," Julia said proudly, repeating her grandmother Mahler's frequent boast.

"You didn't cry *often*," Papa corrected. "All babies cry sometimes."

"Did Lena cry?"

"Lena was a good baby," he told her. "Except in the

beginning, when she had the colic. Poor thing. Mama was beside herself. We all were."

"I didn't have the colic, did I? What is the colic?"

Papa shrugged. "A bad stomachache. Very painful. You could see it in her little face."

"Lena said we had a big house in Munich, with our own kitchen and dining room. And our own servants."

"We had a very nice apartment," Papa said. "Only people like the Kruses have big houses like this. And, yes, for a time we had two housemaids, Elsa and Brigette. They were sisters. But Brigette got married and moved away before you were born. And Elsa didn't want to come here with us."

"Tell me again why we came here?" It was a story Julia never tired of.

"Because I needed to be with my girls," he said. "Because that is what your mama would have wanted me to do."

"And how did Mrs. Kruse hear about you?"

"Mrs. Kruse had tried to hire me away from the Pfistermuehle Hotel many times. After dessert, they would always bring me out so they could compliment the meal. And then try to hire me away."

"But you always said no," Julia put in.

"But I always said no," Papa recited.

"Until Mama died," Julia followed.

"Mrs. Kruse, we know, is a very shrewd woman. A year after Mama died, she and Mr. Kruse were in Munich at the Pfistermuehle and she made the offer again. But this time she said that we could have an apartment and that you and Lena could share her children's nanny and governess. It was very tempting. Grandmother Mahler was growing too frail to look after a toddler."

"So you said yes, finally," Julia said, with satisfaction.

"So I said yes." He tightened the last ribbon on her braid and whirled Julia around to face him. "Are you glad I said yes?"

Julia nodded, although she had never known anything different from the cozy apartment on the Kruse estate that she shared with her father and sister. "And that is how we came to be here," Papa said. "Now run up to the nursery. The staff is waiting for me."

As she climbed the stairs to the nursery, Julia could hear footsteps coming down. She pressed herself against the bannister as she did every morning to let first Henriette Kruse, lost in her own thoughts as always, brush past her, and then Henriette's brother, Robert, who took the steps languidly and with great care.

Even at seven, Robert was never in a hurry; he moved deliberately of his own accord. Julia stared openly as he made his way down, waiting for the broad smile he would always bestow upon her as he passed.

On this morning he stopped for a moment, gave her his usual wide, warm grin and then winked at her.

A prickly heat rose up all the way from Julia's toes to her cheeks. She looked away shyly as he continued past her, so handsome in the dark blue sailor suit that constituted his daily uniform.

Robert had winked at her! Only grown-ups had ever winked at her before and so this deepened the air of maturity that already swirled around him. He was a whole three years older than she was.

Julia watched as he moved the rest of the way down the stairs. Did he feel her eyes on him? He did not turn around.

"Robert!" Julia heard Mrs. Stephens call, an impatient edge to her normally even voice. "We are all waiting for you."

To Julia's surprise, Mrs. Stephens's words had no effect. If anything Robert moved even more slowly afterward. As he turned the corner out of sight, Julia imagined his glacial pace continuing as he rounded the bottom of the stairs, daring Mrs. Stephens to say something, to discipline him. She waited and heard nothing.

Robert would not be rushed.

QUEENS, NEW YORK

January 1945

"It's a wonder you're so tiny, surrounded by all this pastry."

In his buttery-smooth alto voice, those were the first words Paul had ever said to her. Her back to him, Julia was closing the lid over the cardboard box holding the baptism cake she had just finished for the Bello family. Nothing but the best for Cassia Bello's first grandchild, a boy, Armando. She had brought Julia a stack of sugar coupons just for the icing.

"Where do you think she got so many?" Julia had wondered to Mrs. Sciorra after Mrs. Bello left. Mr. Bello owned several clothing factories in Queens, but he was known to have his hand in other businesses as well.

"Who knows." Mrs. Sciorra shrugged. "I try not to ask too many questions."

Julia turned to face the voice. "Can I help you?"

"Paul Burns. Mrs. Bello's driver." He smiled, and Julia noticed deep lines outlining soft blue eyes.

"Is she in the car?" Usually Mrs. Bello came into the bakery to select her cakes or approve the final product before bringing it home.

He shook his head.

Julia frowned. "Mrs. Bello always carries them out herself."

"She's getting the house ready for the party." He was still smiling. "You can trust me with it. I had a good lunch."

It was the first time Julia ever remembered seeing him; although later Paul would tell her he had been watching her from the car for months, watching her through the display window, which had been more lightly stocked during the past few years. Julia usually worked in the back, but since two of the cash-register girls had left, one after the other, to work at the new munitions factory, she'd been helping out in the front more often.

"It's just," she tapped the lid lightly, "Mrs. Bello usually carries it on her lap. They're very fragile, my cakes. One hard turn—"

They were alone. It was a Saturday, just after five. The bakery closed at four. Julia had only stayed to see off the cake.

"Where do you live?" Julia frowned again, not understanding. "You can carry the cake to the Bellos' house yourself, if you like," Paul explained. "Then I'll drive you home."

Julia studied him for a moment. He did not wear a uniform but he was smartly dressed; a crisply ironed white collar poking out from a navy V-neck sweater, impeccably creased gray wool trousers. She looked over his shoulder and saw what was, indeed, the Bellos' cream-colored Cadillac at the curb. Still, she could hear Lena's voice in her head, scolding, "Tell him to bring you back to the bakery at least. You can walk home from there."

But he had such kind eyes, merry eyes. His hair was black, shot through with a few strands of silver here and there; but it was his eyes that made her feel warm inside, a little giddy.

"Come on. How about it?" he coaxed, another slow grin spreading over his face, the grin of someone who already knew what the answer was.

"If you don't mind taking me back here," she told him, forbidding her own smile. "I can walk home."

His cheer faded. "On one of the coldest nights of the year?"

"I don't live far," she told him. "And I have a coat, of course."

"All right then. I'll bring you back here."

Julia went to the back to hang up her apron and get her coat and hat. Mrs. Sciorra would be pleased, she thought. She always said Julia knew how to take care of her best customers. She had learned this from her father.

Paul Burns placed the cake box on the hood of the car and held the rear door open for her. Julia hesitated climbing in—this must be where Mrs. Bello always sat. After she was settled, he laid the box gingerly in her lap, ducking his face in close to hers for a moment. His skin, coarse with a late afternoon shadow, smelled, not offensively, of motor oil and soap.

"Don't worry," he said, winking in the rearview mirror as he started the car. "I'll take it slow. I don't believe you've told me your name."

"Julia. Kruse."

"How long have you been working at Sciorra's?"

"A long time. Almost twenty years."

"Twenty years! That's impossible. I thought you were new. Besides, you don't look old enough to be working anywhere for twenty years."

"Almost twenty," she corrected. "I started young. I usually work in the back, but I'm often needed in the front these days."

"So you're the one who makes the cakes Mrs. Bello is always talking about. The reason she says Sciorra's makes the finest cakes in New York."

"I have been their cake decorator for a long time," Julia admitted.

"That birdcage cake you made for her fundraiser in Forest Park. That was brilliant. She talked about that for weeks."

"That was years ago and it took a lot of sugar. It will be a long time before I make anything like that again."

He nodded. "She hasn't had a party like that in a while. But Armando, the little prince, he calls for something special, even in times like these."

"Well, first grandchild," Julia allowed absently, staring out the window. She so rarely rode in a car. Meringue snowdrifts in the alleys between the storefronts—remnants from a heavy storm the weekend before—shone almost blue in the waning light.

Later Paul would tell her that Mrs. Bello was never so careful about the cakes after she left the store, that she usually put them in the trunk or beside him on the front seat. "She never carried them on her lap," he told her. "But you were so worried. Never say Paul Burns doesn't recognize an opportunity when it's staring him in the face."

"An opportunity to make me look silly," Julia said.

"An opportunity to drive a beautiful woman around in my car."

"Go on," she said. "Mrs. Bello is very beautiful."

"Mrs. Bello is a grandmother. And my boss. And she doesn't fill my car with the scent of vanilla and sugar."

It was true; Julia hadn't worn perfume for years. Not since the bottle Robert had given her, the one with the lilies of the valley on the label, had run dry. She'd never replaced it. At first, she'd thought she'd eventually choose her own scent from the bottles at Merkens Drugstore, stopping by after work to try out fragrances with exotic names like Shalimar, Narcisse Noir, Tabac Blond. They were expensive though, and she was trying to save her money. Then, one Mother's Day, Johannes brought home a poem he had written from school. "My mama," it began, "always smells like cupcakes."

QUEENS, NEW YORK

Late January 1945

Mrs. Sciorra cleared her throat. "Your young man is here." She stood in the doorway, both hands thrust in her apron pockets. "He wants to know if you have time for a quick bite. I told him yes."

"My young man?" Julia froze over the cake she was decorating. "Here? Now? I said I'd go to dinner with him Friday. That's four days from now."

"I don't think he can wait until then. So, go."

"But I'm not ready," Julia cried. "Besides, I'm in the middle of something."

"You've been working on that all morning and you'll work on it more later. Put it in the freezer and go."

"But I don't know what I'd say." Julia touched her braided bun. "And I need to fix my hair."

"Your hair. No. Your hair is *bella*," Mrs. Sciorra hovered behind her. "*Bella, bella, bella.* Out of place in all the right places."

"Then what will I say to him?" The back of Julia's neck tingled. "Mrs. Sciorra, I'm not ready for this."

"Ready? What's 'ready'? Take off your apron, put on your coat, and you're ready. Go!"

Reluctantly, Julia stood to untie her apron. "What if I make a fool of myself?"

"That," Mrs. Sciorra assured her, "is not possible." She touched Julia's cheek. "He wants to spend time with you. Not study your sentences."

"Are you sure?" Julia said.

"Absolutely," Mrs. Sciorra told her. "Now. Take a deep breath. In and out." She demonstrated, her slender hand on her striped apron. "In. And out."

Julia did as she said. The tingling did seem to subside.

"Coming! Coming!" Mrs. Sciorra called. "She's coming!"

"How long?" Paul looked at Mrs. Sciorra when Julia came to the front. "An hour?"

"An hour? Pssh. At least." Mrs. Sciorra waved her hand. "What's an hour?"

An hour, Julia thought, could pass very slowly if you couldn't think of anything to say.

In and out, she told herself silently as she let Paul help her into her coat.

In. And out.

"So how many awards have you won, for these cakes?" They sat in a dark booth at the back of Merkens.

"I don't know. I don't count. The last competition I won was in 1942. February. They've been on..." she searched for the word, "on 'hiatus' since then."

"So you're the reigning champion?"

She felt his steady gaze wash over her like a blast of heat. He was so attentive. Julia couldn't recall ever talking to someone who seemed so interested in what she had to say.

"I suppose. For the duration, anyway. I miss it. Now I only get to work on them when people bring me rations for a special cake."

Paul grinned. "Like a baptism cake."

"Like a baptism cake. I still practice, but I have to use the same sugar paste over and over, until it gets so dry it crumbles in my hands."

"So is this something you go to school for?"

"Some do. I learned from my father. And books. On my own. Mrs. Sciorra has sent me to some classes. But I've never been to pastry school."

"Your father?" Paul waited.

"He was a chef in Germany. He baked too; pastry was his favorite, although he would never admit it. Master chefs don't bake; that's women's work." She caught herself running her fingertips along a spot on the wooden table where someone had carved the initials JR SN inside a jagged heart, and she willed herself to look at him, directly into his face, into his eyes, those eyes. They were a soft chalky blue, a newborn blue. His gaze held her like an embrace. "But I learned from watching him. Techniques, recipes they don't have here. It makes me more valuable."

"A chef at a restaurant?"

"For many years. The head chef at the Pfistermuehle Hotel in Munich," she told him. "After I was born and my mother died, he became a chef for a prominent family outside Stuttgart. It was a better situation; he could be home for my sister and me. We could take our lessons with the family's governess, alongside their children. That was part of the agreement." She hoped he would not ask the name of the family.

"How did he lose her? Your mother?"

"Fever. Childbed fever. She lived four days after I was born."

"Oh." He winced. "I'm so sorry."

"It's all right. I never knew her," she told him. She thought she saw tears in his eyes. She hadn't wanted to upset him.

"For you," he said, "but also for your father."

She looked at him again and saw in his face a simple, unadorned pain, a personal pain. This seemed odd, she thought, for a middle-aged bachelor, handsome as he was. It was one of the most undistilled expressions of grief she'd ever seen, unsettling almost, until she remembered where she'd seen it before.

"My wife died in childbirth," he explained. "And the child, with her."

"Oh." Julia straightened. "I'm sorry." Then, without even thinking about whether it might seem forward, she found herself putting her hand over his. Papa. This was where she'd seen such grief. In her papa's eyes, on Christmas Eve, after they'd opened their presents and Julia would catch him watching her and Lena, the joy that had seemed to overflow only moments before utterly gone. Times like these, even when Julia was small, she knew he was missing Mama and there was little she could do but rise up from the wrappings and take his hand.

"It was many years ago," Paul said. "Still."

"My father never got over it," Julia told him.

"You never do," Paul said. "But you do go on. You do." He straightened. "And is he gone too? Your father."

Julia nodded. "Years ago, also. Very suddenly. His heart."

"So we are both alone over here," Paul said.

Julia didn't answer this. She had Lena, she supposed, although she wasn't sure if Lena, so far away right now, counted. And she had her son, Johannes, who most definitely did count. She removed her hand from his, which was surprisingly soft.

"How long have you worked for the Bellos?" she asked finally.

"I don't know. Twenty-five, twenty-six years, I think. I've been going in to the Grumman factory Sundays too, for the last couple of years. I detail the planes before they're sent off. Doing my part. It's a lot like detailing the Cadillac. Though if this keeps on long enough, they may even start drafting old fellas like me."

Julia wondered how old he was. Older than she was, she guessed, but beyond that she couldn't tell. "They say it might be over by summer."

"Last summer, they said it might be over by now," he said.

"Well, I hope they're right this time. It is turning around." She thought of Johannes, stern and somber in his uniform, in the photograph in her wallet, where it would stay, for now.

"The Pacific'll take longer. Stubborn blokes, they are." Then he paused. "You must have family in Germany."

She swallowed. "Not really. My sister's here. But the people we lived with, yes, I wonder about them. I worry. It was my country."

"Your sister?"

"Lena. She used to be a nurse for Bell, in the city, but now she's out in California, Stockton, taking care of soldiers. What about you? You said you were alone here."

"Actually, I do have an older brother. Patrick," he told her. "We came over together. The rest are all still outside Galway."

"You don't sound so Irish," she told him. "You look Irish, though. Black Irish. Anyhow, English. Irish. Tends to sound the same to me."

He grabbed his shirt over his heart. "Ah, no, please. Not that." He paused and leaned in toward her. "I'm going to have to assume you have no idea what you just said."

"I'm sorry." She laughed in spite of herself. She had begun to feel as if a ball of light had taken root deep in her chest and now it was starting to thrum and glow. "I'm not a good judge of accents."

"Besides, you don't sound so German yourself. And you don't look it either. Unless there are more dark-haired lasses in Germany than I thought."

"Oh, there are more than most people think," she told him. "But our governess was Scottish. Mrs. Stephens. English governesses were the best kind. Only the most prominent families had them. She taught us English from the time we were wee."

"Wee? Yes, Scottish. Well, that's a little better."

"She had to go back after the war started. The Great War. I miss her terribly, still. She was like a mother to me."

"Ah, yes, the Great War." Paul frowned.

"Did you fight?"

He shook his head. "Too young. Too young for that one, too old for this one. I could have lied about my age, but I was married by then. Married at seventeen."

Julia laughed again, softly. If he only knew. She had also been seventeen.

"Rash, yes, I suppose. But I came here young and grew up quickly. By seventeen I felt like an old man. Little did I know—"

"You don't have to explain," she told him.

She thought about telling him about Robert, but it felt too soon. She didn't want to change the mood.

The hour was passing quickly now. With Robert, even in the beginning of their courtship, she always felt she had to be so cautious, that she might say the wrong thing and his easy, generous smile would instantly disappear.

"Well?" Mrs. Sciorra said as the bell over the bakery door signaled Paul's departure.

"It was nice," Julia said. "Not so hard as I thought. To make conversation."

"See! I told you," Mrs. Sciorra said, following Julia to the work room, where she put her apron back on.

"He's a good listener," Julia said, steadying her hands as she resumed piping. Even with the white cake before her she could still see his open face, gently asking, gently receiving. Julia wasn't sure she had ever felt more listened to in all her life.

STUTTGART, GERMANY

June 1910

It was Mrs. Stephens who had told her father how smart Julia was. The older children had had another governess, Miss Oliphant, who eventually returned to England to get married. Mrs. Stephens arrived to take her place.

Mrs. Stephens, who always seemed, Julia thought, a little lonely, sometimes stopped by the apartment after the staff had dinner to enjoy a brandy with Papa. Sometimes she'd bring a cardboard puzzle for Julia to work on and a book for Lena to read; both girls were fond of her, each in their own way. Lena lit up when she heard the knock at the door, taking Mrs. Stephens by the hand and leading her into the living room, getting out the brandy and snifters herself.

Julia coveted Lena's books more than anything else. She'd do her puzzle quietly on the floor in their bedroom while Lena took her book to bed, working slowly on pictures of farm scenes or castles that were so easy she ended up doing them over and over, waiting for Lena to fall asleep, the soft telltale thud of the book dropping to the floor. Sometimes, if she was feeling impatient, she was even bold enough to slide it from under her sister's sleeping hands. Which was how it happened that one night her father looked in on his youngest daughter to find her reading *Der Streuwelpeter* in bed.

"Such hair he has," Papa said as she moved over so he could lean in and kiss her goodnight, referring to the main character's long blond mane streaming out behind him.

Julia nodded. "No one likes him because of it. He's messy."

"How sweet of Lena, to read it to you."

Julia corrected him. "I'm reading it to myself."

Her father laughed. "Well, then, let me hear you 'read' some to me."

"When the rain comes tumbling down," she began confidently. "In the country or the town. All the little girls and boys. Stay at home and mind their toys."

Papa looked bewildered. "Well. Keep on then." He kissed her forehead.

"It's very strange," she heard him tell Mrs. Stephens in German. That was how they spoke to each other; he knew very little English. "But I believe Julia may be…reading."

The next night, Mrs. Stephens returned with a new book, one about a duck that Julia hadn't seen before, and asked her to read from it.

"Well, she needs to start lessons now," Mrs. Stephens told her father after Julia finished the book. "She doesn't need to wait until she is six."

Later, Julia watched as Lena removed the five books she owned from their bookshelf and spread them out under her pillow. "You." She shook her finger at her. She wore one long braid down her back; that was all she would sit still long enough for Papa to make. "You are forbidden to touch my books ever again."

Fortunately, Mrs. Stephens began bringing both of them reading material, children's pamphlets, monthlies, the occasional book, so the shelf began to fill again. Julia was careful to keep whatever she was reading under her pillow as well. Books tended to disappear if she wasn't careful.

"I wouldn't bring Julia any more books," Lena once told Mrs. Stephens. "She just loses them."

"I do not," Julia protested.

"Then where is *Ten Gray Kittens?*"

Julia pulled the small cardboard book out of her apron pocket. "See!"

"In your pocket?" Lena replied with disdain. "Where you'll get crayon and cocoa all over it."

"Girls, girls," Mrs. Stephens said, soothingly. "Let's not fight over this."

Lena stomped off to their bedroom. Julia pressed herself

into the corner of the sofa to read until her sister fell asleep. Sometimes when she did this, she closed her eyes and pretended to be asleep too, all the while listening to her father and Mrs. Stephens whispering stories to each other. Mrs. Stephens had lost her husband and her son to malaria when they lived in Bombay with the Foreign Service. Her stories were better than anything Julia could read in a book. The best part, though, was when Papa lifted her up, carried her off, still feigning sleep, and tucked her into bed.

"I am careful," Julia insisted. "I am."

"We know you are, liebchen," her father said, reaching over from the table where they sat to stroke her head. "Don't mind your sister."

But how could she not mind Lena? She was always offending her older sister; her very existence was an offense.

"You smile like such a baby," Lena had said bitterly once, after Easter services, as they stood having their photographs made in front of the cutting garden. "Always waiting for everyone to say how pretty you are. How *adorable*. It's disgusting."

Lena was the one with their father's dark blond hair and green eyes; as her sister grew older, Julia noticed the youngest footman's glances would linger over her.

"Baby," Lena whispered. "Baby. Baby. Baby."

"Closer," Papa said, moving his hands toward each other while the box camera swung gently from his wrist. "Put your arms around each other. Yes. That's it."

Lena reached for Julia's shoulder, her hand resting on her forearm, while Julia slipped her own arm around Lena's waist. She felt her sister's fingers dig hard, too hard, into the bare skin below her dress sleeve. Her eyes watered as the shutter clicked.

Matters only worsened when Julia joined Henriette, Robert, and Lena at their lessons, leaving Marie Therese in the top floor nursery and kind, indulgent old Nanny Kepler all to herself.

Julia had been so excited to become a part of their schoolroom, to learn more about everything there was to learn, to become a better reader, because stories were so delicious, and, of course, to spend all day with the other children, especially Robert, who made room for her to sit beside him on the very first day.

Henriette sat on the other side of him and Julia noticed that his cheeks flushed bright red when Mrs. Stephens suggested that sitting between two young ladies might help him be more still and concentrate on his lessons.

Lena sat by herself at the far end of the long schoolroom table. The oldest by several years, Mrs. Stephens gave her special lessons.

By the end of the first week a whole new world of words had broken open for Julia. Suddenly everything made sense and she found herself gliding effortlessly ahead of even Robert and Henriette in their reader. Mrs. Stephens began to call on her to read aloud more often than anyone else. Henriette was too shy and reading seemed a kind of necessary evil for Robert. He did it well enough, but he really came alive during the nature walks Mrs. Stephens led them on once a week, bringing home a pail full of rocks and seeds and pinecones that he would identify and assemble in boxed collections.

One Friday they were dismissed at noon. Mrs. Stephens asked Julia to stay behind for a moment. "Julia," she told her, rummaging in her great canvas carpet bag. "I'm so glad your father agreed to let you start your lessons early. Soon you'll be reading as well as Lena. Here." She pulled out a dark blue, cloth-bound book. "I want you to have this, as a reward for all your hard work."

Julia took the book from her hands. It was a heavy hardback, heavier than the cardboard picture books lined up on her shelf. She read the gilt-embossed title out loud. "*Der Schweizerische Robinson*. Thank you." She wasn't sure what else to say; this was the kind of book even the Kruse children only got for Christmas or on their birthdays.

"My son loved that book when he was your age," Mrs. Stephens said. "He too was quite an early reader."

Julia pressed the book to her chest.

"May I start reading it right now?"

Mrs. Stephens nodded. "Of course."

On the way out of the classroom, Julia noticed Lena lingering in the hallway, pretending great interest in a painting of a country gentleman and his horse.

Julia paid her no attention. She was eager to start her book.

When they took dinner in the apartment that evening, Julia wasted no time in telling Papa and Lena all about the shipwrecked family and their tree-house home.

"What an adventure," Papa said. "I hope you'll have more to tell us tomorrow."

"You can borrow it after I finish," Julia told her sister, who was curiously quiet. "May I be excused? I'm close to the end."

"Of course, liebchen. Your mama would be so happy to know both her girls are such good pupils."

Julia made her way to her bedroom and drew the book from her nightstand shelf, carefully turning the pages to where she had left off. The oldest boy, Fritz, had been about to set off in a canoe he had made himself, to explore faraway parts of the island.

As she settled against her pillow, Julia began to realize that every other page from where she had left off had been carefully scissored out. The last ten pages were gone entirely.

She felt a heavy, cold weight settle on her chest. Who would do this to such a precious object as a book?

Julia knew exactly who. Her eyes stung with tears as she flung the book onto the bed and ran to tell her father.

Crossing into the sitting room, Julia saw Lena hunched over some knitting on the sofa, glowering and sullen, as if she was just waiting for her sister to tattle. Her face was a grim mixture of guilt and envy.

Papa lowered his evening paper. "What is it, liebchen?"

Julia stopped. Destroying a book was an evil deed, one Julia knew would evoke a stern punishment from Papa, not to mention profound disappointment from Mrs. Stephens.

Lena would only hate her more.

"Oh," Julia said. "The ending! I loved it. I just wanted to tell you." She looked evenly at Lena. "You must read it next."

Lena did not answer, but Julia thought she might have seen a brief flash of relief pass over her sister's face.

Julia ran back to the room they shared, closed the door and locked it with the skeleton key. She threw herself on the bed and let the tears come, burrowing under the soft white pillows to muffle her sobs.

What had she done to make Lena hate her so? She couldn't help what had happened to Mama. She couldn't help being younger, she couldn't help being, well, more pleasant most of the time. She couldn't help being who she was.

She couldn't go to Papa or Mrs. Stephens for comfort without telling them what Lena had done. She couldn't tell anyone. But that wasn't the worst part. The worst part was that Lena, whom she looked up to, admired, even loved, in spite of everything, had done something that Julia would never have done to her. That she would never have done to anyone.

Her chest ached with pain and confusion. As the tears subsided Julia tried to cheer herself with thoughts of people who didn't seem to hate her: Papa, Mrs. Stephens, Marie Therese.

Robert. At least Monday would come soon enough, with more learning and books and Robert beside her.

QUEENS, NEW YORK

February 1945

"You barely ate," Paul said as they approached Merkens. "Shall we stop for an egg cream?"

He had taken her to Gebhardt's, a German restaurant. It was such a sweet gesture that she didn't tell him she preferred not to eat German food out; she could make better at home.

"All right." Julia had considered inviting him in for coffee at home but perhaps that was too forward. Perhaps you didn't invite a man in for coffee after the first date, the first official date; it would scare him off. She didn't know the rules for these kinds of situations and she very much wanted a second date.

She set her purse down on the counter and excused herself to the ladies' room.

"Heard from our Hans?" Mr. Merkens asked as she passed him wiping down booths in the far back of the store. He always called Johannes "Hans," our little Hansie at first, and then when he grew taller than both of them, our Hans. Julia had never much cared for the nickname, but Mr. Merkens was such a kind soul, always telling her what a fine young man her son was growing up to be, how proud she must be of him. After he came home on leave from basic training, Johannes had insisted on visiting Mr. Merkens in his uniform.

"He's still building barracks in North Carolina but he thinks they may ship him out soon. To England. They'll need people who can rebuild when it's over, he says."

"Well, you tell him Mr. Merkens said to take care of himself."

"I will," she told him.

"You know him?" Paul said as she returned to the soda counter. She didn't think he had heard them talking.

"Mr. Merkens? Everyone knows Mr. Merkens."

"I usually go to Eddie's myself," Paul explained. "It's closer to the Bellos'."

The soda jerk, a new boy, no more than fourteen perhaps, with hair the color of dishwater and acne-ravaged skin, set their drinks before them. Rosewater and witch hazel, Julia wanted to tell him. That was what Mrs. Stephens had told her was the secret to clear skin. It had worked for Julia and it had worked for Johannes, although perhaps good skin just ran in the family. She did not know. Perhaps she would take him aside the next time she came in alone. She didn't want to make him blush, make his skin any redder than it already was.

"When can I see you again?"

Julia had walked up to the top of the stoop but Paul remained a step below. Propriety. He could never kiss her this way, as much as she wanted him to. She would have to step down again.

It was too obvious but she stepped down anyway and he did…nothing. Yet he had just said he wanted to see her again. These rules were so confusing. Why wouldn't he kiss her?

"I wish I didn't have to work at Grumman tomorrow. I'd take you somewhere, anywhere. To Forest Park or Coney Island."

"They say it's going to rain tomorrow anyway. Maybe even snow."

"How about Monday? Lunch, Monday."

"I thought Monday was when you caught up on your sleep?" He'd told her he drove for Mrs. Bello on Saturdays, if she needed him, and worked at the factory Saturday and Sunday nights. Mrs. Bello sacrificed his services Monday mornings so he could sleep in. Everyone did their part, even the well-off.

"A few hours, a little refresher, ought to do me fine, this once."

"Well, if it's all right with Mrs. Sciorra."

He smiled. "In other words, yes."

"In other words, yes."

"Julia." He took her hands. "Julia, Julia, Julia."

Now, she thought. Now. She could see that his lips were soft and full. She waited. Now.

He lifted her hands, pressed his lips against her knuckles. They were soft, yes.

"Such small hands," he said, as he gently let them drop. He stepped down another step and watched as she drew out her key for the door and willed her hand steady as she fit it into the lock.

"I'll wait here," he told her. "Until the lights come on."

He was a gentleman, she told herself, and that was a good thing. It had just been so long.

Just a kiss. One kiss. Was that too much to ask?

STUTTGART, GERMANY

May 1922

Robert knew. Julia could tell, as his mother made a show of giving them the tickets, of the great surprise, that he already knew.

"New York," Marie Therese breathed. "How exciting! I've always wanted to go to New York."

"Now you'll have a place to stay," Mother Kruse said, wringing her white cloth napkin over her plate.

"I don't know what to say." Robert looked at the tickets as if he'd never seen them before. "It's very generous of you."

"A honeymoon in New York!" Marie Therese pushed the dessert plate that held the remains of her apple strudel aside and leaned in to look at the tickets herself.

"Not just a honeymoon trip," his father put it in. "Robert will be starting at Friedrich's Jewelers on Park Avenue. If he does well, they will let him buy into half the business. We've always wanted to open a store abroad."

Julia looked at Robert. He knew. He knew.

Henriette was quiet, her thin lips drawn into a line. Perhaps she knew as well, although she rarely said much at dinner. Mrs. Stephens used to say Henriette was a daydreamer, off in her own world. Clearly she was here with them now but she still had nothing to say.

"And you'll be near your sister, Julia," Mother Kruse added. "I know that will be a comfort."

Robert reached for her hand under the table, squeezed it.

"I'll help you pack," Marie Therese told her. "And shop. You'll need some new dresses."

"There will be time for dresses in New York," Mother Kruse said. "The ship leaves in a week."

"We'll have a party then," Marie Therese said. "A wedding party and a going-away party all in one!"

Marie Therese. Dear Marie Therese. Julia almost wished she were coming with them. But Julia had Robert. A big country, a big city. But Robert would make it smaller, Robert would take care of her, even if he had kept this from her. Robert could do anything—even elope with the cook's daughter, against his parents' wishes.

There was silence. There would be no parties.

"Thank you," Julia said. "We are very grateful."

"You've known about this," she said later, as they lay in his childhood room. His rock collection still lined the windowsill; the maids were careful to keep it dusted. "Why didn't you tell me?"

"Mother wanted it to be a surprise. I thought you'd be excited."

"I don't like you keeping things from me like that."

"She was going to announce it last Sunday at dinner but then Father was delayed in Hamburg. He was actually there, arranging it. She wanted him to be here."

"But is this what you want?" She folded herself into him. "I thought you were going to tell them you wanted to study geology, instead of business, in Heidelberg."

"A whole new country. All to ourselves," he whispered into her neck. "No one to interfere. Just the two of us. We'll see how it goes."

"I just wish you could have told me. I don't like it when you keep secrets, especially with your mother."

"And soon you won't have to worry about that, across the ocean from her. Besides," he said as he lifted her nightgown. "You didn't seem to mind when *you* were my secret."

No one had known what to do with Julia after her father's heart attack. There was talk of sending her to his cousin's family in Wiesbaden; they had several young children and the wife needed the help.

"Wiesbaden is too far away," Robert told her. He was home

from university in Heidelberg for the funeral. "I won't let them send you to Wiesbaden."

By the end of the weekend, he had persuaded his mother to let Julia stay on in a spare room until the end of spring, while she decided what to do. After all, Herr Mahler had been so good to them. It would only be right to let her stay. And she wouldn't be any trouble. When had Julia ever been any trouble?

By then, he promised, I will come for you.

He had left a note for his mother then, too, telling her that they would be back but that this was the only way they could tell her what they were doing without being stopped. And they were of age now, both of them. They knew what they were doing. He didn't tell her where they were eloping to—back to Heidelberg—but he did tell her that when they returned, they would already be married.

BROOKLYN, NEW YORK

March 1945

Everyone on the boardwalk looked so young. It had been years since Julia had been to Coney Island. Johannes had long been old enough to go by himself with his friends; he didn't need her anymore. It was the first warm night in spring. There were soldiers everywhere, of course, groups of them in their uniforms, surrounded by young girls made up like starlets, their hair perfectly coiffed. Julia touched the smooth braids twisted into a bun at the back of her head.

Paul took her hand in his, his fingers, long and slender, enveloping hers.

"Can we just walk?" she suggested. "It's been a long time since I've been here. And it's such a lovely night."

"It's been a while for me too. I used to come here all the time. Even in winter. Especially in winter."

"In winter?"

He nodded as they passed a dance hall, a restaurant, a merry-go-round trimmed in white lights that were just coming on as dusk turned to full dark. "Most of it's closed, but it's quiet. Nice. I can get a bowl of chowder at the diner and watch the ocean, sometimes the snow on the sand. It's easier to see the water with an empty beach. I like to look at the water."

Boarding the boat with Robert in Bremen was the first time Julia had ever seen the ocean, which had seemed to go on endlessly during the crossing. Too much ocean. She didn't know what people saw in it until Robert had taken her to the beach for the first time. This is the kind of ocean I like, she remembered thinking at the time. White waves cresting over good, solid land.

"So we'll walk," Paul said. "Just tell me when you want to stop."

It was different, of course, without Johannes, without having to keep up with him in the crowd. In some ways, Julia felt as if she were seeing the boardwalk for the first time. A girl with a huge basket of roses came up to them, held one out to Julia. Paul gave the girl some coins and Julia took the rose, thornless, dark red, its tips almost black, a little wilted. She brushed the soft petals against her nose—the scent was not very strong, not like the roses from the Kruse cutting garden in Stuttgart—but the petals felt good against her skin. Cool.

They walked for some time without saying anything. Even though Paul had told her to tell him when she wanted to stop, Julia sensed that he did have a place in mind and that they would walk along in comfortable silence until they reached it.

She looked up at the enormous Ferris wheel as they passed below it, remembered taking Johannes on it when he was about five. How small he had felt, pressed against her side, how quiet it was at the top while they waited, interminably it seemed, for someone to get off at the bottom. The lights of Manhattan had flickered in the distance like tidy rows of stars but the height bothered her so she couldn't really enjoy the view.

"Do you want to ride?" Paul asked, noticing her looking up.

"Not especially. Unless you do."

He shook his head and they continued on. He must have come here with other women, she thought. If he'd brought her.

"Do you always bring your dates here?"

It just came out and Paul looked surprised, but it was an honest question.

"Katie and I came here when we were courting. Not so much after we were married. The polio scares, you know. And then she was expecting."

Julia waited for him to say more.

"Otherwise, no," he told her. "I usually like to come here alone."

And then there were screams as a car full of people on the Cyclone roared past overhead. How Johannes used to beg her to let him ride the Cyclone when he was little, but she never let him. She didn't want to ride it herself and she couldn't bear the thought of him riding it alone.

Lena had joined them that last time. "Fine," she had said. "I'll ride it with him if you want."

Johannes looked at her pleadingly with his dark delft-blue eyes, his father's eyes, and she had to say yes. Whatever went on between them as sisters, Julia trusted Lena completely with her son. Lena didn't love him as much as his own mother did, but Julia believed her sister loved Johannes as much as she had ever loved anyone.

Paul stopped. "How about the Cyclone?"

Julia hesitated. Really, the Ferris wheel had almost been more than she could bear. But things had changed. Johannes was all grown up, not needing her nearly as much as she needed him. What was at stake, really? Nothing. Nothing at all.

"Do *you* want to?" she said.

"Sure." He smiled, his white smile, and she thought how rare it was to have such straight, even teeth. The next thing she knew they were sitting in a car, climbing slowly to the top of a wooden platform, his arms wrapped around her as if he really could keep her from flying off.

She laughed nervously as the car dropped from its great height and took a sharp curve to the right, throwing her full weight against him as he held on. It felt as if their car might careen off into the crowds at any moment, fly over the lights and sounds into the sea, and she didn't care if it did. She didn't know it was possible to feel so safe on a roller coaster.

As the car came to a stop, finally, Paul loosened his grip.

"Your cheeks are bright red," he said as he helped her out of the car. "I wouldn't have pegged you for a roller coaster girl."

"Neither would I," she told him. "That was my first time. But I wouldn't mind doing it again."

"Maybe later," he said, slipping his arm around her. "I have something I want to show you," he told her, as she had known he would.

NEW YORK, NEW YORK

July 1922

They stayed at the Hotel Amsterdam when they first arrived. Robert would start work at Friedrich's the following Monday. Gladys Friedrich, Walter Friedrich's American wife, came to see her every morning to help her settle in and prepare for life as a jeweler's wife. If all went well, Walter would take Robert on as a partner. About ten years older and originally from Munich, Walter Friedrich was glad to be associated with the Kruse name.

"It will be easier once you know where you're living," Gladys said. "I hope it's near us." The Friedrichs lived in an apartment in Forest Hills and sure enough, after looking in Brooklyn Heights and the Bronx, Robert came home that first week to tell her they would be living in an apartment in Queens that was right up the street from Gladys and Walter. It seemed as good a place as any, Julia thought, even though she hadn't seen it. Besides, Lena lived in Queens too, in a duplex in Glendale.

Evenings at the hotel were romantic and adventurous. They dined in a grand, old dining room each evening: veal one night, lobster another. Julia's appetite was only just returning; she'd been too seasick on the ship to enjoy the food.

During the day, Gladys took her shopping. The first morning they'd met, she'd asked Julia to show her the clothes she'd brought. "To get an idea of what you have and what you need."

"I don't know that I need anything," Julia said. She still shopped with Marie Therese every fall and spring; she wasn't some peasant girl. The last time had been in February, just before her father had died.

"Never mind that," Glady said. "Every bride needs a trousseau. I'll have Walter talk to Robert tomorrow and we'll see what we can do."

Two days later, Robert handed her a small stack of bills and told her to pick out some new clothes as a wedding present.

"First," Gladys said, after inspecting the bills—Julia was still getting used to American money and didn't really know how much there was—"We go to Saks to see what's in style. Then, we go to A&S and see if we can find something just as nice but a little cheaper. Someday we'll be able to afford Saks, Walter says. Just not yet."

"The store is named A and S?"

"Well," Gladys said, "Abraham & Strauss. But everyone calls it A&S."

"In Germany, we went to a dressmaker at Westervelt's twice a year and had our dresses made."

"Well, those days are over. For now, anyway," Gladys told her. "Unless Robert's parents are giving him a lot more money than Walter says. Because that, honey, is what's called couture over here. Here we buy ready-made. For now, anyway."

Thursday would be the day they shopped for the apartment, Gladys explained. "And I'm pretty much guessing you need everything."

"But I haven't seen it yet," Julia told her. "I don't know how big the kitchen is."

Gladys snorted, a habit Julia found unladylike but no one else seemed to mind. She guessed it didn't matter if you were as pretty and sophisticated as Gladys, with short dark hair that she curled around her ears just so. "If it's anything like our kitchen, *not very* is all I can tell you. Not very. We'll just get the basics, so you can, you know, fry an egg and make some coffee."

They walked past the crystal glasses and china at Saks. Julia thought she saw her mother's Hutschenreuther china.

"That," Gladys said, "is what you get if you don't elope."

Eloping was something Robert had told her that she and Gladys would have in common. She and Walter had run off to the Poconos to get married, because her parents, who ran a jumble shop in Brooklyn, disapproved of her marrying a German.

"Of course," she told Julia, "that was until they saw how he takes care of me."

"Here's my pattern. Lenox." She showed Julia a white plate with a silver band. "We buy a little at a time. It's important to set a nice table."

"I brought my mother's china with me." This was true; her father had been saving it for her and Lena in a great oak chest.

"Really," Gladys said. "What kind?"

"That is the name," she pointed at the Hutschenreuther, "but I don't see anything that looks like it. Maybe the pattern is too old."

"You can show me after you're all moved in." Gladys ran her hand acquisitively along the silver rim of the one of the Lenox teacups. "When you have Walter and me to dinner."

It turned out the kitchen in the new apartment was even more modest than the Friedrichs'. Their stove at least had four burners. This stove had only three and a tiny oven that would barely fit a Cornish hen.

"Isn't it wonderful?" Robert said. "Everything's brand-new!"

"It's very nice," Julia told him. "Just a little small."

"Well, when you're used to your father's kitchen, everything seems small."

This, Julia had to admit, was true.

He put his arms around her from behind and she closed her eyes, felt her whole body growing warm. If being held like this meant she had to cook in a tiny kitchen, then so be it.

"You'll work magic here," Robert told her. "I know you will."

"The bedroom, though," Julia teased. "That *is* a problem."

He nodded ruefully. The apartment came partially furnished with two single beds in the bedroom.

"Well, it's just temporary," Robert told her.

"Never mind," she told him, slipping out of his arms mysteriously. "I think I know how to fix it."

"You do, do you?"

Julia nodded. After all, she'd bought sheets just that day for a full-sized bed. She did not intend to begin her married life in the kind of bed she'd slept in as a child.

"Tomorrow," she said. "You'll see. Until then, we'll make do."

Lena had helped her pack the hotel room but then she had to work the day of the move. "I'll come by tomorrow, after work, to help you get settled."

"Can you do me a favor?" Julia asked. "Do you know where I can buy some rope?"

"There's a hardware store around the corner from me," Lena told her. "But most places should already have laundry lines set up for you."

"Every household needs some rope," Julia told her sister, surprised to hear a little of Gladys's tone in her voice.

"All right," Lena said. "I'll see what I can do."

"If Robert had looked as far as Glendale or Ridgewood, he would have been able to afford something bigger," Lena said as she stood in the middle of the living room, after a tour that had taken less than a minute.

"It's only temporary," Julia told her. "Once Robert is more established, we will be able to afford something bigger. And when he becomes partner, his parents will buy us a house. That's what he says."

"I'm surprised they didn't set you up in an apartment in the city."

"Robert wants to get away from the city at the end of the day. Besides, the Friedrichs live just up the street. So I'll have some company."

"By the way," Lena reached into her purse and took out a brown package, "here's the rope."

"How much was it?"

"Consider it a wedding gift. Along with Mama's china."

Julia thanked her and set it on the coffee table. She'd have to find the scissors in the box from A&S before she could do anything with it. But she would take care of the beds that night.

The following morning, after Julia rose to make the first pot of coffee of her married life, she found herself beginning to reel and had to sit down on the couch. They'd eaten at the diner around the corner the night before and she found the taste of pot roast rising at the back of her throat. It was the coffee, she decided. She had made it too strong and now the bitter odor was making her sick.

Robert said Americans called the couch a "sofa," but theirs wasn't very soft. The cushions were square and hard and the fabric was scratchy, the color of rust. Even so, sitting there uncomfortably, Julia felt very tired. Her lids felt so heavy she could hardly keep them open. She got up and returned to the bedroom, slipping in beside her new husband as gently as possible. She'd woken too early, she told herself. Just a few more hours' sleep. She'd make him a fine breakfast then.

"I haven't been feeling well in the mornings," she told Lena when her sister stopped by next. "Almost all the way until two or three o'clock and then I'm starving. And this American coffee. I don't know what they do to it, but I can't stand the smell."

Lena folded her arms across the blue bib of her crisp white Bell uniform. "Julia. Sick in the morning? Don't you know what that means?"

Julia shook her head.

"Of course," Lena said. "Why would you? Papa never told his liebchen anything. So here we are."

"What," Julia insisted. "What does it mean?"

"You're probably expecting."

"Expecting? You mean a baby?"

"Of course a baby."

"Expecting a baby," Julia repeated incredulously.

"Oh, for heaven's sake. You elope with that Kruse boy so that you can do what married people do. You spend ten days in a second-class cabin on the Atlantic. What do you think is going to happen?"

Julia had been too ill during the crossing for her and Robert to do much of anything, but they had been married for almost two months before that. Maybe that was why she had been so sick on the ship. Papa hadn't told her much, it was true, but Julia knew that what she and Robert did after they were married was also how you made a baby. She just didn't know it could happen so fast.

"Are you sure?"

"The only way to be absolutely sure is to see a doctor."

"I should tell Robert."

"Have you missed your period?"

"What?"

"Your period. You know, your monthly visitor."

Julia paused. Come to think of it, she hadn't needed to use anything since...well, since she'd been in Stuttgart. "I don't know. I might have."

"Julia! You either have or you haven't. Didn't Marie Therese or Henriette tell you anything?"

"Well, maybe if you hadn't run away," Julia blurted out. "*You* might have told me. Besides, it's not such a bad thing. I am married, you know. These things are supposed to happen to married people."

Lena was quiet.

"So," Julia said softly. "Now you can tell me. Everything."

"First, I'll get you a doctor's appointment. I wouldn't tell Robert until after that."

"Maybe that's why I've been so exhausted all the time," Julia wondered aloud.

"Oh, Julia," Lena said. "Well, the doctor will just confirm it. But you need to see one all the same. I'll get you an appointment right away. I know the best ones."

"Right away?"

"Having a baby is a complicated business, Julia. You need medical care to make sure it's done right."

"How will the doctor know?"

"He'll do an examination. And a blood test."

"Does it hurt?"

"Just a prick," Lena told her. "You'd better get used to it. It's only the beginning."

Julia was quiet, suddenly wishing for her mother in the abstract, or Mrs. Stephens, then remembering why she did not have her mother, which made her feel even worse.

"And you better get used to the idea of having it in a hospital," Lena said, looking directly at her as if she'd been reading her mind. "Because that's what you're going to do."

"I'll ask Robert," Julia said.

"I don't care what Robert says," Lena told her. "That's what you're going to do."

"He's my husband," Julia protested.

"And if he knows what's good for him, he'll listen to me," Lena said.

"Lena," Julia said, "just let me talk to him first."

"Fine," Lena said, "but if he says no, I'll talk to him."

"Somehow," Julia said, "I think I'll be more convincing."

"Really?" Lena bristled.

"Really," Julia said. How many times had Papa told them that honey was the best way to catch a fly?

"Are you going to tell him that if he wants to be certain he still has a wife after all this, he will make sure she goes to a hospital?"

"Well..." Julia swallowed.

"Because I will," Lena told her. "I will."

CONEY ISLAND, NY

March 1945

"Her name was Anne Elizabeth and she was a tiny, tiny thing when the nurse brought her to me. 'Say goodbye, Mr. Burns,' she told me."

They stood before a huge window in Luna Park that opened onto several rows of metal cribs. Glass covers shielded the smallest babies Julia had ever seen. She'd read about these—incubators, they were called, in the newspaper.

"She was covered in downy blonde hair, like a little monkey, she was, I must say. And her eyes were closed, so I don't know what color they were. I think they would have had to have been blue. Katie's eyes were blue too."

"I'm sure they were," Julia said softly. "Besides, all babies' eyes are blue, in the beginning."

"I didn't know what else to do. They said she was too small to survive. That she would only live a few hours, days at most. That babies this small never survived. She was only seven months in the womb. I wanted to stay with her. I asked to stay with her, I begged. 'Mr. Burns,' they kept telling me, 'it's best this way. Just say goodbye.'

"I had just said goodbye to Katie, but she was already gone when I got to her. I wanted to stay with this little one. Odd looking as she was, she was alive. She was all I had left. But I did as I was told. I always do as I'm told. They told me it was best to say goodbye, so that's what I did."

Julia slipped her arm around Paul's waist as he continued, as he told her how he'd come home from the brewery that day to find blood all over the floor of the bedroom, and a trail leading to the front door, where he'd found a note from Mrs. Wooten down the hall to go to Flushing Hospital right away.

Apparently, it was Mrs. Wooten who heard Katie calling and

found her on the floor near the door. The doctors told Paul it was a hemorrhage, that she was almost gone by the time the ambulance got her to the hospital. It was too late, even, for a transfusion.

"So they took the baby, hoping to save her, I guess," he told Julia. "Hoping she'd be a little bigger than she was. But she was too small. Of course she was; Katie was small herself. The tiniest wrists and hands, like a bird. Like you. Of course the baby was small.

"I just wanted to hold her. I thought maybe she'd open her eyes for me. But the nurse said no. I was so young. I did what I was told. I kissed her hot, wet little forehead, creased with wrinkles as if the skin on her face was too big for her. Then I kissed her again and again until the nurse turned around and walked away. I thought my chest would tear apart as she left with her. I really did."

He explained that his wife had chosen her name, Anne, after Paul's mother, and Elizabeth, after her own.

"They gave me a week off from the brewery, but the wake and the funeral took up most of that. Katie was gone and Anne Elizabeth had just disappeared. Like she had never been a moment on this earth. But she was. I saw her. I kissed her little wrinkled forehead.

"Most of the men from the brewery came and the wives, if they had any, brought dishes and I ate well for months, it seemed, because I could only eat a little bit every day, what I managed to wrap up and bring to work. Lunch was the only time I could eat. Every morning it was like waking into a nightmare, my stomach in bits. Hungover too. After work, I went to Bridie's and then I just drank."

"I've never seen you drink," Julia said.

Paul seemed unable to do more than glance at her as he told this part of the story, keeping a steady gaze on the rows of infants, some of them still and sleeping, some of them restless, stretching, kicking off their blankets.

"Bridie's was on the way home. First few days I just stopped off for a couple of pints but it was so much better than home that I stayed every night as long as I could. If I was too far gone, someone would call Patrick and he'd come and take me home. I usually woke up in the clothes I'd slept in.

"Patrick let me carry on like that for months; I guess he thought it'd run its course. Then one day he met me, right after work—he must've had to get off early from the shirt factory, where he was a foreman. Still is. 'You're coming home with me tonight,' he told me.

"Laurie wasn't home when we got there; she was at her mother's, he said. He had a few things to say and he thought I'd prefer she wasn't privy to it. It was time to stop, he told me, or I'd end up like Da. I told him I wasn't anything like Da. For one thing, I had been on my way to being a good husband and father, and I had better reasons for hitting the pints than he ever had, running off to Liverpool to work and never coming back, the money stopping after a year. There were six of us; we all went to work after that, except for Claire. She was only five.

"The money stopped because he died, Patrick told me. They found him in an alley behind a pub he favored, facedown in his own sick. Mam was so ashamed, he said, she'd rather we thought he'd abandoned us all. She swore him not to tell. I asked him if he would rather that I was dead, because Bridie's was the only thing between me and a bullet through my head. He said the drink would kill me, that the drink wasn't kind to us. I'd seen him at Bridie's for a pint, here and there, I told him, and he said that he knew how to handle it. When I turned to leave, he said, 'Katie would never have wanted this.' I told him that Katie would never have wanted to be dead."

But he didn't go to Bridie's that night, Paul told her. He just walked the streets, thinking about what his brother had said. Patrick was right; Katie would have been mortified. Her own father, kind as he was, not a mean bone in his body, had a tendency to come home without the table money often enough that she'd made Paul swear, swear on their wedding rings even, to be careful about his drinking. And he had been.

Julia thought about her father's nightly brandy with Mrs. Stephens, the tiny scarlet snifters, the gold liquid. It would have been so easy for him, she thought, to pour another and then another. But as far as she knew, he never did.

"The doctors told me that Katie died, the way some women do, because the sac that held the baby's food and oxygen was so low, covering where the baby would have to come out, so low that the slightest labor pain could start her bleeding. There was no way of knowing it was like that until it was too late, even though Katie was so faithful about going to the doctor, insisting that her baby was to be born in a hospital, where it was clean and safe. No way of knowing that one day she'd just up and bleed to death.

"Later, Mrs. Wooten told me that she'd asked her to call her doctor and an ambulance to take her to Flushing. And then Katie'd said, 'Please don't let me die.' 'That's always bad, when they say that,' Mrs. Wooten told me. She'd had a sister die in childbirth. They know something. And she was right. It was the last thing Katie ever said."

Paul told her he never went back to Bridie's after that, or to any of the other corner bars in the neighborhood, that it was hard at first, that he passed the first few nights feverish and shaky, even had to call in sick a few days. But working was the hardest. The odor of hops in the air always. He could hardly stand it.

So he began to look for work elsewhere. When the foreman found out, he arranged to have Paul transferred to deliveries, said there was an opening there and they didn't want to lose a good man like him. He delivered to restaurants and pubs, found out he liked the driving. Then Prohibition came along. He had to start looking again; the Bellos needed a driver. He'd been with them ever since.

"I didn't know anything," he told her. "Katie was the one who read. I was just a young sod with a smart, pretty wife who took care of everything. I gave her my money; she took care of the rest. After she was gone, I realized it was up to me. I started to keep up better. Started to read—the paper, the business section, auto magazines, books even. And one day, I was reading the paper in the car while Mrs. Bello was getting her hair done when I saw a story about a girl who'd won the Little Miss Glendale Beauty Pageant, this six-year-old girl. Anne Elizabeth would have been six too. There wasn't a day I couldn't have told you how old she'd be if you asked me. Even now. Twenty-seven. She would have been dark-haired, like me, or auburn, like Katie. Little Miss Glendale was a blonde. But that wasn't the most important thing about her. No, the most important thing about Little Miss Glendale, the article said, was that she was born at home, two months too soon and the midwife told her parents to keep her wrapped in blankets in a shoebox next to the stove. Don't expect too much, the midwife told her parents, but sometimes if you take care of them and keep them warm, they live. And she did. She became Little Miss Glendale.

"A shoebox. A shoebox! And they told *me* to say goodbye. Katie was right about a lot of things, about a lot of things, Katie knew better, but not about having babies in hospitals. Not always. No one at that hospital told me I could try to save my baby."

It wasn't until some months later, he told her, that he read about the incubators at Luna Park.

"About this fellow, this doctor, right here." Paul pointed to a white-coated man with round black eyeglasses and a bristly gray moustache, leaning with a stern, matronly nurse over one of the glass cribs. "He takes these babies that are born too soon and he saves them. The hospitals, most of them, wouldn't believe in him, said it was too expensive. So he starts building these places and charges admission. And he's proving it to them. I read a little while ago that Queens Hospital is thinking about putting some of these machines in. Finally. No wonder everybody thinks hospitals are where people go to die."

"You never know," Julia said softly, still hugging his waist. "My mother had me at home, with a doctor, and she still died. You just never know."

"I used to come here more often," he told her. "Pick a wean and follow it until it was released. I haven't been in a while." He smiled wistfully at her.

"I don't know," Julia said. "Some of them look pretty good."

"I think one of his tricks is to put the bigger ones up front. But they still need the heat, the special vitamins and medicines. They're little glass wombs, is what they are. He even hires wet nurses."

Julia remembered Helene bringing the baby to her, the insistent tug on her breast. The tug. She shuddered.

"Cold?" Paul said.

"A little."

He slipped off his coat and arranged it over her shoulders. It felt warm from his body and she pulled it close.

They watched the babies for a while, watched the nurses cradle them and rock them and feed them, babies sleeping, their fists to their mouths, babies crying. Julia was no longer undone by a baby's cry, but still, she was glad that she couldn't hear through the glass.

She would have to tell him soon. About Robert. Johannes. Everything.

But not now. Not yet.

QUEENS, NEW YORK

August 1927

Even though Julia had seen a few photographs of her mother, her parents in their wedding finery, and one of Margrethe, dark hair piled upon her head, cradling an infant Lena, Julia always imagined her as the fairy from the Hans Christian Andersen tales her father read to her, the woman with the great blue wings and long golden locks, hovering in a flowing green robe and waving a star-tipped wand. It wasn't until one morning, soon after Johannes was born, as she gazed upon him in her arms, filled with such love that she thought her heart might tear open, that her mother became real.

Lena. Her mother had felt like this about Lena. With her second daughter, with Julia, of course, there had been no time for her to feel anything. They had shared the world together for only a few days, while her mother's fever raged and the doctor, as the story went, stayed at the house, sleeping on the sofa for two days until he finally told her father that there was nothing more he could do.

If she could have, Julia would have asked her mother if all the feelings she had after her second son, Nicholas, was born were normal. The sorrow she felt at the way her bond with Johannes had been, it seemed, forever broken. The way he looked so huge to her when the nurse, Helene, led him to her bedside each morning after his breakfast. Nicholas had stolen some of their closeness, this tiny, red-faced baby who was always hungry. And yet, when she nursed Nicholas, she resented all of them—Robert, Helene, Johannes, even—and longed for her family to just go away and leave them to themselves. There was no time for the luxury of falling in love the way there had been with Johannes. There was only the trying. And the exhaustion from the long labor and the pain from the surgery.

"Will I ever feel like myself again?" she'd asked the nurse who examined her incision before she left the hospital.

"You should just feel lucky," the nurse told her, washing the long purple scar up and down with antiseptic soap. "You and the baby are healthy. A hundred years ago you both would have died."

But Julia did not feel lucky, especially at home, with Helene hovering over her and Nicholas tugging constantly at her breast, denying her even two full hours of sleep, with her nightgown continually damp and cold, and Johannes sequestered so far away in the other rooms, Robert sleeping on a cot in the kitchen. For the first few weeks, Lena even felt compelled to come during her lunch hour and mutter over her scar, even though by Helene and the doctor's accounts, it was healing perfectly well.

In all her life, even after Papa died, she had never felt more alone. Still, even if she had been able to summon her mother from the heavens long enough to ask if this was what having a second child was supposed to be like, Julia realized her mother wouldn't have been able to tell her.

She wouldn't have known.

"It's best to take it slow," Helene had told her when she explained her plan for the outings that were part of Julia's recovery. "First down to the bench outside the building and just for a few minutes. The next day a little longer and the day after that, a little longer. If that goes well, we'll all go to the park together. There are benches you can sit on there."

Julia disliked being spoken to as if she were a child, but she had to admit that sitting in front of the apartment building that first day, gathering the strength to stand and return inside, she'd overestimated her stamina. Would her life ever go back to the way it had been, free from all the aches and exhaustion? Free from Helene? Just the four of them. Julia, Robert, Johannes, and Nicholas.

There were pain pills for the first week but then Helene said she would have to taper off. "You don't want to become an addict," she said cheerfully. Helene was always cheerful. "Do you?"

Aspirin barely touched the pain, but Julia took it obediently every three hours. "You must stay ahead of it," Helene told her as she counted the pills out of the jar. "Or it will be much worse."

And she was still bleeding. Occasionally, an innocent movement, a shifting of position, would trigger such a gush of blood that Julia's head spun. Helene said this was normal but it worried Julia. This had not happened after Johannes was born.

She regained some of her strength the second week, so Helene decreed she could go out on her own, to the delicatessen around the corner, although she couldn't buy much. She wasn't allowed to carry anything heavier than the baby. After weeks of this routine even the delicatessen grew tiresome, but it was better than nothing, better than being stuck in the apartment all day.

A few days before her six-week checkup, Helene told her that if the doctor gave his permission, she could take Johannes for an outing on Fresh Pond Road for a little while afterwards. "He does need a new winter coat," Julia agreed. It was already late September, and the air was cooling down rapidly.

She might have first suspected when Helene persuaded her not to take Nicholas along in the pram. Julia had been looking forward to taking him out along the avenue, showing him off a bit. Of course she was partial, but he was a pretty baby, with his dark curls and bisque skin. Helene was right; it would be difficult to manage them both. So she nursed Nicholas twice as long as she usually did and then she and Johannes set out.

"If you're a good boy," she told him, "we'll stop for a soda on the way home."

"When is Helene going back to her own house?" Johannes wanted to know as they sipped their egg creams, a handsome blue wool toggle coat wrapped in brown paper lying beside Julia in the booth. Johannes had wanted to wear it home but the day had turned out unseasonably warm, the sun shining brightly through the fluttering orange and red leaves when they passed the large oak tree in the playground of PS 121.

"Very soon," Julia told him. "I'm almost all healed. That's why we could go out today."

"Good," Johannes said.

"Don't you like her?"

"She's all right," he explained. "But I'll be happy when it's just you and Papa, Nicholas and me."

"She has been a great help," Julia admitted. "I don't know what we would have done without her. But," she leaned across the booth and whispered, "I'll be happy when it's just us too."

"I could have taken care of you," Johannes told her.

"I'm sure you would have done a good job," Julia assured him. "But she is a nurse."

The house was quiet when they returned. "Nicholas," Johannes sang out, waving the celluloid rattle he'd picked out for him at the Jack and Jill shop. "Nicholas! We have a sur-prise for you."

"Shh." Julia closed the front door carefully. "He's probably napping."

If he was, Julia thought, it would be a miracle. Nicholas rarely slept longer than three hours, and they'd been gone almost that long. She tiptoed back to the bedroom, gingerly turning the doorknob and opening it just a crack.

The bassinet was empty.

She waved Johannes away sharply. "Go wait in the living room."

Something must be wrong. Something must be wrong with Nicholas.

Maybe she just didn't see him. She ran to the bassinet. The blankets were gone.

"Helene!" she called. "Helene!" She waited. Perhaps she was giving him a bath.

But there was no one in the bathroom, no one at the kitchen sink. She ran back to the bedroom, noticed the top drawer of the changing table protruding a few inches. She gave it a pull and it flew open.

Empty. The top drawer. The next drawer. The last.

She threw open the doors to Robert's chifforobe. Empty. What else had Helene stolen? Or perhaps Helene and the baby had been kidnapped, the apartment ransacked.

"Look, Mama," Johannes called from the kitchen. "There's a letter here."

The envelope was propped up on the napkin holder, her name written on the front in Robert's tiny, precise print.

"Who's it from, Mama?"

"Go to your room, please," she said.

"Mama? What's wrong? What is that?"

"Johannes, please!" She sank onto the red chair at the kitchen table, waiting until her son was gone to rip open the envelope with shaking hands.

Dear Julia,

By the time you open this letter, Helene, the baby, and I will be on a steamship to Germany. Beyond that, I cannot tell you where we are going because I know you would want to find us. There would be no point in asking you to wait, to think it over, to see things our way.

I am sorry. There was no way to prepare you for this that would not do as much or more damage than has already been done.

When two people find each other the way Helene and I have, there is no other choice. For it was destiny that brought us together. Why else would you have such a difficult labor? Why else would the agency send such a nurse as Helene to us? A nurse who could care for you and make you whole again; a nurse who also spoke German and comforted me in my loneliness. A loneliness that has been an ache in my heart for some time.

We resisted for weeks. We tried. But in the end, destiny is impossible to deny. Julia, sometimes choosing not to resist destiny causes pain, the kind of pain you are no doubt feeling right now. Understand we have made this difficult choice to avoid causing you any further pain, the pain that announcing our intentions and staying in New York, in America, would have caused you. Besides, I have long felt that America, despite bringing Helene and me together, is not where I belong. And the life of a jeweler is not either, though I tried to make it so.

Leaving both boys would have been hard for me, Julia, but harder for you. Harder for you to make a new start with two children to provide for. I would not have taken them both from you either, though I was tempted. You must tell Johannes, when he is old enough, that it pained his father very deeply to leave him behind. He is a sweet boy, a smart boy, my firstborn. He will make you proud; I have no doubt of that. I could not take him from his mother. He would have never recovered. But Nicholas. Nicholas will never know.

Helene will be a good mother; you must admit that, Julia, you have seen it with your own eyes.

You would never have been able to choose which child to keep. Someday, God willing, you will understand. You have Lena here. She will take care of you as you make a new start. It is possible for both of us. We are still young. Remember the Pater Noster that Mrs. Stephens taught us so well.

Verzeihen Sie uns unserem Eindringen, während wir denen verzeihen, die gegen uns übertreten.

Robert

Verzeihen. Forgive. He had underlined the word three times, as if it were a command.

There were fourteen ships departing New York harbor for Europe that day. Five for Germany alone. Julia stood at each dock in turn and searched the waves of people as the first, second, even third classes boarded, before running to the next departure.

Couples, families, single men and women filed past her, ears and noses, ears and noses, ears and noses, but none of them was Robert or Helene, none of them carried the bundle that could be Nicholas. She strained to hear above the crowds; please let him cry, please let him cry. Cry, Nicholas. You must cry.

They're smothering him, she thought. Or else why wouldn't he cry? All these people, all this noise and commotion must be frightening him.

Surely Robert's straight straw-blond hair would stand out here; that's how she would find them. Or Helene's pale, ale-colored hair. They would look like they belonged together. And she would not stop them, she did not care, as long as she had Nicholas.

So many dark-haired people, like her. She never realized how many dark-haired people there were in New York. Nicholas was born with a soft, full cap of dark hair, just like Julia's, just like his grandmother Margrethe. "It'll fall out, of course," Lena had said when she first saw him. "Come in blond, like Johannes's did and everyone will think you're his nanny, not his mother."

But Nicholas was hers, he was. He was hers.

Perhaps they had disguised themselves. Of course! She must look harder. She must not cry, so she could see.

They had to be on the last boat. Why wouldn't he cry? Was Helene holding her hand over his mouth? Did they see Julia, pacing at the gate, and turn the other way? They had to be on this one. She had watched every boat board. Every single one. It had to be this one.

She ran to the front as a man started to pull the gate closed. "No," she panted. "No. My baby is on this ship. I must get on."

"I'm sorry, ma'am. Only ticketed passengers now."

"Let me through!" She grabbed hold of the iron gate with both hands and shook it hard. Surprised, he let go for a moment. Julia drew up her skirt and ran through.

"Nicholas! Nicholas!" she screamed as two uniformed men moved deliberately toward her. At the last moment she zigzagged out of their reach and kept running.

They were raising the ramp but slowly; she could make it. *"Nein! Nein! Nein!"* she screamed, her voice growing jagged and hoarse. She lurched toward the ramp and tripped on an uneven board, fell forward, and tried to pick herself up.

He was crying. She could hear him crying. He was on the boat and she could hear him crying. He had heard her and he was crying for her; he wouldn't let them hide him from her. Her breasts stung as a dark stain bloomed across the front of her dress.

Then someone had her by the shoulders, the elbows. *"Nein! Nein! Nein!* Let. Me. Go." She tried to shake him off but then someone else had her feet and she felt herself flying, flying, just inches above the dock. There was a hand on her arm, just above her elbow, and she tried to bite it but she couldn't reach her head all the way around. *"Nein. Nein. Nein. Mein Baby schreit fur mich."*

She tried to say the words in English. *My baby is crying for me.* She knew them, but they would not come.

PART II

QUEENS, NEW YORK

Late February 1945

They never showed close-ups of the German soldiers in the newsreels. American mothers weren't looking for them. Julia always searched, even though she had no idea what Nicholas would look like now. Still, she knew she would recognize him because she was his mother. She would just know. Even though he wasn't supposed to be fighting yet; he wasn't old enough, just seventeen. He could have lied about his age. Would Robert let him do that? Would it matter?

He was not a Nazi; of that she was sure. Not her Nicholas, he could never do that, it wasn't in his nature. She did not know how she knew this; she just did. She'd heard all the things the Nazis were doing and she couldn't imagine it. Not her Nicholas. Some of it was propaganda, of course. American propaganda. They'd spread the same lies during the Great War. When this was all over, they'd see. It was only Hitler doing all these things, Hitler and a handful of his men. The German people were proud; they would fight for their country, but they weren't murderers and rapists. Soon everyone would see. They were good people, the Germans. Good people who had been tragically misled.

They were waiting for *To Have and Have Not* to come on at the Ridgewood Theatre. The newsreels were showing footage from the Battle of the Bulge, American GIs marching German prisoners of war through snowy fields with their hands over their heads. It was the coldest winter on record, the announcer said, and the Allied troops were freezing; the supply planes couldn't get through the snow and fog to drop the winter supplies the soldiers needed. Julia watched the German soldiers march in their coats, boots, wool pants. She smiled. At least the German boys were warm.

"Off to kill some Krauts," that's what the men said in

Merkens or at the register at Sciorra's when they talked about their sons. German boys were the same as American boys, she wanted to tell them. Boys. Just boys. No one should be killing anyone. Except Hitler. She prayed every night that Hitler would die, just like she used to pray, in the early years after he left, that Robert would die. Then it would all be over. For once, she wasn't alone in her prayers. What must it be like to have millions of people, all over the world, praying for your death?

Recently some gangs of boys had painted swastikas on the doors of a block of homes in Glendale. There had been some broken windows. But no one had bothered her. The Flood girls across the street were still kind to her, smiling and waving as they went in and out of the house, even though all three of their husbands were in Europe. They knew Johannes was at Fort Bragg, that he could be sent over at any time. They didn't know about Nicholas. Except for Mrs. Sciorra, no one did.

Paul squeezed her hand when the war newsreels came on, even though he didn't know about either of her sons. He recognized that Germany had been her country once and that was enough. He seemed to understand how complicated it all was; he was an American and yet he was still Irish; he didn't tend toward the kind of manic flag waving Julia saw in everyone else around her, even if he did do his part for the war effort. It wasn't so simple as killing Krauts or Japs. It was war, something to be gotten through, although it was beginning to seem as if it would never end.

In the first few years after losing Nicholas, Julia began to think, Well, it can only get better. Nothing can be worse than what has already happened. Then the clouds of war rolled into Europe, billowing, black but glacially slow. And then, Pearl Harbor. What could be worse than worrying about your child during peacetime—did he have enough to eat, was he healthy, was he loved?

Dresden. Dresden. The word made the skin at the back of her neck go cold and damp.

It was always possible for things to get worse.

QUEENS, NEW YORK

October 1927

"You think you are the only person this has ever happened to?"

Lena stood at the end of her bed, her arms crossed over her nurse's uniform. It was dark outside; she must have just gotten home from work.

"There are a lot of people who are worse off than you in this world, you know," her sister scolded. "And somehow they get out of bed and go on with their lives."

Julia blinked at her. *Who?* she wanted to know. Not because she needed proof, but because she needed to know how they did it.

She turned away from her sister, faced the wall, the faded yellow roses on the wallpaper. "I want my baby," she whispered to the roses. "I just want my baby."

"This can't go on," Lena sighed as she left the room. "This isn't a boarding house."

Julia considered how long she had been there, a few days, a week perhaps, no more. She could hear Johannes playing in the front room. As long as he was all right. She closed her eyes and tried to think. First she was on the docks, the people streaming past, searching for bundles, straining to hear Nicholas cry. And then she was at a police station.

"Now, ma'am, we have to know. Do you belong to someone? Who should we contact? You got a husband?"

The voice was kind; he handed her a cup of tea.

"Julia Kruse." She took the cup. The voice came into focus; a burly, older man with a moustache, his blue uniform coat unbuttoned over a plain white shirt. "I was trying to find my husband. He took my baby. On a ship."

"To where? Where was he going?"

"Germany."

"Germany. Jeez," the officer said, as if to himself. "How many ships for Germany every day?"

"My baby," Julia said. "Nicholas. They took him."

"They?" the officer said. "Wait a minute. Who's they? I thought it was just your husband."

"Helene. She was my nurse. They took Nicholas."

"A nurse." He paused over this information. "Were you in…a hospital?"

"No. No. We've been at home. I just had a baby and she was our nurse."

"Are you sure she is with them?"

"Yes." She reached into her pocket and handed him the letter.

He glanced over it quickly, let out a long sigh. "Is he a German citizen? Because if he is, I'm not sure what we can do. Now, if he's an American…"

"Can't you telegraph the ships? Tell them what to look for, a German couple and a baby. A tiny baby. Not two months."

"I'll talk to my supervisor. But in the meantime, is there anyone we can call? Anyplace you can go?"

Home. She'd left Johannes with Mrs. Canady, a neighbor. There was no one home to call.

"My sister. My sister, Lena Mahler. You can call her."

Julia closed her eyes again, the ache of remembering all of it. She would get up tomorrow, she would go back to see the supervisor. He would be able to do something. Surely. They could meet the ship in Germany. Arrest them. Bring Nicholas home.

Sometime during the night, she felt Johannes crawl into bed beside her. She put her arm around him, felt the fine, satiny hair at the back of his head. Johannes.

"Mama?" she heard him whisper in the darkness. "Are you awake? Mama? I want to go with you."

"Go with me?" Had she spoken her plan to go back to the police station aloud? She didn't think she had. "Where?"

"Aunt Lena says if you don't get out of bed, she's going to

take you to a hospital. I want to go with you, Mama. Please don't leave me behind."

"Shh, liebchen. I'm not going to a hospital. I won't leave you." She tried again to think what day this was, how long she had been in this bed. "Johannes."

"Yes, Mama."

"What day is tomorrow?"

"Saturday."

Saturday. Lena wouldn't have to work. She could stay home with Johannes. Julia would go back to the police station. Lena would be happy she was getting out of bed.

"Mama. Where are Papa and Nicholas? Why are we here?"

"Papa and Nicholas," she said slowly, trying to think. "Papa and Nicholas went on a trip."

Johannes sighed. "That's what Aunt Lena said. But she didn't say where."

"To Germany. To see Grandmother and Grandfather."

"Why didn't he take me? Nicholas is just a little baby. Papa took me last time."

They had been back to Germany once before, to visit Robert's family. Johannes had been not quite three. He had a good memory, Johannes did.

"Nicholas hasn't been to see them yet," she said. Perhaps Robert was taking Nicholas and Helene to his parents, Julia thought suddenly. Perhaps they could reason with him.

"He should have taken me instead," Johannes sulked.

"Don't worry," she told him. "Go back to sleep. I would never go anywhere without you."

Johannes sighed heavily and turned toward the window. "I remember. Aunt Marie Therese gave me toast soldiers every day at breakfast. Nicholas can't eat toast soldiers yet. I should have gone."

"I'll make you toast soldiers," Julia told him.

"With cinnamon sugar and butter," Johannes murmured.

"With cinnamon sugar and butter," Julia said, but he was already asleep.

"Well, the dead have awakened," Lena said upon finding her breakfast, one hard-boiled egg and two slices of toast, buttered and plated, waiting for her on the kitchen table.

"The coffee is almost done," Julia said.

They were silent for a few moments. Julia stood at the counter while Lena ate.

"You should eat something," Lena said between mouthfuls.

"Not yet," Julia said.

In sleep she had forgotten everything. Waking brought on a new dread that destroyed her appetite. This was the way it would be for weeks, months even, until eventually she would be able to awaken with the same knowledge she had gone to sleep with.

Nicholas was gone.

"Is Johannes still asleep?" Lena wanted to know.

Julia nodded.

"Of course you'll live here," Lena said abruptly, poking at the last toast crumbs and then licking them from her fingers. Papa had often admonished them not to do that; it wasn't what ladies did. Ladies like their mama. Julia remembered how Lena would glower at him and do it again when his back was turned.

"That is very kind of you but—"

"No buts. What do you have? Let's count. A toddler. One. No husband. Minus one. No job. Minus two. You'll live here so my nephew has food to eat and a warm place to sleep."

"I could get a job," Julia offered, setting Lena's coffee before her. Cream. One sugar.

"If you like." Lena waved her hand over the steaming cup. "Doing what, I don't know. But you'll live here, and we will raise Johannes together."

"Thank you." Julia watched her sister eat. This was all she could think of to say.

Lena drank her coffee. She was openly fond of Johannes. No matter that he was the offspring of a sister who had brought her the only grief she'd had in her life, whose dirty diapers she'd had to change, whose runny nose she'd had to wipe, and who was now her responsibility once again. Somehow, in Lena's eyes, Johannes rose above his hapless parents.

"I'll have to do something about the apartment," Julia said.

"When is the rent due?"

"In a couple of weeks, I think." Robert took care of all the bills, but she thought the rent was always due on the fifteenth.

"That gives you a little time. Pack up what you need and sell the rest."

"I was thinking about going back to the police station today."

"The police station?"

"Talk to someone about having them arrested."

"Arrested? They're probably almost there by now."

"There must be some way to get a message to the ships. To stop them when they arrive."

"You think the police are going to listen to some immigrant woman prattling on about her missing baby? I'm not even sure they'll believe you."

"Lena, please. I have to try."

"Fine. Try. If I were you, I'd start packing up your apartment."

"Can I leave Johannes with you?"

"When you work," Lena explained. "Your time off is sacred."

"I know. And I'd bring him," Julia said. "I just don't think he should be there when I talk to them."

"All right." Lena accepted this. "We'll find something to do."

"He's not much trouble. He'll just play with his cars."

"We'll go to the park," Lena said with another dismissive wave of her hand. "He needs some fresh air."

"It's up to you."

"But you should eat something," Lena instructed. "You don't want to faint again."

"I'll have something before I go," Julia said, though it was more likely she'd bring a few pieces of toast with her. "And I'll be back in time to make some dinner."

"Do what you like," Lena said. "If you have time, why don't you stop by the apartment on your way back. Pick up some clothes and a few more of Johannes's things."

"If I have time," Julia said, but she didn't think she could face the apartment today.

Lena, it turned out, was right. The officers on duty, none of whom she recognized as the one who had brought her there days before, told her that she would have to talk to the chief, who was extremely busy, who was, at that very moment, out on a critical case. Maybe he would be able to see her, maybe he wouldn't.

She waited. They were kind enough to bring her cups of tea, these officers, even though she, like her sister, preferred coffee. Still she drank the tea so as not to offend; she found it settled her stomach anyway. And she waited.

"Look, miss," the chief explained when she finally got in to see him. Walker was his name, Chief Walker. "If we pursued every domestic disturbance that came through these doors, that's all we'd be doing. All day, every day."

"This is a kidnapping," Julia told him. "Not a domestic disturbance."

"Maybe it's just for a visit. Did you have a fight, maybe? Were there problems in the marriage?"

"It's not just a visit. He took one son and left me with the other. He left a letter." She pushed it across his desk.

Chief Walker held up his hands as if he was afraid to touch it. "I believe you. I don't need to see it."

"Do you have children?" Julia asked.

"I have not found a Mrs. Walker yet," Chief Walker said, resting his hands on his considerable paunch and looking at the floor, "but I have nieces and nephews. Five of them. My brother Billy's kids."

"Do you have a sister?"

"Boys was all my mother had," he explained. "Three boys. You know what they say."

Julia waited. She did not know what they said.

"There's a special place in heaven for the mother of three boys. God rest her soul," the chief continued. "Because that's where she is."

"Officer Walker, please. He was only six weeks old," Julia repeated. She felt tears coming again and she didn't stop them. Robert was sometimes helpless before her tears. It was probably why he'd left the way he did.

"Look," the chief said, not looking at her and staring instead at the glass door to his office, as if he could will someone to come through it. "Go back out there and Officer McGinnis will take a report. But there is no way we can contact those ships; we don't have the jurisdiction. We have no way to proceed in a case like this. Give it a few months. If he still hasn't come back, I don't know, come see us again."

He got up and opened the door. "McGinnis!" he yelled.

"It will be too late by then," Julia said, trying to maneuver in front of him, at least get him to look her in the eyes. But he was a large man, broad-shouldered. He towered over her and if he didn't want to look at her, he didn't have to.

"McGinnis. Get this woman's story."

"Yes, sir," the young man said. He was younger even than she was, Julia thought, his neck above his shirt collar sporting a bright red razor burn. No wife, Julia guessed, as she followed him to a desk in the corner with a typewriter and a chair beside it.

His Adam's apple vibrated as he cleared his throat. "Name," he said dully, his bony fingers poised over the keys.

She sighed. "Julia Kruse."

On the walk home, Julia suddenly thought of Mrs. Stephens. Mrs. Stephens! They exchanged letters a few times a year, small Christmas gifts. Mrs. Stephens always remembered her birthday—Julia didn't even know when hers was, though she'd tried to find out. Mrs. Stephens, who had taught Robert, Henriette, Marie Therese, Lena, and Julia but who had a special fondness for Julia. Mrs. Stephens, who sometimes sat companionably with her father and a glass of brandy in the front room after the girls went to bed. There was a time when Julia had been sure Mrs. Stephens would marry her father and she'd have a mother at last. But the years went on, and then the war began and Mrs. Stephens had to leave and it became clear that she and her father had been just friends after all.

Mrs. Stephens would know what to do. She always did.

When Julia arrived home, Johannes was playing on the braided rug with the tin train Robert's parents had sent the Christmas before. She glanced at Lena, who had the *Daily News* spread out beside her on the sofa and was peeling her daily apple with a paring knife over a plate in her lap.

"We went by the apartment," she said. "I had a feeling you wouldn't have time."

Julia sank into the deep green Morris chair near the door.

"Not much success, I take it? I suspected as much."

"They took down some information," Julia said. "They want me to come back in a few months."

"What took so long?"

"I had to wait to see the chief."

"Anyway," Lena continued without looking up. "We took a taxi back. I brought you and Johannes some clothes, let him pick out a few toys. It shouldn't take long to pack up. You should call someone about selling the furniture. Your bed, probably, and the living room set. The boy's bed and some of the dressers, that's all that will fit here."

Julia thought of the living room set they had saved for in that first furnished apartment, the overstuffed sofa and loveseat with the blue velvet shadow stripes they had picked out when they moved to something bigger, where Johannes had his own room and she had a larger kitchen and, finally, a four-burner stove. They had been trying to save for a house, but something always came up.

While they talked, Johannes scooted over to play at Julia's feet.

"See," Lena said, "didn't I tell you she would come back?"

Johannes remained silent.

"He came undone when he woke up and you were gone. I told him you were coming back."

"I should have woken him before I left," Julia admitted. "But I was afraid there'd be a scene."

"Yes, well," Lena said, "there was."

Julia reached down and stroked his shoulder. "See," she said, "Mama's back. Mama will always come back." She looked at Lena. "Do you have any stationery?"

"Stationery?"

"I have some letters to write."

QUEENS, NEW YORK

Late February 1945

Paul came in for coffee after the movie, followed her into the kitchen, followed her, she noticed, into whatever room she was in, didn't wait, as Robert had, to be brought things. "Moonlight Serenade" had begun to play on the radio in the living room.

"It's been so long since I danced," he said.

"I don't even know how," Julia told him. There had been dancing on the ship long ago, but Robert was not interested. Marie Therese and Henriette took dancing lessons in town but she had not joined them.

"Nothing to it, really," he told her. "I used to dance a lot." He put his arm around her waist, reached for her shoulder. She bumped into the kitchen chair, wood scraping across wood.

"I don't know." She tried to back away. He had danced before. She never had.

"You just," he drew her closer, "follow me. Like this."

The radio played and he led her with small, light steps around the kitchen. They kept bumping into things, the stove, the counter. The silverware sang in the drawer. Paul did not seem to care. She tried not to step on his feet.

The song ended. "Mairzy Doats" came on, one she disliked, but the music had already begun to seem far away.

"You're doing fine," he whispered, his breath so warm against her ear that her scalp bristled, and then he pressed his lips there and she began to shiver. She let go of his shoulders and reached for his face. He pulled her closer, his hands at her hips until there was no space between them. The song played distantly. She stood perfectly still; afraid to move, afraid he would loosen his gentle hold. She did not want him to let go. Ever.

"Paul."

He relaxed slightly. "I should go."

She shook her head against his chest, the soft wool of his sweater brushing her forehead.

"I should. I…"

"No." She shook her head harder, insistent. "Stay."

The percolator began to bubble. She turned it off.

It was some time later before either of them said anything. The radio played on in the living room.

"Julia." He ran his hand along her bare waist, let it rest on her thigh. "Julia, Julia, Julia."

"Paul." There was no sense to be made of this. None at all. She might as well smile.

"Marry me."

Julia was silent. She waited. She knew. These were the things men said when they were happy, content, when they wanted to feel that way forever. Just before they fell asleep. It had been the same with Robert, who would smile and turn away from her, always, drifting into a solitary sleep, a place where she could never follow.

"Marry me," he said again, his eyes already closing. Although he did not turn away.

When she woke again the yellow roses on the wallpaper were remarkably close, Paul breathing softly at the edge of her bed. She'd been dreaming. In the dream, Paul had been standing beside the bed, recovering his clothes with infuriating care, explaining that they had made a mistake; he would have to go. Later he would come to Sciorra's and stand at the counter, picking up Mrs. Bello's bread as if nothing had ever happened, while she stood beside the display case wanting to scream, to pound his chest.

Paul turned and folded himself around her again, patted her arms awkwardly in half-sleep until he found her hands and took them in his. Julia closed her eyes. These are his hands, she told herself. Real and warm. It was dark outside. There was time, still, to dream something else, for now.

She blinked, followed a rectangle of headlights across the wall, then another. The lights are real, she tried to tell herself. I am still here. In my own room. And I am not alone.

For how much longer she did not know. She still had not told him anything.

QUEENS, NEW YORK

October 1927

Dear Mother Kruse,

By the time you receive this letter, Robert will have arrived in Germany. Perhaps he is already at your home. With Nicholas and Helene, Nicholas's nurse. Robert left Johannes and me and returned to Germany with her. And Nicholas. They took Nicholas.

You must understand how it grieves me to be without my son. How torn apart your grandson is to be without his father and his brother. Whatever your feelings are towards me, it is for him that I appeal to you to help us. To convince your son to return to us, or, at the very least, to return Nicholas. Perhaps even you could bring my son back to me if Robert does not want to come. You must understand. You are a mother.

I tried to be a good wife. I thought I was. I was ill after Nicholas was born, weak after a long labor and then surgery. You must understand. The doctor said both Nicholas and I would need a nurse. I am as surprised— no, shocked—at what has happened, as you must be. But more than anything, I am desperate for my son. We are living with Lena now. Nicholas will have a perfectly fine home with us.

Please tell me that you can help us.

Yours,

Julia

Dear Mrs. Stephens,

I hope this letter finds you well. I know it has been some months since I have written. Forgive me; a great deal has happened. I told you I was expecting another child. Nicholas was born in August, a healthy boy, and big, so big and me so small that I labored for two days and he finally had to be removed in an operation. The doctor says we are both lucky to be alive.

Since then he has been doing well, in spite of his auspicious arrival. Johannes was getting used to being a big brother.

Mrs. Stephens, I need your help. A terrible, terrible thing has happened. It is difficult to write this. We needed a nurse after the baby and I came home. Helene. She had been with us for six weeks. A few days ago, I went out with Johannes, for a doctor's appointment and to buy him a new coat. It was the first time I had been out of the house for such a long period since I'd been home. I was just starting to get my strength back.

When I returned, Helene, Nicholas, and all his things were gone. There was a letter from Robert. They were taking my baby and going back to Germany to be together. They did, Mrs. Stephens. They really did. They took my baby.

I went to the docks to try and find them but I couldn't. I do not know what to do or where to turn. I have been to the police and they insist there is little they can do in these cases. In Germany, the name Kruse might carry some weight, but here I am nothing but an immigrant woman with domestic troubles. Apparently, in America it is a man's right to pull his baby from his mother's breast and cross the ocean with him and there is nothing I can do about it.

Mrs. Stephens, there has to be something. Lena is no help. We are living with her and she would just as soon move past this as quickly as possible. She never liked Robert and she's not terribly fond of babies. I am appealing to you for help. I don't know what you can do but you are so much closer to them than I am here. You speak the language. You can go to Stuttgart and find out where they have gone. You can appeal to Mrs. Kruse. She always listened to you. I suspect it was your high opinion of me that kept her from disowning Robert when we eloped.

Mrs. Stephens, please. I have no one left. Write me soon and tell me if you think there is anything you can do. If you need money to pay your way, I have jewelry I can sell. Please.

Love,
Julia

P.S. As soon as I can save enough money, I will come over myself. If *you cannot find* him, perhaps we can try together.

QUEENS, NEW YORK

November 1927

Robert had taken her engagement ring with him; she'd had to take if off when her fingers swelled in the late stages of her pregnancy. It was a sapphire and diamond dinner ring of his mother's; he must have thought it belonged in the family. Or, she thought, he had sold it to fund their passage. But he left her the string of pearls he had given her the day Johannes was born and the diamond Hamilton watch he had presented to her just weeks ago, after Nicholas' birth.

The pearls meant more to her because Robert knew how much Julia had longed for a set. Lena had inherited their mother's wedding pearls, though she never wore them. Julia had made a fuss over the watch, too, but puzzled over it later. She didn't wear a watch. Perhaps Robert thought she should.

It didn't matter now. She was taking both pieces to Holcomb and Son's to see what she could get for them.

"You know," the younger Holcomb told her, examining the watch under the same kind of glass that Robert used in his work. "If you pawn these, you might be able to buy them back someday."

Julia was determined. "I can get more if I just sell them." She knew he recognized her as the wife of another jeweler; they all knew each other. But jewelers were also discreet. They had to be, Robert had once told her, to sell men gems for their wives and their mistresses. Or in this case, to buy them back. It was written right there in Holcomb's disarmingly pallid face. *Why was Robert Kruse's wife selling her jewelry? Was his store in trouble?* But he never said a thing. She knew he wouldn't.

The deal netted her almost a hundred dollars, which would tide them over until she could find a job. If Julia was very careful and if she found work soon, there might even be enough

left over to seed a trip to Germany. She carried her purse, full
of bills, home with the utmost care, feeling for the first time a
sense of hope, of control, perhaps, returning to a world that
had been churning for weeks.

Johannes and Lena must have been out at the park because
the mail was still on the floor in the hallway under the mail slot
when she got home. Julia fanned through the letters, hoping,
as she had each day, that there would be a reply from Mrs. Stephens or her mother-in-law. The gas bill, the grocer's bill, a sale
at the uniform shop in Brooklyn, and then, at the bottom, her
own letter to Mrs. Stephens, dirty, smudged. Stamped: *Deceased.
Return to sender.*

Julia lowered herself onto the hall steps that led to the upstairs apartment.

Motherless though she had always been, contending with the
shock of Papa's death as just a teenager, it had somehow never
occurred to her that Mrs. Stephens was mortal. Tall, strong, full
of life, surviving the deprivations of the Great War with her
usual aplomb, Mrs. Stephens would never die.

Julia was still on the hall steps, the letter in her hand, when
Johannes and Lena returned home.

"It says Mrs. Stephens…is deceased." Julia stood and followed them into the apartment.

"Really?" Lena hung her cape on the peg next to the door
and reached for Johannes's coat. "How old was she?"

"I don't know," Julia said, carrying the letter into her bedroom. "Papa's age, maybe."

She closed the door to Lena and Johannes murmuring in the
living room, heard the radio click on. She brought a shoebox
down from her closet, emptied it of her church shoes, which
she lined up on the closet floor, transferred the bills from the
purse to the box and returned it to the shelf. Then she opened
her top dresser drawer and began to arrange the letter on top
of the others she kept there.

Dear Julia,

I'm glad to hear you are settling in. You must tell me more.
What is the neighborhood like? Are there parks? I know
you have found the library. How does Robert like his job?
You will see by the envelope that I have moved. The
family in Glasgow no longer needed me and I have some
friends in London. I am living in Carshalton and care for a
four-year-old girl, Penelope, in the afternoons—the family
is still getting established and can't afford me full-time.
It's just as well; I'm not as young as I used to be and I'm
finding it harder to keep up with the little ones. Penelope
is very active, too, for a young lady. Good-natured but so
much energy. Or perhaps it is my lack that makes it seem
so. Do not worry about me; with my husband's pension I
have enough to get by.

    I will close this letter hoping to hear more from you
soon.

Love always,
Mrs. (Judy) Stephens

Dear Julia,

I hope Johannes enjoys his Hamley's bear. It is a copy of
the giant one at the Regent St. shop; his head nearly brush-
es the ceiling of the first story. Every child must have a
stuffed bear from Hamley's.

    I so enjoyed the photograph. He is beautiful, the perfect
combination of you and Robert. I can't wait till you send
me the next one (just a wee hint); they change so much the
first year. Enjoy your happiness, dear, sweet Julia. You certainly deserve it and it would please your father no end to
know how well you are doing. How is Lena these days? It
must be a comfort to be near her again. Your father would
be so proud of his girls, making their way in America.

    I have stopped taking care of Penelope. She has begun

school and I was ready for some rest. Mr. Stephens's pension will be enough to get by if I am very careful. So perhaps I will be able to visit, now that my days are freer.

I always wanted to see New York. But I have a lot of pennies to pinch before then. I appreciate the invitation.

Love always,
Mrs. (Judy!) Stephens

Dear Julia,

Congratulations! Another baby! I wonder if this time it will be a girl. You'll know soon enough. I always wanted more children, you know, but it wasn't to be. Mr. Stephens and I got started too late, I think.

I noticed the new address. Tell me about your new place. Is it more spacious? Will Johannes have his own room? Have you got your bigger kitchen?

I'm glad Lena will be there to help you; you'll need it. I am still saving for a visit but it goes very slowly. Everything is so expensive here. Inflation, they say. Is it like that in America too? Mr. Stephens's pension doesn't go very far some months. Everything costs. Paper. Stamps. Medicine. But I'm not writing to complain.

Love to Robert and Johannes and Lena. Take care of yourself.

Love always,
Mrs. (Judy!) Stephens

After they started corresponding, Mrs. Stephens began asking Julia to call her by her first name, Judy, but Julia could never bring herself to do it. She felt a little guilty about it now, that she hadn't granted her at least that, but "Judy" just didn't feel right. Besides, it was important to Julia that the world have a Mrs. Stephens in it, even if she was thousands of miles away.

QUEENS, NEW YORK

March 1945

Julia stood naked in the soft yellow light of the bathroom, Paul asleep in the other room. He was a restless sleeper, startling and tossing, but never waking himself, only her. She didn't mind, she'd woken alone for so many years; she wasn't sure she would ever tire of opening her eyes in the dark to his warm body draped over hers.

He had never seen her body in the full light, only in the slivers the headlights made through the blinds, and now she stood appraising herself: small, round breasts, not as firm as they once had been, but firm enough, prominent deep brown nipples from pregnancy, nursing. Before that they had been pale, indistinguishable from the rest of her breasts, and even in the years between Robert and Paul, Julia would look with pride at this dark mark of motherhood. She moved her hands from her breasts, fingered the fine white line, so much whiter than the rest of her skin, that ran up to her belly button, where Nicholas had come from, where he'd had to come from, his head so large; it was the only way. The line that said, Yes, he had been there, she had carried him inside her. This person, this boy, an ocean away, who had once rooted for her in the bassinet beside her, had not been a dream.

She worried more about the striated white scars in the small pouch of skin between her hip bones, felt the tiny ripples beneath her fingertips and wondered if Paul could feel them too. These marks she was not proud of, remembering the day she had stepped out of the bath when she was full with Johannes and had watched the steam clear from the mirror to see deep purple flames spreading like fresh bruises up her belly. She had been so frightened, so startled that she had rushed to see Lena at work, asking her sister to follow her into the examination room and insisting she lock the door behind them.

"Yes, yes, those are perfectly normal, I'm sorry to say," Lena had said, shaking her head at her sister's mottled belly. "Your skin can't stretch any further. Fortunately it won't be much longer."

"Will they go away? After the baby comes?"

"The purple? It will fade. But your body will never be the same. What can I tell you? This is what happens."

She never let Robert see her in the full light after that, couldn't bear the thought of him wincing away from those terrible flames, even after they receded, finally, to the slightest scars, like tiny white mouths.

"Julia? Are you all right?"

"Yes." She snapped out the light and stepped, blinking, into the hallway where Paul stood. "I was just—awake."

"Come back to bed." He took her hand. "You know what I think?" he said as he led her back to the bedroom.

"What?"

He paused behind her at the side of the bed, ran his hands up her thighs, along the sides of her waist, up to her breasts.

"I think you were disappointed, not relieved, at that doctor's appointment."

"You do, do you?" she murmured. How could he know this, know her so well after just a few months?

"Yes." He stood behind her. His fingertips were soft against her nipples and then on the skin between her breasts; she took his wrists in her hands and followed him down to her belly where he stopped for a moment.

"Let's try again."

"That's ridiculous. Really. I don't know why I even thought…" She held her breath, her hands riding his along the skin between her hip bones.

"So? So what if it's ridiculous. It wouldn't be the only thing."

"Do you know the very first time I saw you?" he said later, sleepily, running his fingers through the loose skein of her hair.

"No," Julia said.

"November 15. It was a Wednesday. Mrs. Bello was inside ordering bread and dessert for a dinner party and I was waiting outside, pacing in front of the window, and suddenly where I expected to see one of the teenagers that works at the counter, there you stood, your head bent over the cash register. I could see your hair twisted at the nape of your neck, could see it shining even from the outside."

Your mother had such beautiful hair. You must never cut it.

"I stood there. It looked like satin. I just wanted to touch it. Like I am now. You looked at the receipt, handed it to her. And then you smiled; you were so serious until then but, ah, when you smiled it was as if—" He paused. "Your whole face broke open and it was as if a soft beam was coming out from the bakery, straight to me all the way out there on the sidewalk. I couldn't move. I stood there still until the light went away. Mrs. Bello started to leave, and I had to pull myself from that place on the sidewalk so I could go open her door. And all the while as she got into the car, all the way home, I was thinking, How can I see that smile again?"

"So smiles," Julia said. "These are your weaknesses."

"No," he said. "*Your* smile. You're doing it now, I can see you doing it, even in the dark, I can feel your whole body, smiling. Julia, this can't be the first time someone has told you, you have a beautiful smile."

"It is."

This was never something Robert had mentioned, although he had also been taken by her hair.

"Then I'm luckier, even, than I thought," he said. "But let me finish my story. After that day, I had a very good reason to get out of the car while Mrs. Bello went into the bakery. I'd stand in my spot outside the window wondering, How do I meet her? How do I meet this woman with the smile that reaches all the way into the street?"

"Why didn't you just come inside?"

"Because I always wait for Mrs. Bello outside the shops. Most of the time I stay in the car, reading my paper. I was afraid she'd be startled if I followed her in. But eventually I realized that that was what I had to do. I started to think about what I would have to say for myself if I did. How I would explain it to Mrs. Bello. Also, each time I watched you, I thought, This time I'll see it. This time I'll see the ring. This time I'll see that her smile is already spoken for. It has to be."

"November," she teased. "What took you so long?"

"I am not a fast mover," he told her. "If it had not been for Armando's baptism, if Mrs. Bello hadn't been busy with the party—"

"You mean to tell me," Julia said, "that if Mrs. Bello hadn't asked you to pick up Armando's cake, you'd still be plotting?"

"Not quite," he explained. "She didn't ask me. But she kept fretting about how she and Annabella and her daughter, Cristina, were going to get everything ready in time for the guests."

Annabella was Mrs. Bello's cook and housekeeper who, Julia had decided years ago, must dislike baking because the Bellos had had a standing weekly order at Sciorra's as long as she'd worked there.

"I suppose I should be grateful that Annabella does not like to bake."

"Oh, I don't think she minds baking, although she is a better cook. Mrs. Bello just prefers Sciorra's. And for that, I am grateful. That and this war, I suppose, which took away their register clerks."

Julia shivered for a moment. Paul rubbed her shoulder. "I'm sorry. I didn't mean that the way it sounded."

"Julia."

"Yes."

"I am sorry."

"I know. It's all right."

"I can't help it. I'm happy. I'm happy to have found you in the midst of all this. After Katie, I decided that kind of happiness must not be meant for me but I'd do all right on my own. But you—what about you?"

Julia paused. "I suppose I'd decided I'd do all right too, on my own."

"Julia. I'm not the only man who's ever pursued you. I'm sure of it. You must have a story. Stories."

"It's not very interesting, really. Hardly worth telling." This was not, Julia decided in that moment, exactly a lie. After all, whether or not a story was worth telling was a matter of opinion.

"But someday you will tell me," Paul murmured into her hair.

"Someday," Julia said. "When you are having trouble sleeping." And then Paul was still, because he was asleep.

Julia brushed the glossy hair at the back of his head with her fingers, watched his full lips tremble with soft breaths. Except for the months after Johannes was born, which itself had been so much like falling in love, she didn't think she'd ever been so happy to just *be* with someone. Even with Robert.

How she could possibly deserve this, something she hadn't even been looking for?

But there was, she knew, always an end or the possibility of an ending. In falling asleep Paul had spared her that once again. For now she would let herself sink into whatever this was, this unsought, undeserved joy, like a hot bath, luxuriate in it, give it back, over and over, because the giving back only seemed to lead to more.

Baths always grew cold though. Always. But she did not have to think about that now.

There had been Robert, yes, but there had also been Papa. Papa, who had loved her and then was gone. Papa, who just days before he died had caught her staring out the window, daydreaming about Robert in Heidelberg and had taken her hand and said, "What is my Julia dreaming about? What is making her smile?"

He didn't know about Robert, at least she didn't think he did, and she felt as if she'd been caught being naughty.

"No, no, don't frown, I'm sorry, liebchen. I shouldn't have interrupted. It's all right. You can have your own dreams."

A few mornings later she had come down for her brötchen and cocoa only to find it wasn't there. Stella eyed her emerging from the back stairway and then disappeared, calling for Niles. It still pained Julia to think of it, how she had stood so stupidly at the long kitchen table, wondering why everyone had gone. Moments later she heard Stella again, crying out, and still she had no inkling what the commotion was, not even when the woman returned to the kitchen, grasping the back of the chair for support.

"Julia, sit down. It's your papa."

After they told her, she had run to the door of his bedroom, but Niles, who must have been stationed there, would not let her in, even as she pounded relentlessly until the doctor came.

"Julia. You don't want to remember him this way. He wouldn't want you to."

The doctor led her to her room. "It was his heart," he told her as he made her drink several teaspoons of dark red medicine and lie down. She remembered those words; Papa had said them once about his own father. "No," she told the doctor, but even as she said it his face and the room faded away.

It was night when she next awoke, her room dark and cold. She could hear footsteps downstairs, an anxious scurrying to and fro, and realized how accustomed she had grown to waking to the sound of her papa's confident stride, so accustomed in fact, that she didn't even recognize it as his until it was gone.

This was how it had been with her: too stupid, always, to know what she had until it was too late, too stupid to know how to hold on to it. First Papa, then Robert and Nicholas and everything that had happened to her so far. And Paul. Paul had not gotten this far unscathed, no one did, but Paul did not know what it was like to be left, the shame, the way it burned still, the way Julia would always be the one who had not been loved enough.

And yet somehow, here was this man beside her, his eyelids,

his cheekbones so smooth, so peaceful in sleep. Such peace. It did not seem as if such peace could exist with what had been before.

But what if it could? What if whatever had happened until now wouldn't matter *because* this had happened? Julia touched his face with her fingertips and he slept on; she turned her lips to his forehead and kissed him to remind herself that he too was real, and he smiled in his sleep the way a newborn does, over nothing.

QUEENS, NEW YORK

December 1927

After Thanksgiving she saw the Help Wanted sign in the window of Sciorra's, the Italian bakery on Myrtle Avenue. It had a beautiful window display, silver and white doilies arranged together in a rich filigree, rows of lushly frosted white cakes, studded with silver dragées. Silver and white, silver and white, nothing but silver and white. There was something pleasing, almost soothing to her about that color combination.

"You have a Help Wanted sign in the window," Julia said as the girl at the register rang up the six almond crescents she had purchased as an excuse to come into the store.

The girl, who was tall and angular with a long, sad face, nodded as she took Julia's money but said nothing.

"Who do I talk to about it?"

Laboriously the girl, who she would later come to know as Annaliese, Mrs. Sciorra's doleful niece, counted out her change, then disappeared wordlessly to the back of the store. Julia waited. And waited. Finally, Annaliese reappeared with a wiry silver-haired woman dressed also in the store uniform, an elegantly cut gray-and-white-striped dress overlaid with a crisp white apron, *Sciorra's* embroidered in black script across the bib. Julia thought she would like wearing a stylish uniform like that.

"Can you bake? What is your experience?" Mrs. Sciorra looked her up and down. She seemed doubtful.

Julia nodded. "Breads. Cakes. Some pies."

"Are you German? You sound German."

Julia nodded again.

"Have you worked in a German bakery? Italian bakeries are different, you know."

She shook her head.

"What is your training?"

"My father taught me. He was a chef, trained at the Munich Culinary Academy. He even taught there sometimes. Before my mother died, he was the head chef at the Pfistermeuhle."

"Never heard of it."

"It's a first-class hotel in Munich. Later he worked for a wealthy family outside Stuttgart, on their estate."

"But your English is excellent. You have an accent, of course."

"My governess was British."

"Governess? And your father taught you to bake?"

"I grew up in my father's kitchen. I have all his recipes, all his techniques." She tapped her head. "Here."

"It might be nice to have some new recipes. I bake the bread myself, since my husband's stroke. But we lost our pastry chef to a bakery in Manhattan. They lured him away." She shook her head. "I can bake, but I'm no pastry chef. Not like him."

"I'm sorry," Julia said.

"Why don't you come in Monday? We'll know by Friday if this will work out, Miss—?"

"Mrs. Kruse. Julia Kruse."

"Mrs. Kruse? Mr. Kruse does not need you at home, to bake for him?"

"There is no Mr. Kruse any longer. I live with my sister and my son."

"How early can you be here in the morning?"

"How early do you need me?"

"Five a.m.," Mrs. Sciorra told her, the slightest of grins playing over her thin lips. "This Monday. You'll help with the bread first. And bring your father's recipes."

"Cookies!" Johannes exclaimed when she brought the plate to the table after dinner that night.

"Where did you get these?" Lena asked, picking up one of the crescents and inspecting it before taking a bite.

"Sciorra's Bakery, on the avenue. They had a Help Wanted sign in the window. I start Monday."

"Mama has a job at a bakery," Johannes repeated. "Aunt Lena has a job at the phone company." He sounded very satisfied with the news, as if this was the way of the world.

"Aunt Lena is a *nurse* for the telephone company," Lena corrected.

"Johannes will go to St. Luke's, to a school they have there for mothers who must work. It's practically free. I already signed him up."

"Working at a bakery isn't the same as baking at home."

"Of course. But it was Papa who taught me, a professional chef. I have to be there at five o'clock Monday morning. I was hoping you could get Johannes breakfast and take him to the school."

"That will add at least another hour to my morning schedule."

"That's when they need me," Julia said. "The good news is that I'll be done at two, so I can pick him up, and by the time you are home you'll have a nice hot supper waiting for you."

"I suppose it can't be helped," Lena admitted. "I can pick up the El at Myrtle Avenue, after I leave the school."

"Johannes will be a big help, won't you?"

Johannes nodded. "May I have another cookie?"

Lena smiled. She had taught him to say "May I" in the past few weeks.

"Yes." Julia deposited another in front of him. "You may."

"Mama will bring home lots of cookies if she works at a bakery," Johannes pointed out after he swallowed, his mouth ringed with powdered sugar.

"You'll have to be careful not to get fat," Lena told him.

"May I be excused?"

"Yes, you may," Lena said.

"Lena!" Julia said, after he left the room. "He's not going to get fat."

"Who knows? He might take after his father."

"Robert was not fat. Brawny, perhaps, robust, perhaps, but he was not fat."

"Well," Lena replied. "I don't know why he left you, but it wasn't because you weren't feeding him."

Julia's hands shook as she washed the dishes, but she didn't care; they were just Lena's plain white dishes—their mother's china still in the packing crates, waiting for the time when she and Robert would be able to afford a proper cabinet. She didn't want to cause a scene that would bring either of them back into the kitchen. Lena got away with saying whatever she wanted because she was impossible to argue with; she was always right. It would just upset Johannes. With the deliberation of rage, she stacked the last plate on the drainboard, wiped her hands on her apron, and hung it to dry.

Dear Judy,

I am so angry sometimes; I don't know what to do. Remember in my last letter I told you that I wished Robert dead. I still do. In fact, I pray for this. At night, I dream I am screaming at him, screaming and screaming and pounding his chest with my fists while he just stands there, ignoring me, in his careful, obstinate, infuriating way. Judy, I frighten myself with my dreams sometimes. I slap him, I pummel him. In my waking hours, I just pray to God to strike him dead. It's true. I do. I wish him dead.

Lena never misses the opportunity to remind me of what has happened. I don't say I didn't deserve it—although I'm not sure what I did wrong besides being too stupid to see what was right in front of my face. But Lena should talk. Why isn't she married? What kind of wife would she be? At least I was married. Lena won't let any man near her. She was awful to Papa. You saw how hateful she was.

I don't want to become like Lena. Full of hate. But it's in my heart now. It is. I don't want Johannes to see it. He doesn't deserve a mother full of hate. How do you hide a heart that is full of hate? How do you find any peace?

When the page was full, Julia did not sign it but slipped it in the back of her dictionary with the others. She did not find it the least bit ironic that she wrote to Mrs. Stephens—even calling her Judy—more now than she ever had when she was alive. She had to. It was as simple as that. She had to do something.

The dictionary had belonged to Mrs. Stephens. She had given it to Julia the day she left to return to England for good, after the fighting broke out. She had already said goodbye to the children in the sunroom the day before; Mrs. Kruse had assembled them there for the news. But that morning she came again to say goodbye to her and Lena and Papa.

"It was my husband's and then it was mine," she said, pressing the heavy volume, with its cracked black leather binding, into Julia's arms. "Now it's yours."

"Some children read fairy tales," Papa said with a wistful smile. "My daughter reads the dictionary."

At this Judy threw her arms around Papa's shoulders and held on for several moments. "Be careful, my friend," she said when she let him go.

Even Lena blinked back tears as she held the silver mirror Judy had given her to her chest.

"I will miss you all so. They are saying it will be short. Perhaps I will be back in six months. A year."

"We can hope," Papa said.

"Or you can come see me," she told them. "I'll take the girls to tea at Harrods!"

"They would like that."

Karl, the second footman, appeared at the door. "We must get to the station, Mrs. Stephens. You'll miss your train."

"Write to me," she cried as he led her away. "When it's over. Write!"

The war would last for four years, longer than anyone had expected. Enough time for Julia to grow from a shy, bookish child to a shy, bookish fourteen-year-old who blossomed with the attentions of her seventeen-year-old schoolmate. By the time she was fifteen, she and Robert had begun to meet alone in a crowded stand of trees at the edge of the estate.

A new governess was hired to continue their schooling, German this time, so there would be no more English lessons. A year later, Lena ran away, first to Amsterdam and then to a volunteer nurse corps in London, eventually making her way to America when the war was over.

They were buffered from the war. There were shortages, but they didn't starve. Papa simply had to be more creative with what they had. With his assistant at the front, Niles, the estate gardener, stood guard over the kitchen garden with a gun many nights, but Julia never heard any shots.

Even though they were conscripting the youngest men by the end, Robert never had to go.

Julia had worried about this from the beginning, but her father explained that he would probably never go, that the Kruses had more than enough money to keep him out of the fighting.

Robert told her he wanted to fight for his country at first. But as the casualty lists soared, he spoke of it less and less and concentrated on his studies.

QUEENS, NEW YORK

March 1945

Julia hadn't realized how much she'd missed cooking for someone. Lena had been gone almost a year, Johannes far longer than that. The bakery was her sanctuary; it always had been. After Robert left, no matter how her heart ached, no matter how her mind rattled and buzzed with plans to retrieve Nicholas, she could always look forward to the satisfaction of working with her hands for hours each day, hours that calmed her frenzied brain and resulted in beautiful cakes and pies, even if these were temporary, destined to vanish into crumbs.

At home, too, she took great pleasure in the rituals that fed her family. Lena had done needlework she had learned at their mother's knee; Julia had chopped vegetables perfectly, precisely, lovingly, just as Papa had taught her. Such comfort she had found, in the days after he died, going down to the kitchen each morning, pulling her apron over her head and doing what needed to be done. Outside the kitchen, her head spun with the problem she had become: what to do about Julia, where should she go? Inside it, the staff merely looked upon her with concern and sympathy and held their tongues as she turned long, lumpy, dirt-caked carrots into piles of orange coins for the stew, coaxed balls of semolina and potatoes into tiny pillows of dough. After she and Johannes moved in with Lena, she consoled herself with Sundays spent pounding and turning the bread dough for the week and carefully turning meat for the sauerbraten that had been marinating for days.

She hadn't made sauerbraten since the last time Johannes had been home, but after the third time Paul took her to Gebhardt's, she'd impulsively offered to cook for him. "After all, we can't keep going out so much," she said and then immediately regretted being so forward.

"I thought you'd be tired of cooking all day every day. Besides, I don't have much else to spend my money on."

"The bakery is for baking and decorating, not cooking. Cooking is different. I want to cook for you." Too, she was vain about her cooking; she knew it was good. She liked showing it off.

"Far be it from me to turn down a home-cooked meal."

Now the house was filling once again with the warm, close scent of yeast and sugar, salt and water, and she was standing at the kitchen counter listening to a Benny Goodman tribute on the radio and running her hands over the smooth soft dough, reminding her always of worn cotton bed sheets laundered many, many times. Without thinking she had made her usual recipe and as a result, she was now shaping eight slender loaves. Of course, he would take some home with him.

She had turned in a flutter of rations for the silverside of beef marinating in the refrigerator for the sauerbraten, for the brown sugar and the butter for the apple strudel. It wasn't, to be honest, much of a sacrifice; she didn't really cook for herself anymore. In fact, she was content to exist on toast and coffee for days at a time. Her uniform was looser on her, it was true, but to her mind, meals were occasions to be celebrated and until recently there had not been much to celebrate.

She set the table that afternoon with her best linens and her mother's silver and china, and the ritual and rhythm of laying out the forks and knives and glassware just so had lulled her into a kind of reverie that followed her into the bath, where she ran her razor along her white calves with painstaking care and the water turned from hot to warm to cool.

Later, as she brought the good wineglasses down from the top shelf of the china cabinet, something heavy and metal fell to the floor, and when she looked down she saw that it was Johannes's napkin ring. She leaned down to pick it up and sat on one of the dining chairs to study it, running her fingers over the back of the bear cub that curved over her son's monogram. Johannes had used it all the way up to the time when he'd left for Fort Bragg even though she'd offered to buy him another, one that was more befitting a young man. But Johannes had said no, this was the one he wanted to imagine while he was away.

Johannes, at five, spinning the napkin ring on the table with his index finger until Lena told him to please stop. Johannes frowning and laying it back on its side. Johannes, at ten, politely removing his napkin, unfolding it in his lap, and setting the ring to the right side of his plate as Julia had taught him, leaving the spinning boy behind forever, as children seemed to do, shedding themselves over the years the way snakes shed their skin, becoming all new people. How many people had Nicholas become? So many, if her memory of Johannes's childhood served her. She had missed them all but consoled herself that she had also been spared the grief of watching them go.

Johannes. What would he think of all this? Of his mama setting the table for a suitor. She stood on tiptoe and put the ring back from where it had fallen, high up on the top shelf and out of her mind.

The last step was the apple strudel; she finished this in her robe, handling each pastry sheet delicately so that it wouldn't tear, brushing between each layer with golden melted butter and then folding the sides to envelop the filling.

After the strudel was in the oven, she pulled out the fitted chiffon blouse she'd bought on the avenue the day before. It was mint green, not a color she ordinarily would have chosen, but the compact saleswoman insisted the shade set off her hair and her eyes. Wearing a uniform each day, fond as Julia was of it, didn't give her much of a wardrobe beyond housecoats and a few dresses for the weekend. Paul had already seen her in every dress that she owned.

"Collarbone and cleavage, collarbone and cleavage," the clerk had said, peering over her bifocals as she stood behind Julia, admiring the blouse in the dressing room mirror. "You can't go wrong."

Julia smiled. Gladys used to say the same thing when they

went shopping for clothes as she tried to coax Julia to buy the less modest, open-collared blouses that were the style back then, with their plunging necklines and dropped waists. Flapper dresses. She fingered the top button on this blouse, which fell to just above her breasts.

Dear, sweet Gladys, who had checked in on her from time to time after Robert left—even after they had moved in with Lena—until she and Walter themselves moved to Long Island where he was opening another store. Gladys, who lived now in a mansion out in Great Neck, where they had been blessed with five darling black poodles but, she wrote in her letters, sadly no children.

Yes, Gladys would approve.

Julia filled the sink with warm water while Paul brought the dinner dishes into the kitchen, watched the plates slide with a satisfying clank under the suds.

"Let's let them soak," Paul said, reaching for the radio above the sink. "Our Love is Here to Stay" drifted into the room.

"You're a fast learner," he whispered in her ear as he took her hands and twirled her around the kitchen. They danced to "Begin the Beguine" and "Paper Moon" and "What am I Here For?" and then Paul danced them over to the sink.

"Shall I wash or dry?" he asked as he let go her hands.

"Dry, if you want to. You really want to?"

"Sure," Paul said. "It'd be a fine thing if I didn't know how to do my own dishes, now, wouldn't it?"

"Well." Julia steadied herself and reached for her apron, feeling the heat rise to her cheeks. "It's kind." Aside from Johannes occasionally, she had never in her life had company doing the dishes. Robert always made himself scarce and Lena had her shows.

"Nonsense. Why would I want to stand here watching you by yourself at the sink? Even if it's a pretty sight."

"This is nice," she said as they stood shoulder to shoulder, their arms brushing as she stacked the dishes in the rack, he reached in to dry them, and she pointed out which cabinet they went in. "It's usually a lonely job."

Paul grinned. "We always took turns at home, all of us. Many hands make light work, Mam always used to say."

"Is she still alive? Your mother?"

"Until two years back. Pneumonia. Just like that, too, I'm told. She was always so strong. I think we thought she'd never die. We still thought we'd get her over here after the war was over, right up until the end. At least that was our plan. I'm not sure it was hers. We'd tried to bring her over before that, but it was always one thing or another. The girls were over there, having their babies. She couldn't leave them; they needed her."

"You miss her."

"You always miss your mam. But she had her hands full back home. Better that Patrick and I were over here, taking care of ourselves. She was proud of us, she said. And we sent her money when we could. Me more than Patrick, what with him having his own weans to feed."

Julia watched his eyes brighten as he spoke of his mother, watched his face go soft. Just as it had when he spoke of his late wife.

"What?" he said. "You're staring."

"Nothing."

He ran his dish towel over the last plate and slid it into the cabinet on top of the others. "There now. All finished," he said softly, pulling her to him as he gently loosened the apron strings at her side. "And not a moment too soon." He slipped the apron over her head. "I'm Getting Sentimental Over You" faded as he danced her out of the kitchen and down the hall.

Sometime during the night, she reached out and he was gone. She heard noises in the bathroom. The faucet would start and then it would stop. She wrapped herself in the top sheet and went to see what he was doing.

"Paul."

The door was open a crack and he opened it further. He was

standing in his underwear, freshly shaven, drying his face with her hand towel.

"It's so early. Are you getting ready to go?"

He shook his head.

"Why did you shave?"

"Your skin was so red when I left the last time."

"You're not leaving?"

"I wasn't planning on it. Do you want me to?"

"You were just shaving?"

"Yes. I cleaned up after myself. I didn't leave a mess." He gestured over the sink. "See for yourself."

"No, that's all right." She laughed. It was just—it was odd. Robert had never shaved just for her. Although he did not seem to have as much facial hair as Paul did. Perhaps he did now, she thought.

Suddenly Julia felt self-conscious standing there in the bed-clothes. She turned and went back to the bedroom.

"I had hoped I wouldn't wake you," he said as he crawled into bed beside her. "You were sleeping so peacefully."

She shrugged.

"We can go back to sleep if you like. Or not. Julia?"

"Yes."

"Is something wrong?"

She was thinking, trying to make sense of everything, of what they were doing, but she didn't want to talk about it. His face was so close to hers; she turned and held it in her hands.

"I'm fine," she said, running her thumbs over his cheek-bones, the skin as smooth as sifted flour under her fingertips, and then he turned and she slid beneath him, pulled his face down, closer, felt his lips—again, those lips—and then his hands at the sides of her hips, lifting her up.

Having Robert inside her always made her feel complete in a way that nothing else ever had, so much so that at first, when he would finish, she would plead, "Stay," but he never did, he always pulled away. Eventually she stopped asking.

And now again, that wholeness, that fullness, but more than

that, the way he had pulled her in—she realized how much she had missed it. How could the girls at the bakery speak of this as just another chore? Maybe they were all just pretending not to like it.

And then he stopped and he did stay, for just a moment, and she felt something flutter and then break open in her that made her grip his shoulders as if she might be carried away.

"Julia."

She let go. There were red marks where her fingers had been. "I'm sorry."

He smiled. "It's quite all right." He was tall but his build was slight compared to Robert's. She felt his hip resting against the side of her thigh, and the sensation made her eyes well up with tears. He was still there.

"You know what this means," he said. Still, so close. His breath was sweet with the apples from dessert.

She shook her head.

"We are no longer alone in this world. We belong somewhere. We belong with one another."

"Is that what it means?"

"Let me hear you say it."

"What? That we belong with one another?"

"Yes. Say it again."

She looked at him. "We belong with one another," she said, then she added, "You know, I don't usually do this. I'm not the kind of woman—"

"Nor am I that kind of man. But we've been around the block a few times, both of us, we're grown-ups, for God's sake. And I am in love with you, Julia. I think I have been ever since that November day." He paused and she realized he was waiting and that she wanted to say it. "I'd forgotten what it was like."

"I know," she said.

"Ah," he interrupted. "You feel the same."

She nodded.

"You know what they say?"

"What?"

"The only cure for love is marriage."

"I'm not sure I like that saying."

"It depends on how you look at it. Patrick was the one I first heard it from. When he fell for Laurie. I've never seen anyone with such a bad dose. When I saw them together, I thought, That's what I want too. And then Katie came along and I had it, for a little while, anyway."

"How long were you married?"

"A year and a half. Nineteen months, to be exact. We courted about a year before that. I was already working at the brewery, but she was sixteen and we wanted to wait for her to finish the business high school. She was smart as a whip, that lass. A reader, too, like you. She loved to read. She brought her shopping cart to the library. She didn't always fill it. But just in case."

Julia imagined a dewy redheaded ghost pulling a cartload of books.

Suddenly Paul pushed himself up on his elbow, the faint glow of the streetlamp reflecting his hair, black and silver and seal-like. "What about you then? What is Julia's story? I want to know. I wonder, When will Julia tell me her story?"

She sighed and turned so she didn't have to face him. "Oh, you know some of it already. And it's late. Or early."

"You said you loved me. I suppose I should just count my blessings for tonight."

"I did, didn't I?"

"You did."

"I do."

"Then I'll wait for the rest. I am nothing, you will learn, Julia, if not a very, very patient man."

"Are you?"

"I am. Just wait. You'll see. And while I may be just a chauffeur, I'm a good one, a very good one, and I was a good husband. I know how to love a woman. I remember."

QUEENS, NEW YORK

December 1927

The two sisters who ran St. Luke's Nursery took to Johannes like so many more maiden aunts. "When Elyse dropped her sandwich on the playground today, Johannes gave her his," they told Julia almost in unison when she came to collect him, their voices rising together in wonder. Or, "We had a new girl, Virginia, who cried all morning. Johannes sat with his arm around her in the cloak closet and told her it would be all right, that mamas always come back."

According to Lena, he did not even cry on the first day. Julia was relieved but not entirely surprised; she had spent the whole weekend preparing him. "On Monday you will go to the school with the toys and the other girls and boys to play with. Mama will come to get you at two o'clock." She drew a large clock face on the back of a grocery sack and showed him what two o'clock looked like. "Mama will always come and get you."

Still, he had little to say on those first walks home when she asked him what he'd done that day.

"Play," he'd tell her.

"Play?" she'd repeat. "What did you play with? Who did you play with?"

He'd shrug, often dragging a winter-fallen branch he'd picked up along the sidewalk. "I can't remember."

"Tomorrow, you must remember," she'd say in exasperation. "Tomorrow your job is to remember one thing to tell me when I come to get you."

He always nodded solemnly but still forgot.

All of the children who went to St. Luke's had mothers who needed to work. Elyse's mother was a widow and a pharmacist's assistant at Merkens. Virginia's family had moved up from Georgia looking for work; both of her parents had taken jobs at the sweater factory on Catalpa Avenue. Abe's father was finishing a teaching degree at Queens College while his mother waitressed at a diner.

The sisters treated the school as if it were a mission, making it as homelike as possible. Julia was grateful. All the parents were. Their children were happy there.

Still, Lena spoke of St. Luke's with a mild disdain, as if it were a kind of necessary evil Johannes had to endure.

"But he likes being with the other children," Julia pointed out one night. "And he has more toys to play with, and paints and clay. Things we don't have here."

"Perhaps," Lena said knowingly. "But the best place for a child that age is with his mother."

He never asked again about Robert or Nicholas, although one day when she went to collect him, one of the sisters said, "Johannes says he has a little brother."

"Yes," Julia said. "Nicholas. He is with his father. In Germany."

"Oh," the sister said, looking stricken. "I must apologize to him then. I scolded him for making up a story."

"No," Julia said. "He's not."

Dear Judy,

Johannes goes to school now. He seems to like it well enough, although Lena thinks he's too young. But he's only there for five hours every day. The rest we spend together. When I first started working at the bakery, Lena told me that she was afraid he'd get stout if I brought home too many sweets. Now she tells me she thinks he is too thin. "He's a good eater," I tell her. "He's just active. An active, growing boy."

The other evening, when he left a rind of ham on his plate, she insisted he finish everything. He told her he was full. "Not too full for cookies, I suppose," she said to him.

"Well," Johannes admitted, "there might be a tiny spot left for cookies. Just one cookie."

I told her he never eats the ham rind; he doesn't like them.

"You should make him," is what she told me. "Then maybe his shoulder blades wouldn't poke out against his shirt." I didn't really blame him. Who likes the rind of the ham? But she went on. "I wonder what his teachers think, such a skinny boy."

I told her he brings plenty of food in his lunch and he eats it all. "Perhaps there's something wrong with him," she said. "Perhaps we should take him to the doctor."

Judy, he is a slender boy but there is nothing wrong with him. And I told Lena that. I told her if I thought he needed to go to the doctor, I would take him.

But it didn't end there. She took him herself! When I went to collect him at school, one of the sisters, Miss Mary Ann, said she was glad there was nothing wrong with him; that Lena had brought him in late after a doctor's visit to find out why he couldn't gain weight. Apparently, the doctor agreed with me.

"I wouldn't worry too much about it," Miss Mary Ann said. "I've seen skinnier."

But that's the thing, I wasn't. I wasn't worried about it.

I was furious by the time Lena got home. Furious. Of course, she had nothing to say for herself. She said she thought it was child abuse not to take a boy this skinny to the doctor to make certain nothing was wrong with him.

"But nothing was!" I told her. "And I knew that. I know my own child."

"All the same," she told me. "Now we can be sure."

Honestly, Judy, sometimes I don't think I can stand a minute more in this house; Lena's self-righteousness permeates the very air I breathe. I earn enough that Johannes and I could probably get by on our own. But I wouldn't be able to save. And I need to be able to save to find Nicholas. I wouldn't be able to live if I couldn't save for that.

QUEENS, NEW YORK

Late March 1945

"I could get used to this."

It was early on a Saturday and Julia had woken to the smell of coffee and the soft clatter of a cup and saucer being set on her bed stand.

"I think you already have," Paul told her. "So let's make it official." Julia smiled over the rim of her coffee cup. "I mean it. Soon."

"I just—I don't see the rush. We're still getting to know one another."

"We're not young anymore," he murmured into her neck. "That's the rush."

"We're not so old," she said.

"Easy for you to say," he told her. "You're younger than I am."

"Not so much, I hate to tell you."

"You'd be surprised, I think," Paul said. "But please, Julia, please. Think about it. It could be such a nice life, you and me. Waking up together every morning. I could make you so happy. I already do."

She was silent.

"Say it," he said, after a moment. "Say it."

"Say what?"

"I make you happy. I know I do." Laughing, he took her chin between his thumb and forefinger and moved her mouth up and down. "Say, You make me so happy, Paul."

Suddenly, without warning, her eyes filled with tears. She took his hand and held it still.

"Your cheeks are wet. Why are your cheeks wet? It won't do for you to cry; I'm supposed to make you happy. Unless they're happy tears." After a few moments, he said, "Never mind. You're right. There's no rush. It's Saturday. We'll sleep a little longer. Talk later."

Julia nodded silently into the damp pillow. Paul always made everything sound so easy. But she knew nothing was that easy. Besides, he didn't know the half of it.

So much he didn't know.

They had both been asleep for a few hours when there was a loud knock at the door. It couldn't be bad news. Johannes hadn't been posted yet. But no one ever knocked at the door at this hour on a Saturday.

She put her robe on and ran to the front window.

There stood Johannes, frowning and adjusting the collar of his uniform. Johannes. She steadied herself on the arm of the sofa. Blood rushed from her head like liquid iron filings, drawn to a magnet in the pit of her stomach.

She came back to the bedroom. "Paul. Wake up." She shook his shoulder. "You have to go. You can get dressed and go out the back door, through the kitchen."

She couldn't face both of them together. Johannes, the image of his father, frowning, betrayed by his wanton mother. The realization crossing Paul's face of all the ways she had lied to him, all the sins of omission.

"What?" He blinked and yawned.

"Get dressed, please. You have to go."

"Who is it? Is it your sister?"

Julia was tempted. Oh, she was tempted. But no. No more lies.

"Please go. I'll explain later. Please. There isn't time."

Paul sat up, as if suddenly everything made sense. "Your husband. You have a husband!"

"No," she pleaded. She sat on the edge of her bed and put her face in her hands. Of course Paul would come to this conclusion. She had no right to be offended. "It is my son. My son. I was married once, and I have a son. He's a soldier and he's here now. Please, Paul, just go."

He stood up and stepped into his pants. The knocking continued, more and more urgent. "I should meet him then. I want to meet him."

"Oh no. Please. Not like this." What would Johannes think? What would he think of his mother?

"If he's home," she explained, "it means he's on leave, that they're sending him overseas soon. I don't want him to find me like this. I don't want this to be how he remembers his mother. I don't know when I'll see him again."

"Then I'll go. But I don't want to stay away indefinitely. I want to meet him."

More knocking. "Just a minute," Julia called, "I'm dressing!"

"For heaven's sake, Mama, just put on a robe."

Paul buttoned his shirt. "Are you going to tell him?"

"About us? Paul, he's deploying soon!" She handed him his shoes, grabbed his elbow, and began guiding him to the kitchen.

"All the more reason. I'll come back this afternoon. You can introduce us then. It'll all be on the up and up."

"Fine," she said impatiently, holding open the back door. Anything if he would just leave and give her time to think.

"That's what it'll be, love. I promise. It will all be fine." He kissed her as she stood, blinking back tears, held his hand gently against her cheek. "You'll see."

She watched him take the back stairs, two at a time, and then disappear down the alleyway.

"Mama!" Johannes's voice yanked her back into reality. "Are you all right? I just wanted to surprise you."

"What took so long?" Johannes drew her into his arms as soon as she unbolted the front door. She felt his shoulder blades protruding against his wool uniform, just like when he was little. He'd lost weight.

"The house was a mess. I didn't want you to see it like that." He looked at her for a moment, as if he were about to say something, then let it go. "Never mind," she said, leading him to the sofa. "You're home. For how long?"

"Six days."

"What can I get you? Coffee? Toast? Tonight, I'll make you a crumb cake. I have some coupons I was saving."

"I would love some coffee."

"And then what?" she called from the kitchen. "England, still?" In his last letter he told her they were probably being deployed to England to help get the rebuilding started.

"No," she heard him say. "Germany."

She stood in the kitchen doorway. He wouldn't look at her, running his finger along a pull on the sofa arm.

"Germany? In your last letter you said it would be England."

"Germany first. They need men to guard the prisoners. They're going to have hundreds of thousands after the surrender. And they need people to build barracks for them too."

"What surrender?" She took a tin of coffee from a shelf over the stove. "They're always talking about this surrender."

"It might be any day now. They can't hold out much longer. They're running out of soldiers. They're drafting teenagers. Boys."

"All the more reason. They're getting desperate. That makes it more dangerous. Johannes, you have to go back and tell them you need to go to England. Better yet, I'll go back with you. I'll tell them myself." Julia felt herself getting desperate, the back of her neck cold and damp against her robe.

"Mama. For heaven's sake, listen to yourself. Besides," Johannes said softly, "I asked for Germany. They can use me over there. I can speak the language. Besides, the way I see it, this is my chance."

"Your chance for what? To get killed?"

"Mama. To find Nicholas."

"In Germany? Now? It is chaos there. Johannes, please don't do this. You don't have to do this. Not for me."

"It's not just for you, Mama. It's for me," Johannes said. "He's probably been drafted by now. He's seventeen. What if I can find him?"

"Among millions of soldiers? No. Please, Johannes. I'm

begging you. For me. Don't go. It's so much safer in England. You said you were going to be in England."

"I don't understand. Don't you want me to find him?"

"Can't you find him from England? It's close enough." She couldn't look at him.

"I'll be all right, Mama. I'll be safe. Think how much safer I'll be than if I'm in the Pacific. I've always wanted to do this. It's our chance. Finally."

Safe. What did he know about safe? What did any of these boys who hadn't gone over yet know, acting as if war were a movie on a screen you could walk home from at the end? They all thought they would live forever. But Johannes would go, she couldn't stop him. He had made up his mind, she could hear the resolve in his voice.

Robert was right. She could never choose between them. Sooner or later, the choice would always be made for her.

QUEENS, NEW YORK

December 1927

"We should call him John now," Lena said one Saturday morning, buttering a triangle of toast. "He is an American, after all. He will fit in better."

"I don't know." Julia hesitated. "So much has happened. To add a new name—"

"The sooner he gets used to it, the better."

"Well, you can call him whatever you like," Julia told her. "To me, he is Johannes."

"I'm going to call him John. And so will you, if you don't want to confuse him."

"But he's named after Papa," Julia said, although as soon as the words came out of her mouth, she realized this reasoning was futile.

Lena remained unmoved.

"John," Julia said, testing the name on her tongue. She didn't particularly care for it. It was too short, for one thing. It didn't feel finished.

"The English form of Johannes," Lena explained.

Julia opened her mouth to speak, then thought better of it. For heaven's sake. She knew it was the English form of Johannes.

"Johannes," Lena called into the living room where he had gone to play after finishing his oatmeal. "Come here, please. We have something to tell you."

"Do you know what your name is in American?" Lena asked as he stood before them.

"American?" He looked at his mother.

"In English," Julia explained.

He shook his head.

"John," Lena informed him.

"Oh. John," he repeated.

"Since you were born in America," Lena said. "We have decided to call you John."

He looked at his mother again.

Julia sighed. "Never mind. Go back and play."

"I named him myself," Julia said, after he was gone. "Robert agreed, but I chose his name." Perhaps Lena didn't understand what went into selecting a name, how seriously most parents approached the task.

Or perhaps she did.

QUEENS, NEW YORK

November 1929

They settled accounts after dinner every Friday. Julia gave Lena her part for rent and food, Lena watching her count out the bills on the table in front of her and then placing them in the black leather wallet in her purse. Then, while Lena and Johannes sat in the front room listening to the radio—recently a new show, *The Shadow*—Julia took her own purse, went to her bedroom, and closed the door. It quieted her heart to feel the pillow of bills growing in the shoebox she kept at the top of the closet—who knew paper, accumulated, could acquire such a weight? On nights when sleep would not come, she imagined carrying the box to the port authority, pictured the ticket master's face as she handed it to him. Then she would imagine herself moving through the streets of Stuttgart, Heidelberg, Munich, toward Nicholas, the same way that Johannes's pencil moved assuredly through a maze, as if it knew by instinct exactly where it was going.

On this night she knew immediately something was wrong when the box lifted too easily from under a stack of sweaters.

It was empty.

She flew down the hall in her stocking feet to the living room, where Lena sat on the sofa and Johannes sat at her feet beside the radio.

"Lena, I need to speak with you." Her heart stamped against her chest. There was no doubt in her mind that her sister knew where her money was and she was determined to get it back.

Lena waved her away. "Shhh. It's almost over."

"Now. I need to speak to you *right now*. In the kitchen."

Julia went to the kitchen table and waited. After a minute or so, she called her sister's name again.

"All right, all right. I'm coming."

"I've been saving money," she told Lena as soon as she crossed into the room.

Lena stood stiffly at the table. Julia watched as the recognition of what she had been called in about slowly passed over her sister's face, her eyes flashing defensively, her lips tightening into a line before she opened her mouth to speak. It was an expression Julia knew all too well and usually didn't care to invoke. "I know," Lena said with excruciating care. "I know you've been saving money. I've only asked that you give what you could afford to this household. Meanwhile you've put away more than two hundred dollars. Two hundred dollars!"

"What I give you *is* what I can afford. If I'm going to find Nicholas, I must save money."

"I know why you're saving it. Not for your own son, just in the other room, but for some child you haven't seen in three years. Who you wouldn't even recognize."

"I will find him. I have to. I don't know why you don't understand that."

"Really," Lena taunted, as if they were still children. "How? How will you possibly find him?"

"If you must know, I plan to hire a detective once I get there. Lena, where is my money?"

"How do you know I have it?"

"Lena." This was ridiculous. "Just tell me where it is."

"All right. It's in this house."

"Where?" Julia's heart surged. If she could just have it back in her hands again.

"I was going to tell you soon. It was going to be a surprise. We're not renters any longer. We own this house."

"Lena, no. You don't possibly mean—"

"Mrs. Wacholder came to me last week. Since her husband died, she's been wanting to sell. She gave us a great deal, Julia. Only four thousand. That's less than we've been paying in rent and it comes with the upstairs apartment."

"We. You mean you."

"It's our house. I can have your name put on the deed. The down payment was four hundred. I only had half of that."

"How did you know I had it? How did you know where it was?"

"I guessed. It was a good guess."

"Lena, you stole it. You stole my money."

"It wasn't stealing. It was for you, Julia, for Johannes and me. We own real estate now, Julia. We own this little house. Well, the bank owns it. But we'll own it someday."

"You didn't ask me. Why didn't you ask me? That's stealing."

"Because I knew you'd say no. Because I knew I'd have to spend weeks convincing you, and Mrs. Wacholder didn't give us that long. Did you want to move? Because Johannes is happy here; he has his school, his little friends, his room."

"No." It was true, she couldn't imagine moving, but then she hadn't even been consulted. "I had plans for that money. Important plans."

"More important than owning your own house? While people are starving and sleeping on the streets?"

"Yes." Julia stood so she and Lena were eye to eye. She would not back down this time. "More important than that."

"Julia. Even with a detective, how could you possibly have found him? And what if you did? You were going to take a three-year-old away from the only family he's ever known."

"That's just it," Julia told her. "The longer it takes, the harder it becomes. Lena, he's my son. And he was taken—no, stolen— from me. No one seems to think twice about stealing from me."

"Shh." Lena put her finger to her lips. "You want the boy to hear you?"

"Why not? What will it hurt for him to find out?" Julia took a deep breath. "Lena, I know you don't understand, but I *have* to find him. I couldn't care less about Robert, but I have to find Nicholas. Find out what has happened to him."

"You said Helene was good to him," Lena offered.

"She seemed good to him. I don't know. She also stole a child from his mother. Who knows what else she's capable of?"

Julia tried to catch Lena's eye but her sister knew enough not to look at her, instead inspecting her hands, as if her neat, evenly clipped fingernails required urgent attention.

"Well, yes. We know you're not always the best judge of character." She folded her arms across her chest. "Besides, I'm sure he's fine. Don't be so dramatic. You just want what you want. That's how it always is with you."

"Lena. That money is the only thing that's been keeping me alive."

"The only thing? The only thing? Honestly, I don't know how you can say that when there is a living, breathing little boy in the other room who also needs his mother."

"I didn't mean it that way." Now Lena was starting to twist her words. It always seemed to come to this. "Not the only thing. Lena, please. You just don't understand."

"Because I don't have children? Maybe not. But I know what it's like to lose someone. That I do know. With no hope of getting them back. Ever. And you just have to get past it. You have to let it go."

"Lena, I know. But it was different with Mama."

"Really? How would *you* know?"

"Because Nicholas is still *alive* somewhere." And because, Julia wanted to add, she *was* his mother and that made it worse and Lena knew nothing about such things. But she said nothing. Talking to Lena when she was in this state, talking to Lena in most states, felt like shouting down a bottomless well. "As far as I know. But I don't know where. It's…it's worse, really."

"I think you should be careful what you say," Lena said tartly.

"Lena, she was our mother, yes. But this is my baby. *I* am supposed to be taking care of *him*. I feel it in my bones, in my skin, every day. It's like walking around hollow, with my insides scooped out."

"He's three years old," Lena pointed out. "Not a baby anymore."

"He will always be my baby," Julia said through gritted teeth.

She blinked back hot tears but she would not cry; not in front of the sister who had always called her a crybaby.

Lena sighed. "Well, the money is gone. I can't get it back. If you're so upset about it, the mortgage will be less than the rent. Ten dollars less. You can have half of that. And if the upstairs apartment stays rented—you can save even more that way."

"As long as you don't decide there's something else you need my money for." The tears were coming now; she was helpless to stop them. Angry tears. Deserved tears. Not crybaby tears.

"And you wonder why I didn't want to tell you?"

There was nothing more to say and Julia had no intention of standing there crying. She started toward her bedroom.

"I'll see the lawyer Monday about putting your name on the deed," Lena called after her. "I was going to do that all along."

Julia closed the door and curled up on her bed, sobbing quietly into a pillow already yellowed with tears. It would never have occurred to her to take something that wasn't hers, from her sister, from anyone. How could Lena do it so easily, justify it so handily, as if she had been doing it all her life?

Because she had been. How Julia missed the furtive looks that sometimes passed from her father to her when Lena was being unreasonable. The looks that said, "What can I do?" and "I *know*, liebchen," and "It's not you." What she wouldn't give for just one more.

She would not give up. Someday she would find Nicholas or he would find her. And he would need to know that she had never stopped trying. She would have to prove this to him and she would have to keep her money safe, protect what was hers.

First thing Monday morning, she would ask Mrs. Sciorra where she did her banking.

QUEENS, NEW YORK

October 1930

"Johannes is doing fine," his first-grade teacher told Julia at their meeting. Her name was Miss Chalk, a fact Johannes took great pleasure in. A tall, big-boned woman, her face was open and pleasant; Julia understood why her son was so fond of her. She leaned back on the edge of a great oak desk, while Julia sat in a student desk in the front row. She was fascinated by the way the wooden lid lifted up on its hinges to reveal storage for books and pencils, the space for an inkwell at the far top right, empty because, as Johannes explained, they did not learn to use pen and ink until second grade. Mrs. Stephens had taught the five of them at a long wooden table. Julia had never seen such a desk.

"He's very well behaved. I don't feel I know him yet; he's very quiet. But that will come. It's only October."

"Johannes?" Julia repeated. "Did you just call him Johannes?"

Miss Chalk looked stricken. "That's his name, isn't it?" She leafed through her papers. "Yes, right. That's his name. At any rate, he seems to be a bright boy. He's picking things up very quickly. He already knows the alphabet."

Julia nodded. "I read to him. We go to the library every Saturday. As much for me as for him," she added.

"Your English is very good," Miss Chalk said. "I suppose I shouldn't be surprised. So is your son's."

"He was born here," Julia explained. "And I began learning when I was very young. Not much older than—" She paused. "Johannes."

"You speak English at home?"

"Yes," Julia told her. "My sister especially. Her English is even better."

"What language do you read to him in, may I ask?"

"If it's one of my own books from home, German. If it's

a new one from the library, English, of course. He likes *The Adventures of Peter Rabbit*. We read that in English."

"Really?"

"Is it a problem?" Julia asked. "Should I read only in English?"

"It doesn't seem to be. No, he's a lucky boy," Miss Chalk explained. "Some of the mothers never learn a word of English all their lives."

"Well?" Lena asked as Julia hung up her coat. She had made it clear that she'd also wanted very much to go to the meeting. "I'd go along," she sighed from time to time in the days before. "But someone should stay with the boy."

"She was very kind," Julia said, sitting in the chair near where Johannes played with a regiment of tin soldiers on the floor. "I can see why he likes her so much. She said he is a good boy—what was the word? Deportment. She said he has good 'deportment' and he's very smart. He's doing well in all his subjects."

Johannes smiled shyly from where he lay on his stomach orchestrating a battle.

"Of course." Lena clasped her hands to her chest. "I knew it!"

"There was something strange, though," Julia said.

"What?" Lena asked. "What is it? They want him to skip a grade. I knew it! I told you they should start him in second grade."

Julia shook her head as she leaned down. "Your teacher calls you Johannes?"

"Mama," he began as if it was obvious. Without looking up, he made one of the tin men hop after another with a bayonet. "There are four boys named John in my class. So I told Miss Chalk my real name. To make it easier."

"Well." Julia grinned at her sister. "All in all, I was very proud."

"Yes, of course." Lena cleared her throat and looked away. "Very proud."

QUEENS, NEW YORK

April 1945

Paul glanced over her shoulder as Julia let him in. "Where is he? Is he here?"

Julia shook her head while he followed her down the hall to the kitchen. "He just went out, to see some friends. He'll be back later. I thought we should talk first."

"Did you tell him about us?"

"Paul. Sit down, please. Let me get you some coffee."

"You didn't tell him."

"I didn't have time. He had a lot of news. Upsetting news. I thought he was going to England, to rebuild. But, no. He's going to Germany. He asked to go to Germany."

"Well." He pulled up a chair to the kitchen table while Julia poured him coffee though he hadn't asked. "Better than the Pacific."

What was it with these men? A war zone was a war zone if your child was going to be there.

"What'll he be doing?"

"Getting ready for the surrender, the great surrender that never happens. Building barracks for the POWs. Building. That's what he's been doing for the past two years."

"What's his name?"

"What?" Julia found it hard to concentrate on what Paul was saying, the collision of these two worlds was clouding her mind.

"His name. This son you managed to keep from me. What's his name?"

"Johannes."

"All right. You have a son named Johannes. That's a rather big piece of information, isn't it? A son."

"Yes. Johannes," she said. "After my father. But please don't call him Hans. He doesn't mind so much but I hate it. His name is Johannes."

"And *his* father? What happened to his father?"

"His father, Robert, is in Germany." Julia paused, still thinking carefully about what she would and would not tell him. "We came here together, twenty-one years ago, but then he went back. Johannes and I stayed."

"You didn't want to go back?"

"It was not our choice. Robert left us here. I had no one else. Lena was here. I stayed."

"I just don't understand." Elbows on his knees, Paul held his face in his hands. "Why you didn't tell me this. Why you didn't think you could."

"I didn't know how." She was telling the truth but that didn't soften the guilt. He looked stricken, betrayed.

"You didn't know how? After I told you everything?"

"You told me how your wife died, your baby died. My husband left me. It's not the same."

"Was he crazy? He must have been out of his mind."

"Paul."

"A beautiful wife. *And* a son. A family. A family!"

"I don't know what he was. I don't know why it happened. You must understand, it's so hard…to tell anyone."

He looked up, met her gaze. "You forget. My father left us too. And he *was* crazy. Crazy for a pint. Did he drink, your husband?"

Julia shook her head. "No. Not really." No, she did not even have that excuse, nothing like drinking to hide behind. Robert had stopped loving her; it was that simple. Paul knew loss, he did, but he didn't know how it felt to be left because you were no longer loved. No longer worthy of love.

She wished he would stop talking, just for a moment, so she could think. Think about what to do, whether to tell him the rest. *How* to tell him the rest.

"So I know what it's like, a little, Julia. To be left. To grow up without a father. Ma, she tried, she really did but—"

"Paul," she whispered, closing her eyes. "Can you be quiet? For just a moment."

"I'm sorry. I'm just trying to tell you. All right. I'll stop."

Maybe it was just too fast. It was all too fast. She felt faint, her arms and legs rubbery, buzzing, and she lowered herself into the chair opposite him.

Acting too quickly. She'd made that mistake before. Seventeen years just she and Johannes and Lena and now so much happening all at once. What would Lena think? Thank God she was in California.

"Julia," Paul pleaded. "What? What are you thinking?"

"Nothing," she lied. "I don't know." Really, she was thinking how deeply she wanted to tell him *why* Johannes wanted to go to Germany, needed to tell him, while at the same time, knowing that she must not do it. How do you tell someone this? How would he see her then? How would she hold up against the lovely auburn-haired Katie, forever nineteen? No. She wouldn't tell him. She just couldn't.

"I'm sorry about what I said. I did want to tell you that. About you having a husband. I don't know what got into me. It just came out," Paul said.

"Well, I did have. In a way. But Lena checked into it. After seven years of abandonment, a marriage is dissolved. She wanted to make sure I could marry again, if the opportunity arose."

"Why didn't you? I'm sure you had the chance."

"I was very young when I married. I had hardly been in the world." This part was easy enough to explain. "I didn't understand the way all that works here. I didn't want to. I just wanted to work on my cakes and go home to my son. It was all I could do."

"Yet you let me court you."

"I wasn't paying attention; it happened so quickly. Lena is in California, Johannes is in North Carolina, and suddenly I am out front and there you are." She had let her guard down, was what she wanted to say. And now she was trying desperately to raise it back up again. It wasn't too late.

"And here we are." Paul got up from the sofa, tried to pull her from the chair where she sat but she wouldn't move. He sat back down. "Now what?"

"I don't know. It was all right while he was in Fort Bragg; it didn't seem like it would hurt anything, but now, now it seems like tempting fate." As the words came out she began to feel less dizzy; the world righted itself, her arms and legs became solid again. She felt herself gaining some control.

"Being happy together. That's tempting fate? Julia, that's crazy."

"Maybe after the war is over," she said, thinking aloud.

"Julia, you've said it yourself, we don't know when it's going to be over. Maybe he'll just be happy. Happy for you."

"Happy?" She looked at Paul. How could he possibly understand?

"Happy that someone is taking care of his mother. One less thing for him to worry about, so he can concentrate on the work he's there to do. One less thing to distract him from staying alive. Think of it that way."

"He knows I don't need taking care of," she said, a little indignant. "I took care of both of us for seventeen years."

"Of course, you did. That's not what I meant. But if he's *your* son, I'd wager he'd just be happy for you."

"For so long it was just the two of us. Why complicate everything, just before he leaves?"

"I don't think you're giving him enough credit. And it's not *that* complicated."

But it was. Meeting Johannes would be just the beginning. The beginning of her transformation from someone who had been left, unloved, which was bad enough, to someone who did not deserve her own child. Slowly it was becoming clear to her what she must do.

"Paul, you don't even know him. You don't even know us."

He sat up, looked away as if he'd been slapped, and she was instantly sorry. Maybe he *would* understand, she considered briefly. Maybe it was worth the risk. But then. The rubbery feeling started crawling up her arms again. She hugged herself to make it stop.

"Please, Julia, let me try. Let us meet one another."

"Not just now." She couldn't look at him, those blue eyes, those beautiful, pleading chalk-blue eyes. She didn't deserve them. "Maybe when it's all over."

"Are you ashamed then? Ashamed of me? Of us?"

"No." She wasn't ashamed of them, not really. She was ashamed of everything else, the past that threatened to come roaring back, like a giant wave.

They were silent a few more moments.

"He'll be back soon," she said, finally, still avoiding his gaze.

"And you really want me to leave."

"Yes."

"Well, then." He stood for a moment then made his way, slowly, to the hall. Without thinking, she glanced up as he passed and saw that his eyes were, unbelievably, full of tears. "If you need me, Julia, you know where to find me. Where you can always find me."

She did not answer. If she opened her mouth to speak, she might call him back. She might run to him, humiliate herself. She pressed herself against the chair with all her might.

The front door opened and then closed. She exhaled, exhausted.

It had been so long ago. Her memory of that time had faded almost to a figment. But it was still there. Images of those early days after Robert and Nicholas were gone, of trying to function, to get out of bed and make Johannes his toast and jam, bathing and dressing herself as if she were underwater, the skin around her eyes burning with the salt of relentless tears. How she used to wish she were covered with bruises, her skin so mottled with purple, black, and brown that strangers in the streetcars, on Myrtle Avenue, would stare, their eyes full of sympathy and understanding. New marks would replace the old ones whenever the shower of what had happened washed over her again, over her whole body, from her scalp to her toes.

Then she wouldn't have to tell anyone. Telling was so hard. From the bruises, they would just know.

Perhaps Lena was just being smart, refusing to let Papa love her after Mama died. Julia had always thought it was foolish, even felt sorry for her older sister, the way she perpetually nursed her wounds like a cornered animal. Maybe it was Lena who was the smart one in the end—Lena, leaving them both behind as soon as she could, running away and bobbing her hair, knowing just how it would devastate Papa; Lena, choosing—instead of the maternity and children's wards the other nurses clamored for, full as they were of the fecundity and fragility of life—to spend her days taking the temperature of hypochondriac operators at the phone company; Lena, who was probably at this moment instructing rows of faceless soldiers on practicing field hygiene and avoiding venereal disease, continuing to ensure that the worst thing that could happen to her already had.

QUEENS, NEW YORK

November 1931

How many times had she collected him from school now? A few hundred, at least. Johannes was in second grade, after all. Yet each time her heart beat a little faster as she watched the children come pouring out of the black iron gates of St. Matthew's Elementary, fluttered until she found his fair head in the crowd.

"Can we stop at the playground today? *Please.*"

"Not today. I'm making sauerbraten tonight. It's complicated."

"I can walk home by myself." He stood a little straighter. "Joseph and Andrew do."

"I know," she told him. "But I am not Joseph and Andrew's mother. I am your mother. And I don't think you're old enough to walk home by yourself. It's still six blocks from the playground."

He sighed, his chin sinking to his chest for a moment in recognition that this was not a battle he had ever won.

"So, what did you learn today? What can you tell me?"

He brightened. "Well, you know how we have been reading about Joseph and Margaret and their sister, baby Joan?"

Julia nodded. They were the children in the stories from his reader.

"They went to visit their grandparents at their farm out in the country. They got eggs from the chickens and Joan tripped and fell in the pond but Joseph pulled her out."

"How nice. A farm," she said, taking his hand as they reached a stoplight.

"That's not all," Johannes said. "Guess what happened when their daddy—that's what they call their papa—came and brought them back home?"

"I don't know. What?"

"There was a new baby waiting for them! Peter. He had come while they were gone!"

"Really. Another baby," she said absently as she watched the traffic light for a safe time to cross. It was late November. The day was brisk and windy and a group of workmen at the corner struggled to raise a gold garlanded star and a strand of Christmas bulbs above the street.

"So I was thinking. I keep praying and praying for Nicholas and Papa to come back but they never do. Now I know what the problem is. We never go anywhere."

Julia absorbed this news silently. "I've never heard you say that prayer," she said finally.

"I say it in my head. Aunt Lena says we mustn't talk about it, that it only upsets you."

"I see."

"Joseph and Andrew are brothers. I don't tell them I have a brother too. I don't think they'd believe me."

"It's just as well," she said. "It would be hard to explain."

"We need to go away, Mama. Then when we get back, Papa and Nicholas will be here. I think that must be how babies come."

"Johannes." She stopped and they faced each other, reflected in the windows of Bohack's Grocery. She still held his mittened hand. She needed to hold his hand to tell him this.

"Yes, Mama."

"Nicholas isn't a baby anymore."

"He's not? How old is he?"

"He turned four on August nineteenth."

"Four! That's old enough to go to the playground with. That's old enough to play catch. So when can we go away on a trip? Aunt Lena should come too. I think the house might need to be empty."

"It doesn't matter what we do, Johannes. He's not coming back."

"But why?" He stamped his foot and, uncharacteristically,

whirled away from her for a moment, his arms crossed stubbornly over his chest. He always reminded her of Lena when he pouted like this, they made the same sour face, pursed their lips together in the same way.

Julia took a long breath, exhaled. She knew this time would come, had prepared herself for it, had rehearsed just how she might tell him, explain what had happened, in such a way that would cause him the least pain possible. He was the innocent bystander in all this. He should not be made to suffer. "When Papa left, he gave you to me. He didn't want to leave you, he told me so; but he knew I couldn't bear for him to take both of my children. So he took Nicholas and he gave you to me."

"Where is he?"

"In Germany, I think. That's all I know."

"It doesn't make any sense."

"I know. It doesn't."

"I don't remember much about Papa. And Nic was just a baby. But I still miss him. I wish I had a brother."

"I miss him too. Every day. But I am glad I have you."

"Well, maybe we could still go on a trip. And when we got home, maybe there would be another baby brother waiting for us. If we can't have Nic."

"Why do you want a little brother so much? What if it was a girl?"

"No." Johannes was resolute. "No girls. We don't need any more girls. It has to be a boy."

"All right." Julia laughed. "No more girls."

"If I had a brother, I could show him how to do things. I could show him my toys and teach him how to play with them. Very carefully, of course. And only if I said it was all right."

"Well," Julia told him as they came upon their block, Sixty-Second Avenue. "I think you're going to have your toys all to yourself. We're not going anywhere. And besides," she bent down and whispered, "that's not how babies come, actually."

"No? Then how do they come?"

She sat down on their stoop and drew him close.

"Someday I'll tell you. When you're older."

"We could still go on a trip." He paused and then his face lit up again. "We could go to Germany!"

Julia took his face in her hands. "Johannes. A trip to Germany is very expensive. But I will tell you—and this is a secret. You mustn't tell Aunt Lena. I have been saving my money to go. To find Nicholas."

"Can I go too?"

She paused. She had never considered this. "Yes. I suppose you could."

"How big is Germany? As big as New York City?"

"Bigger," she told him.

"As big as America?"

"No," she said, "not that big. Saturday, when we go to the library, we'll get out the atlas and I'll show you."

"Well, if it's not as big as America, we should be able to find him."

Julia stared into Johannes's eyes, his father's indigo eyes, like the Blue Willow pattern on Mother Kruse's breakfast dishes.

"Maybe," she told him. "We can try." She let go of him and he bounded up the steps. There was so much more to say. But he already knew enough.

Later, after the supper dishes were put away and Lena and Johannes were listening to their show, Julia got out her dictionary and opened it to B, where she kept her Bank of the United States passbook. Two hundred eight dollars and forty-six cents. Lena was right, she had been able to save faster since they bought the house, even with Johannes's school to pay for. But third-class passage was up to eighty-five dollars the last time she checked. Now she would have to double that.

At night, before she fell asleep, the numbers floated like a cartoon inside her head. This much for train fare. That much for food. That much for a cheap, safe place to sleep. The private detective was the biggest variable. She had to save enough for that. She had to be ready to go when she got there. But she wasn't sure how much one would cost.

It could go on for hours, sometimes, the numbers, the calculating, the figuring. She'd think of some new expense, some new way to save a few more pennies and then she'd be wide awake until she'd gotten up to write it down. Most of the time, though, it was a way to get to sleep. She went over the budget until she had it memorized. Depending on the cost of the investigator, the trip was as close as a year, as far away as two or three.

She never dreamt about the passage, only about the arrival. Stepping off the ship in Bremerhaven and making her way straight to the *polizei*, where she would ask for detective recommendations. The *polizei* would know who to hire.

She'd never traveled by boat that she wasn't seasick, so she preferred not to think about the journey itself. Besides, what was five days of sickness at sea? Getting there was all that mattered.

QUEENS, NEW YORK

December 1931

It had been cloudy all day, cloudy, cold, and damp. There was even talk of flurries. Julia could taste it, the wetness in the air as she walked out of the bakery to get Johannes from St. Matthew's. First she had to stop at the bank, though. It was Friday. Friday was banking day.

It was the Sciorras who had recommended the Bank of the U.S. They kept their nest egg there, Mrs. Sciorra said. Excellent customer service, she said.

Julia had been worried when some of the local banks started failing. She considered withdrawing for a time. Then she received a letter from the bank president. The Bank of the U.S. was a national bank, he told his customers. It was on solid ground and in no danger.

So she waited. It was hard to resist the pleasure of watching her money grow. She anticipated the satisfying thump each week as the teller stamped the addition of not only what she had deposited but also the interest.

In fact, she had been tapping the passbook in her coat pocket, wondering what all the noise was about when she turned the corner and saw the crowds gathered around the front door. Thick black chains snaked around the brass handles, so it was impossible to get in. It was the middle of the day.

There was a hand-lettered sign in the window. "Closed until further notice."

This was not possible. The letter had come from the president just a few months ago. Her money was safe. Everything was fine.

Someone started shaking the door, rattling the chains. Then the sound of glass shattering, and, finally, sirens. Julia stood frozen, just watching, waiting to see if any of the men climbing through the windows were coming out with anything. She would climb up there too, if it would do any good.

But no one came out until the police came and broke through the chains and started leading people out. "But they have my money!" an older gentleman in a flat cap cried as a police officer led him away.

Julia watched from across the street. This could not be happening. It simply could not. The bank president had told them their money was as safe as if it was in Fort Knox. Fort Knox. Even Lena didn't know what that meant. Julia had had to go down to the library and look it up. And then she felt satisfied.

She couldn't stay any longer; she had to get Johannes and get home while she could still stand.

"Mrs. Walker gave me another star today. If I get stars all next week, Mama, I will have enough for a St. Matthew's pencil. Just like Joey has. He said he would give me his since he already has two. Wasn't that nice? But I said I wanted to wait until I could get my own. We played stickball today and I got three hits. I don't have homework except my spelling words but they have to be in cursive, so can I go to the matinee tomorrow, Mama, please? Can I go to the matinee with Joey and Andrew? It's a triple feature. Mama, what's wrong? Say something."

"I'm just tired," she told him.

At home, she went directly to her room. "I need to lie down," she told Johannes as he set his schoolbag on the kitchen chair. Usually she made him a glass of milk and a plate of crackers to hold him over until dinner.

"What about dinner? Mama? *Mama?*"

She closed the door and lay on the bed, still in her coat. She felt for the leather passbook in her pocket and drew it out.

Two hundred forty-seven dollars, stamped in black ink. There. And gone.

Despite everything, they had been lucky so far. Lena's job at Bell was secure; she was the head nurse. If they needed to let any of the medical staff go, and so far they hadn't, she would be the last one. Mrs. Sciorra had volunteered that Julia wasn't going anywhere, even though she hadn't had the nerve to ask herself. "The only way you'll go," Mrs. Sciorra told her, "is if I go. If we have to shut down the bakery."

That didn't seem likely. Business was down, yes, but Sciorra's found an even keel in the teachers, the police officers, the firemen, those who'd kept their jobs and who kept returning for their daily bread. So they baked fewer cakes and more bread. But Mrs. Sciorra said Julia would stay no matter what. "When this is all over," she said, "people will buy cakes again. And they will want Julia's cakes. I don't want them to get them from Schulberg's. Because he would hire you in a minute. He's said so himself."

Why, why hadn't she taken the money out when she considered it? Every day a list of bank failures in the paper. But not the Bank of the U.S. Even Mrs. Sciorra had said once that they had a lot of overseas assets, that they were safe. She would know, Julia thought.

But there was that passbook, the smooth reassuring texture of the leather cover in her coat pocket. Besides, she couldn't leave money in the house where Lena might find it.

"Bank of the U.S. failed, I heard," Lena said casually later over the meatloaf leftovers Julia had managed to put together. Too casually. Julia looked across the table at her, tried to catch her sister's eye as she pushed her green beans around on her plate, but Lena wouldn't look at her. More proof. Lena knew. She had seen the passbook somehow. She knew.

"Maybe now you'll finally give up," she said and then lifted a forkful of beans into her mouth.

Julia put down her napkin and pushed her chair back. "I've not been feeling well. I'll clean up later."

"She was in her room for an hour today," she heard Johannes explain as she closed her door. "I hope she's all right."

Later Johannes came to the door with a plate of cookies. They always had cookies; she brought leftovers home from work.

"Aunt Lena and I cleaned up from dinner," he told her. "So you don't need to worry about it."

She took a cookie, held it in her hand, but could not bring herself to take a bite.

"That was sweet of you," she said.

"Are you all right? Maybe you should see Dr. Crawford."

"I'm just sad. I got some bad news today. That's all."

"What bad news? What happened?"

She looked at him, his eyebrows furrowed with concern. He was eight years old. An old soul, Lena had said once. Maybe she should tell him.

"Nothing," she said finally. "Nothing for you to worry about. I just need some sleep. I'll be fine in the morning. You'll see."

"Is it about Papa and Nicholas?"

What could she say? It was always about Papa and Nicholas. "Well," she told him, "that sometimes makes me sad, yes."

"Me too," he told her. "Joey's father plays stickball with us sometimes. He used to play on the Yankees farm team. Did you know that?"

"Yes." Julia smiled in spite of herself. Johannes had told her this many times.

"I think he tries to be extra nice to me when we're all playing. Joey and Andrew must have told him that I don't have a father. But I hate it. I hate it when he does that. It just makes me feel sick, here." He rubbed his stomach. "A lot of times, I just feel sick when I see him coming to play."

"I'm sorry," she managed, even though listening to him say these words momentarily took her breath away. If she ever saw Robert again it would be all she could do not to scream into his face, not to slap him silly, not just for what he had done to her but for what he had done to Johannes, to his own son. She tried to catch a breath.

"He's never coming back, is he?"

"No, liebchen. I don't think so." She drew him against her, hoping, perhaps, to absorb some of his sadness, saturated as she was with her own.

Johannes sat up, suddenly exuding energy and hope apropos of nothing, the way children do. "But we'll find Nicholas someday, right? Wait till he sees what he's missing. He doesn't even know. I'm going to teach him to play stickball and handball. I'll bet he'll be good at handball."

"He probably will," she said weakly. "If you teach him."

"Well, you should try and eat something. I hope you feel better." He patted her hand and left. She looked at the alarm clock ticking on the nightstand. *The Shadow* was coming on.

Julia forced herself to sit up. She would begin again, somehow. She had to. Not just for her but for Johannes and Nicholas. Even though she had never had much of an education in mothering, she was sure this was what mothers did, what Mrs. Stephens and what her own mother would have done had it been necessary. For both of her sons, she would never give up.

"We were going to buy a little house upstate someday," Mrs. Sciorra said, dabbing at her eyes as Julia came in from the cold air to the heat of the bakery. "And I still have one more daughter to marry off. Maybe she'll wait. Neither of them have jobs anyway." Her eyes widened as she regarded Julia with sudden recognition. "Oh," she said. "Your savings. For your beautiful boy. You should never have listened to me."

"You didn't know," Julia said. "How could you have known? They kept saying it was safe."

"Well, at least he's young," Mrs. Sciorra said. "You have time. But if I were you, I'd keep my money under my mattress."

"I had another son," Julia began. "He, too, was beautiful," and with that the words came pouring out, for the first time, really.

Mrs. Sciorra grew more stricken the more she told her, until finally she took Julia in her arms and they both sobbed, intermittently, huddled together, this wiry woman with her steel-gray bun, the tiny woman with the thick, dark braids coiled at the nape of her neck. "Oh, you poor thing," she kept saying, over and over. "You poor thing."

Julia didn't know how long they had been standing there when Flora came in from the front of the store. "Mrs. Sciorra, the flour man is—" She stopped when she came upon them in their tearful embrace. "The flour man is here," she said as she turned and left.

They burst out laughing. "What a sight we must be," Mrs. Sciorra said. "What a sight. Never mind." She gave Julia's hand a squeeze and wiped her eyes with the corner of her apron. "You'll tell me more later. I have to see the flour man."

QUEENS, NEW YORK

April 1932

Dear Judy,

The money is gone. For days those words assaulted me every morning, before I opened my eyes. The garbage truck clanging in the alley before dawn: the money is gone; the money is gone.

It is so hard to write these words. I have wanted to write them for months. But I wasn't ready. Writing it makes it real. There is nothing left to do but start again. I keep the money at Sciorra's now, in a drawer under a box of old receipts. No one knows about it. A small envelope of bills.

It was a quiet Christmas. Johannes wanted a sled and they had them on sale at Macy's in November. Lena brought it home and hid it in her closet. It was a lovely sled, with gleaming red painted blades. I've never seen anything like it. All the Kruses' sleds had wooden blades. Do you remember?

Then, we had a heavy, early snow at the beginning of December. Ten inches. Johannes's school was closed even, for three days.

We should give him the sled now, Lena urged me. We don't know if it will snow like this again.

I said no. It would spoil the surprise. I wanted to see his face when he found it under the tree Christmas morning.

You are making a mistake, Lena said.

But I was sure it would snow again; I was sure of it. That early snow was an accident; it never snows like that in December. And Johannes's face, Christmas morning, *was* full of joy even as the ground outside was dry and hard.

He kept it in his room all winter, waiting. There were flurries. Great white flakes drifting in the dull air and

Johannes jumping and twirling at the window, "It's snowing, it's snowing. Wait till Joey and Andrew see my sled."

But it didn't stick. Twice I had to watch him run to the window in the morning to see that the snow had melted, the sidewalks dry and gray, like a rebuke.

Lena would stand behind him, shaking her head. She didn't have to say anything. I kept waiting for her to tell him that she wanted to give him the sled before Christmas but that I refused. She didn't. I suppose I should be grateful for that. She might, still.

But she was right. I waited too long. It is so hard to know what to do sometimes, Judy. Sometimes she acts like he's her son too, like she has the same say as I do and when she does, I react. I do the opposite. *I* will decide when he gets his sled; *I* am his mother.

And so there it stands still, against the wall beside his bed, the red painted blades gleaming.

FORT BRAGG, NORTH CAROLINA

February 1945

"I'm not sure I understand. Your whole unit, the one you've trained with, the one you've worked with these past few years, is going to England. Those are the orders. And you don't want to go with them?"

Johannes shook his head. Colonel Strickland had asked to meet with him after he'd turned in his request and now they sat across from each other in the colonel's office.

He took a deep breath. "I have a brother in Germany. Four years younger. I haven't seen him since he was a baby. I was hoping—"

Colonel Strickland stared at him, puzzled, but let him go on. Johannes was fond of Colonel Strickland and if one thing made him hesitate about making his request, it would be that he would no longer be working for him. He was from Alabama and had a slow manner of speaking that made everything he said sound careful and deliberate. Whenever they sought him out for advice on a construction problem, he would listen to all the options, gather all the information, and then take his time, pondering as he called it, until he came to a decision. He had a wife and two young sons that lived off-base in Fayetteville, and Johannes often thought how lucky they were to have such a father.

"I was hoping to try and find him, bring him home, before he comes to any harm."

"Sergeant Kruse, I'm not sure how you would do that or if it's even possible."

"I've done some checking with the International Red Cross. They say they can help."

"You realize he may have already come to harm, depending on where he lives. They've lost a lot of civilians. Do you know where he is?"

"No, I don't."

"How did he end up over there?"

"My father took him when he was a baby and went back to Germany. He was born here, though, and so was I. So he's actually an American citizen."

Colonel Strickland considered this for a moment, resting his clefted chin on steepled fingers. "What about your mother?"

"My mother raised me. She's still in New York."

"All the more reason to think this through, son. We've secured a lot of locations over there, but Germany is still a lot more dangerous than England. Hell, they're bombing us in their own cities. And you're all the woman has."

Johannes nodded. "I know. I know. But I've wanted to do this my whole life, sir. It's all I've ever wanted."

"Look, Sergeant Kruse, I realize that right now, your whole life seems like a pretty long time but from my end, you're not even halfway through it. Things may be winding down over there but they're just winding up for us. I've got to be sure I set things up to make sure my boys get home safe and I've got to follow orders. Fortunately, in this case, they're the same thing, which is mighty rare in this war."

"Yes, sir. I understand, sir. But after Camp Ritchie, I'm sure I'd be of better use in Germany."

"True enough. But you'd also be leaving the other men. You've made a good team for over two years. That's an eternity in the army." The colonel sighed, lifted the request form Johannes had given him from his desk, looked at it, and then set it back down. "I'm going to need to ponder this for a few more days. I'll have to let you know later in the week."

"Yes, sir."

"That will be all, soldier."

Johannes stood, saluted, and took his leave, silently praying as he headed out into the warm hallway near the mess kitchen, that Colonel Strickland would see his way clear to sending him to Germany. It was beginning to look like his last chance.

After boot camp there had been some deliberation as to whether to send him to foreign language school to continue developing his German or to make him a part of the Engineer Corps. Ultimately, it was decided that there were enough men who had studied German in college and who were further along in their language studies to suit the army's needs. Besides, he already had skills they could use immediately in the Corps— he'd excelled at engineering, construction, and drafting at the technical high school. He loved building things with his hands.

The news disappointed him at first—German language school seemed, after all, the fastest ticket to where he wanted to go—but his superiors assured him that there were Corps units deployed all along the European front, building landing strips, POW camps, repairing the bridges. A posting on the continent seemed inevitable. But then his unit became so practiced at erecting the buildings needed to process the thousands of soldiers who streamed through the camp that his superiors worried a new unit would be too hard to bring up to speed. Johannes and his men were ordered to remain stateside until Fort Bragg had reached capacity.

He had been called into Colonel Strickland's office once before, less than a year earlier, when he was sure that he would finally get his orders abroad. The work had slowed down considerably for the crew he led.

"Looks like you and your men are in for a change of scenery," the colonel explained. "And one that will take advantage of your language facilities as well."

Johannes sat forward, almost as if to follow his heart, which rose and thumped against the cage of his breast. "The European front?"

"Well, no, not exactly, although that's still in the cards down the line; it depends on how fast things go this fall and the kind of winter they have over there. No, you're headed to a special operation in Maryland. Camp Ritchie."

"I don't understand. How will my German help me there?"

"Camp Ritchie is a special operation. Top secret. They've got a model German city up there, right down to the houses, the streets, the beer halls. They're training soldiers in the German way of life, in the organization of their military. They bring in actors who speak German and they use it to train special ops for working in-country, for translation and interrogation. They want to put you through the training—and they want you to help continue the building there."

Johannes sank back in his chair. He would not go to Germany. He would build a pretend Germany in America. It was almost insulting.

"You look disappointed, son."

"I have to admit," Johannes explained. "I thought you were going to tell us we were finally getting posted abroad."

"Patience, son. It's still good training," the colonel continued. "This is only a short-term assignment. That way when they do send you overseas, you'll be ready."

"Do you think we will be sent to Germany eventually?"

"Honestly, son, your guess is as good as mine. France, England, Germany, Belgium. From the reports I'm getting, it could be any one of those places. We'll know more in the spring. In the meantime, you've got some packing to do. You leave in the morning."

QUEENS, NEW YORK

April 1945

Julia sat in the living room in a silence only occasionally interrupted by the swoop of a car outside. She had turned the radio on, low at first, but she couldn't bear to listen to the war news so she turned it back off.

Johannes had gone to bed not long after dinner, saying he had not slept well on the train the night before. She peered through the crack in his bedroom door and saw that he was already asleep, his pink lips parted the way they had since he was a baby, his sweet pink lips, her beautiful boy. He was a man, yes, a young man, but sleeping like this he was just a boy, a child, his features as calm and smooth as those of the baby she had held, until he grew out of her embrace.

If she could have done it without waking him, she would have climbed into the bed beside him and wrapped herself around him, but that was not possible so she stood and held him with her gaze as long as she could. He was always her child in sleep. How could she let him go? But it was not her choice; nothing, it seemed, ever was.

She stood in the kitchen in her nightclothes kneading a circle of dough, pushing the heel of her hand into it and turning it, over and over because she did not know what else to do. The bread received all her nerves, the electricity up and down her arms, dulled the uneasy wad of fear just below her breastbone that kept her from sleeping or even sitting still enough to read. So she floured and kneaded, floured and kneaded until the bread under her fingertips was smooth, soothing, like a worn quilt. Until the phone started to ring.

The phone hardly ever rang and never at night. But now it rang and it rang and it rang, and even though part of her yearned to speak to him, to hear his voice, she was afraid that if she answered it, she would not know what to say, that she would make things worse. She always made things worse.

After several minutes, after flour streaked her face from wiping away tears that dotted the bread, the ringing finally stopped and her breathing steadied. She could knead bread all night if she had to. She could knead it until she collapsed and sleep finally claimed her on the kitchen floor.

And then it started ringing again. It wasn't Lena. Lena would never let it ring like this. The ringing echoed in her ears, in her skull, all she had to do was answer it and she could have what she wanted and, at the same time, if she answered it, there would be even more to lose.

"Julia. Julia, listen to me. I'm sorry but I had to call. I had to talk to you. Listen to me."

She held the receiver in her hands, transfixed at first by his voice, that voice; it held her but she must not give in. She opened her mouth and choked out a sob.

"Julia, please. Please."

"Paul. You don't understand."

"But I want to. I want so much to understand."

She heard Johannes's door creak open and then footsteps.

"Mama? Who are you talking to?"

"No one." She dropped the receiver into the cradle. "A wrong number."

"Mama. You've been crying."

She shook her head, pushing the surge of tears back into her chest, down into her stomach. "The phone startled me. I don't get many calls."

"Mama. Please." He took her into his arms. "It will be all right. I'll be safe. Safe enough. Building. Translating. And I'll bring Nicholas home to us."

He patted her back, softly, and she remembered how she would comfort him when he was small, gathering him, crying over a fall or a broken toy, into her lap, and he would pat then, too, tapping her back with his tiny palm. Here, even now, standing over her, was that same small boy who thought he could bring his brother back by going on a trip. It was so ridiculous she had to laugh, a strange, light laugh that escaped from her like a bubble to the top of a soda bottle.

"And now you're laughing? Mama, what has come over you?"

She felt a strange smile escape her lips, too, and she reached up and touched her son's face, her fingertips tracing the skin along his cheekbone that was always so soft. "Oh, Johannes. I didn't mean to laugh. It just came out. I don't know what else to do."

∽

It took every ounce of control Paul had in his body not to drive back to her house after she hung up the phone, to sit instead in his chair in the front room of his apartment at the Bellos', her sob echoing in his ears, and think about what to do. How to show Julia, still, that he believed in them, that there was a way out of this, whatever this was.

He did not know. He still could not understand why she hadn't told him about her son when he had told her everything about Anna. There was something about her manner that went beyond awkwardness, that seemed suddenly skittish, almost desperate.

Whatever it was, it had to be surmountable. He had to at least try.

It was Mr. Sciorra who answered the first time Paul called. His words were drawn out and slow and Paul remembered that he'd stopped working after a stroke, but he managed to make out from them that his wife was at mass—of course she was at mass, why hadn't he thought of that?—but she would call him back, so he waited. He waited the entire agonizing afternoon—he didn't want to seem a nuisance—only to learn that Mr. Sciorra had failed to give her the message.

"Paul Burns?" Mrs. Sciorra said. "What can I do for you?"

"Well, it's Julia—"

"Is something wrong? Is she all right?"

"Actually, she's fine… I mean, she's not ill, and I don't mean to bother you at home. I was hoping you might be able to help me. Her son came home on leave. He wanted to surprise her, I think, but it's only upset her and somehow because of this she never wants to see me again."

"Johannes?" There was a pause on the line. "She definitely wasn't expecting him or she would have told me."

"Johannes. Yes. I'm afraid I didn't know about him, or her husband. Her ex-husband. There were things she was going to tell me, she said, but she wasn't ready yet. This must have been part of it."

"Oh, Paul. Yes. It is. It is."

"All right. She has a son and an ex-husband she didn't want me to know about. Yet. I don't think that's insurmountable—"

"That's not everything."

"How bad can it be?"

Mrs. Sciorra sighed and there was another interminable pause, but he didn't want to interrupt her. Calling her at home was forward enough. "All right," she said finally. "I will talk to you, but not now. Come to the bakery tomorrow night. After closing. At seven. Can you come at seven?"

"Of course. Whatever you say."

"Good," she said. "Seven is good. That will give me some time."

Julia slept soundly, exhausted after all the crying, and when she woke up Johannes was still asleep. After he got up, they ate the bread from the night before for breakfast.

"It is a little dense," she observed as he spread margarine over a second slice. "Too much flour maybe. Too much kneading."

"It's delicious," Johannes said. "I've missed it. There's nothing like Mama's bread in the mess, anywhere."

"It's my papa's recipe."

Johannes nodded. "I know."

"I wish you had known him," Julia said, standing behind him at the stove. "He would have loved you. I wish you could have known your grandparents."

Johannes sighed. "I know."

"Lena will hate that she missed you."

"Aunt Lena is where she needs to be. Besides, I like it when it's just you and me."

Julia smiled. "Do you have any plans today? Do you want to do anything?"

"Not particularly," Johannes said. "It's a nice day. A walk would be good. Would you want to come with me?" His voice was tentative and Julia realized it was probably because of last night, because he thought she might burst into tears again. But she was cried out for now, so there was little chance of that.

"I would," Julia told him, trying to sound happy, trying to sound brave, to be brave, for him. "Where do you want to go?"

Everywhere, it turned out. Dressed in his uniform, Johannes wanted to go everywhere, to retrace the steps of his youth through the entire neighborhood, past St. Matthews, where they stared up at the windows of his grade-school classrooms decorated with snowmen and paper snowflakes, down Myrtle Avenue, stopping in every shop where he might know someone to say hello.

They stopped for lunch at Merkens and Mr. Merkens looked at Julia expectantly at first, as if he might have wondered where Paul was, but he never said anything. Instead he insisted on serving them himself and giving them their lunches free and clapping Johannes on the shoulder whenever he set anything down on the table.

"If anyone'll give Hitler hell, it'll be this one," he said and winked at her.

Julia nodded while Johannes grinned and blushed and basked in the attention, and in that one wink their entire history unfolded, from the day she and Robert had first walked into Merkens with Johannes in his carriage, until that moment.

But Julia wanted more. *More* history. She wanted Nicholas,

of course, she would always want Nicholas, but she wanted Johannes too. She wanted Johannes to come home, to meet a girl, to get married, to grow old. Older than she was now. She wanted all of it but most of all, she wanted more time for him, more time with him. Whatever she had had, it was never enough, and she would always feel it slipping away.

She felt it lying in bed at night, breathing in salt and sweat at the back of Paul's neck, tasting it, stroking silvery black curls between her fingers as he slept, as he rocked over her, felt the nagging sense, whenever there was too much happiness, that she was on the verge of losing it all.

Lena, scolding, "Focus on the son you have. Not the one you lost."

She was focusing on him now. He was the choice she had made, if she had any choice at all. Some happiness was better than too much, was better than none at all.

Julia always arrived first at the bakery, early in the still-dark, warming the ovens, starting the brötchen Sciorra's was now known for, and the dough for the baguettes so they would be fresh for the morning customers, while Mrs. Sciorra came in an hour later to finish the sesame loaves after their second rise and start on the cookies and the cakes. This morning she was earlier than usual, which was just as well, since Julia had lain awake staring at the ceiling at her bedroom for the second night straight and now, after two hours in the growing warmth of the kitchen, she could hardly keep her eyes open.

"I haven't slept well," she explained as Mrs. Sciorra donned her apron. "The brötchen is out and the baguettes only need a few more minutes. If I could just close my eyes for a few minutes, I'll be fine for the rest of the afternoon."

"Of course," Mrs. Sciorra said, searching her face. She shook her head. "Look at those dark circles. Are you coming down with something?"

"Johannes came home this weekend. He's on leave until next Friday."

Mrs. Sciorra frowned. "And this is keeping you from sleeping?"

"He's on leave because he ships out after that. To Germany."

"I thought he was going to England."

"So did I. But they've ended up with far more prisoners than they expected in Germany, and they need buildings to keep them in. Johannes is happy. He plans to find Nicholas. I am not happy." Julia felt the tears coming on in spite of her exhaustion. "I wanted him to go to England. I wanted him to be safe. Now both of them will be in the middle of the war."

"Come now, come." Mrs. Sciorra led her to the desk at the back of the workroom. "Rest will help. You need to rest. Should I see if Paul can bring you home?"

"After Johannes came home, I had to call it off. I've been thinking about it for a while. It's bad enough he had to find out about Johannes. I don't want him to find out about Nicholas too."

"Julia, he was going to find out eventually."

"I don't want him to pity me and I can't imagine he won't. I don't want anyone's pity."

"Pssh. He'll think you are strong. Surviving after all this."

Julia shook her head. "It will change how he thinks of me. I will always be the one who was left, who was taken from. What did I do to deserve that, he'll wonder? Better to end it now, before all the complications. I must concentrate on Johannes." She was determined. "That is what I must do."

"Right now you need to rest." Mrs. Sciorra lowered her into the chair. "Everything will look different after you have had some rest."

The young man at the table in the back of the bakery did not look like Julia, that was true; he was tall and fair-haired, with dark blue eyes, but Paul would have recognized Johannes anywhere. The uniform helped, but he plainly favored his mother in his affect, in the way they both held their heads with a kind of coltish grace, bowed, just slightly, as if they were both continually humbled by the world. He could not help but like him instantly for this.

"Sit. Please, sit." Mrs. Sciorra gestured at the table as she filled a plate with biscotti and set it before them. "It seems," she said, taking a place at the head of the table while Paul and Johannes faced each other on either side of her like penitent children waiting to learn what they had done wrong, "we all have something in common. Si?"

Johannes remained quiet, although his dark eyebrows rose expectantly.

"Julia. Your mother." Mrs. Sciorra turned to Johannes. "We're all very fond of your mother."

Johannes eyed Paul, waiting for him to say something.

"It's true," Paul admitted.

At this Johannes opened his mouth to speak, but Mrs. Sciorra continued. "This man," she gestured to Paul, "thinks no one sees him sitting in the Bellos' car, gazing through my front window, thinks no one sees him hesitating at my front door to look a little longer at the woman who is suddenly all the time at my register. But I see him. I know that look. So I am not surprised to come in one day and discover that same man wants to take my cake decorator to lunch, and then to dinner. I have known this man for many years and never have I seen this look on him."

"It was that obvious?" Paul said.

"Well," Mrs. Sciorra told them, "I notice these things. Not everyone does but I do. And I notice when someone looks that way at Julia. Julia, who is like a daughter to me. Every woman should know that gaze. I have known it myself."

Johannes finally spoke up. "I'm sorry. Shouldn't we be introduced?"

"I was about to do that," Mrs. Sciorra said. "After I explained why you were both here."

"Paul Burns." He put out his hand. "I've been...calling on your mother."

Johannes shook it tentatively. "She hasn't mentioned you."

"She didn't tell me about you until after you had arrived, Saturday. She didn't seem to want us to know about one another."

Puzzled, Johannes turned back to Mrs. Sciorra. "With all due respect, if she didn't want us to know about one another, why are we here?"

"We all want Julia to be happy," Mrs. Sciorra went on. "Johannes thinks this will happen if he goes to Germany and brings his brother home. Paul hopes this will happen if he and Julia can just be together. But I know Julia. Whatever she thinks, she will never be happy unless you both know about one another. If you both know about one another, all the rest will fall into place." Mrs. Sciorra took a deep breath, braced her arms straight against her lap, and looked up at the ceiling. "Mio Dio, if I am wrong, strike me down quickly and be done. Johannes, your mother is beside herself because you are going to Germany. I have never seen her like this. I had to send her home today."

"I know. She's not been sleeping. But she'll get used to the idea."

Mrs. Sciorra put her hand up. "No buts. We must get this all out. You can explain yourself later. You are happy to be going to Germany. Why are you happy to be going to Germany?"

"Because that is where I'm most needed and because that is where I might find Nicholas."

"Si. Your brother."

Paul straightened. "There's another brother?"

"Yes. Nicholas. My father took him back to Germany when he was a baby."

"Your father just took him?"

"And Helene. My father and Helene took him," Johannes corrected.

"Helene? Who is Helene?"

"Mama's nurse," Johannes explained. "After Nicholas was born. There were complications."

"*That's* what it was," Paul said finally. "What she didn't want me to know."

Mrs. Sciorra shook her head. "It was years before she told me. She still doesn't like people to know. She's ashamed."

"Ashamed? That her son was taken from her? What kind of man does that?" Paul said. "I'd want to kill him for that, myself."

"My father," Johannes said softly. "My father did that."

"I'm sorry, Johannes. I'm so sorry." Paul looked into his eyes. "For both of you."

"Thank you," Johannes said, blinking. No one other than his mother had ever said that to him, not even Aunt Lena.

"She's in such a state right now," Mrs. Sciorra said. "She's terrified of losing you, Johannes. She's terrified of you," she turned to Paul, "finding out about Nicholas. So afraid that she'd rather turn you away. That is her way of trying to keep a lid on all this."

"Why wouldn't she want me to know?"

"Never mind that for now. I don't care what Mr. Sciorra says about my meddling, I could not see Julia like this without doing something. There are things you can do, both of you, to make this better for her."

"I'm already planning it," Johannes said. "I've contacted the International Red Cross. If Nicholas is in Germany, I will find him."

"I don't understand," Paul said. "What can I—" He stopped. Recognition passed over his face. "Mr. Bello."

"Si," Mrs. Sciorra sighed. "Mr. Bello."

"Who is Mr. Bello?" Johannes put in.

"My boss," Paul told him. "I'm his chauffeur. The family's chauffeur."

"There are people in Queens with chauffeurs?" Johannes said.

"A few," Mrs. Sciorra said. "Mr. Bello is very well connected. He is, I think, able to get things done."

"How do you know?" Johannes said.

"Both of his sons were drafted, but they work in Washington, for the War Department," Mrs. Sciorra explained. "And whenever Mrs. Bello needs extra rations—for sugar or flour—"

"Or gas," Paul added.

"Poof." Mrs. Sciorra snapped her fingers. "They appear. Like magic."

"What do you think he can do?" Johannes said.

"I don't know but I can at least talk to him," Paul said. "I've never asked him for anything before."

"I thought," Mrs. Sciorra said, "that you might also introduce him to Johannes before he ships off."

"Sure, I'll meet him," Johannes said. "If he can help."

"Let me talk to him first," Paul said.

"I leave on Friday."

"I'll talk to him tonight. I'll give you my number." He paused. "After your mother has gone to work in the morning, you can call me. But we can't tell her about this. We can't tell her we've even met. Not now, not yet, anyway. Not ever, if this doesn't work out."

"I won't," Johannes agreed. "I don't want to get her hopes up if nothing comes of it."

"Johannes is a good boy," Mrs. Sciorra added. "He can keep a secret."

"She's upset enough with me as it is," Paul told him. "No point in having her angry with both of us."

"Oh, she's not too pleased with me either," Johannes allowed. "I never should have told her I wasn't going to England. I thought she'd be happy."

"I don't blame her," Paul said. "It may be winding down, but it's still dangerous."

"But I'm done here. It's my time, finally. They need me over there, with my German. I'm ready to go. And I'm ready to look for my brother. And if I find him, I'm bringing him home."

"What if he doesn't want to come?"

"I'll convince him."

Johannes's jaw was set. So steadfast, so young. Paul remembered looking out at the world with such resolve when he set out for America, so sure of his path that all he needed to do was take it. He knew it wouldn't be easy, but it was straightforward and it led right out of Galway, where there was nothing for him. But it also led away from his mother, telling him to be careful, knowing, as she must have, that she might never see him again and still letting him go.

Perhaps Johannes could find his brother among the millions of soldiers in Europe; he certainly seemed willful enough. And perhaps Mr. Bello did know people who could help them raise the odds. But more likely Mr. Bello also knew people who could keep such a willful young man as this out of harm's way. Out of the worst of it anyway.

It was a good thing, he thought, he had never asked Mr. Bello for any favors before. Now that he was about to ask him for two.

"Mrs. Bello said you wanted to speak to me?"

"Yes, sir." Paul stood in the doorway of Mr. Bello's study where the man often went after social gatherings to smoke his pipe and look out the large plate-glass window into the night.

"Have a seat." He waved his pipe at a chair across from his desk. "Something wrong with the Cadillac?"

"No, sir," he said. "Nothing wrong with the Cadillac. Still a cream puff."

"Good," Mr. Bello replied. "She's got to last a bit longer. What can I do for you, then?"

"I have a question, sir. A problem. I was hoping you might be able to help me."

"Go on," he said, framed by the window and the dark, rain-slicked street beyond.

"I happen to know of two brothers. Americans, both of them. But one is fighting for the U.S. and one is fighting for Germany, probably. If you can believe it. Probably he's eighteen or nineteen, the younger one, in Germany. The older one, you know, the one on our side, is about to be sent over, but he doesn't want to be shooting at his brother, who, by the way, he hasn't seen since he was a baby. He wants to find this brother. Bring him home."

"He wants to bring home a Nazi? That's some souvenir."

"They're not all Nazis. He's still quite young."

"Then how did he end up fighting in Germany?"

"The father took him back when he was still an infant. Left his older brother and mother here. It's a sad tale. They don't know that he's fighting—but they're assuming it."

"So the boy is American but he grew up in Germany?" Mr. Bello took a puff from his pipe and continued gazing over the street. Paul stood behind him.

"Yes, sir."

"Does he even know he's American? Does he know he has family here?"

"We don't know what he knows. He was so young, he probably thinks the second wife is his mother."

"There's a second wife?"

"Probably. At least there's the woman the father ran away with."

"Quite a piece of work, the father is, isn't he?"

"Yes."

"But," Mr. Bello offered, "all this might come as a shock to him. It would to me. He might not want to leave. And if he really is a Nazi, they won't want him over here either."

"Maybe so," Paul said. "But it seems like he ought to know the facts. It's pretty bad for the Germans right now. His brother just wants to get him out of it. And he was born here. That ought to count for something."

"Not if you're a traitor," Mr. Bello pointed out.

"Can you be a traitor to a country you don't know you're a citizen of?"

"How did you get tangled up in this?"

"I know the older brother," Paul said. "And a woman I was keeping company with—she's their mother. She works at Sciorra's. Your wife knows her."

"A woman you were seeing?"

"Yes," Paul said.

"I see."

"You know so many politicians," Paul continued, "and with your connections in the War Department."

"What's his name, this young man? The Nazi."

"Kruse," Paul said. "Nicholas Kruse. K-R-U-S-E."

Mr. Bello went to his desk and wrote it down. "And the brother? The one who's on our side?"

"Johannes. Kruse."

"Well, he hasn't been in office very long, but Henry Latham owes me a couple favors. I helped him get there. I'll give him a call in the morning. See what he can do. And I'll give Anthony a call, he's a deputy with the Army Service Forces in Washington and he may know how to find someone over there. I don't know. We'll give it a try."

"Thank you. I'm very grateful. I know you don't have to do this. But there's one more thing."

"Something else?"

"How would you go about keeping someone safe over there? I'm assuming, perhaps, that there are some assignments that are better than others?"

"I'm sure there are."

"Is that something you can ask Mr. Latham about as well?"

"Who are we talking about? The older one?"

"Well, yes. If there's any way to help make sure Johannes can stay out of harm's way."

Mr. Bello sighed. "It's a good thing I've always liked you, Burns. I'm not a magician. We are in a war. But I'll see what I can do."

"Thank you," Paul said. "I appreciate this. Truly. And if you want to talk to Johannes, he's here on leave until Friday. It can be arranged."

"Well, I'll let you know what I find out. And, Burns?"

He stopped in the doorway. "Yes, sir."

"You think this will win her back. The mother?"

"I don't know," Paul said. "I just want to help, if I can."

"Of course," Mr. Bello said. "But it would be a nice dividend, yes?"

"It would, sir. Yes. It would."

Mr. Bello closed the doors to his study. He had asked to meet with Paul and Johannes both, to report what he had found out.

"What we're talking about here is a needle in a haystack," he began. "But there are things we can do. Apparently, there are all kinds of people over there being searched for, for one reason or another, not always good reasons. There's a list, apparently, that goes out to all the field hospitals, all the POW clearing-houses. Congressman Latham says he can get your brother's name on that list."

"That would be great," Johannes said. "That would be won-derful."

"He'd still have to end up with the Americans somehow. Wounded or captured. You have to hope he's not on the East-ern front."

Johannes nodded. "It's possible, but the majority of the Volksturm, the most recently drafted, are on the Western front. I realize it is still going to be difficult. But it's better than noth-ing."

"Confidentially speaking, Mr. Kruse, as I understand it, you weren't just building barracks in North Carolina. You spent a considerable time in Maryland. This Camp Ritchie I'm just learning about?"

"Yes," Johannes admitted. "I went into the army as a con-struction engineer but once I got there I also trained as a trans-lator and interrogator. Because of my German."

"I wouldn't bring it up if everyone weren't saying we're about to win it. In Europe, anyway."

"I'm sorry," Paul interrupted. "What is Camp Ritchie?"

Mr. Bello turned to Paul. "From what Latham told me, it's a covert counterintelligence operation in Maryland preparing soldiers to understand the German culture, to speak the lan-guage, fight in their villages, interrogate their prisoners. Mr. Kruse here has had some special training that will be useful where he's going."

"Yes, sir, I have," Johannes said. "Nonetheless, I hope this conversation will not go beyond this room."

"It won't. I trust Mr. Burns; I've trusted him for over twenty years, with my family. But with that kind of training, Congressman Latham thinks you are well equipped to work with us to find your brother."

"That's what I've hoped all along, sir."

"So long as we're all on the same page." Johannes nodded vigorously. "You'll be the in-country contact, then. If they find him, they'll notify you immediately and work with you to determine what the situation is. Whether he's really a Nazi or just caught up in all this, CENTCOM will be keeping track of your whereabouts as well."

"I understand."

"They'll keep me in the loop back here and I'll let Paul know if anything happens. But we'll try. We'll see what we can do."

"That's all we ask," Paul said.

Mr. Bello stood and reached for Johannes's hand. "I hope it all works out for you, son. I hope you stay safe. We all appreciate your service."

"Thank you."

"Paul can take you home or wherever you need to go after I talk to him alone for a minute. You can just wait in the parlor. He won't be long."

"Of course."

Mr. Bello closed the door to the study. "I just wanted to let you know—the fact that he's had special training limits where he can be assigned. I still might be able to get him in at the new headquarters in Frankfurt—that he speaks German is a plus there, of course—but they're going to want him wherever they can best use him. The only thing I can guarantee is they won't send him to the Pacific, even after the surrender; his training has pretty much assured him that.

"It's more complicated. I understand."

"He's got a good head on his shoulders. I can see that. Let's hope it keeps him out of trouble."

"Let's hope," Paul said, moving toward the door.

"At least we'll be able to keep an eye on him. That's something you can take back to his mother. Henry Latham himself will keep him in his sights."

"Indeed. Thank you," Paul said as he let himself out, although he wasn't sure he was taking anything back to Julia right now, except Johannes, and he was dropping him off at the end of the street.

They sat in the car in Mr. Bello's garage. "Does your mother know you've had this special training?"

Johannes shook his head. "I couldn't tell anyone. I'm surprised he knows about it."

"Well, there doesn't seem to be much Mr. Bello doesn't know. All the same, it does sound like he can help. Getting your brother on that list."

Johannes nodded. "I'll take anything I can get."

Paul put the car in gear. They'd be at Julia's street in a matter of minutes, but he wasn't ready to say goodbye yet—especially since he didn't know when he'd see this boy again, or his mother. "Do you fancy stopping off for a soda before we go home?"

"I don't see why not." Johannes shrugged. "As long as I'm not too late. She'll get suspicious."

"Just something quick, then."

"Order whatever you want. Doesn't have to be just a soda. You're still a growing lad."

They were at Eddie's—he hated being so secretive but if they stopped in at Merkens someone might see them together.

"Mama's been feeding me well. But I wouldn't mind a banana split."

"Go ahead, then. I don't imagine you get a lot of banana splits in the army."

"No. But it's not so bad. There was a guy at Camp Ritchie who was a chef at some big hotel in New York. I think it was the Waldorf. Anyway, they do the best they can."

The waitress arrived. "A banana split," Johannes said, "and an egg cream. Chocolate."

"Just a coffee, that's all," Paul said.

"I miss egg creams," Johannes said. "Looks like I'm going to be missing them for a long time. Gotta get my fill."

Paul smiled. "Your mother's very fond of them as well."

Johannes nodded. "Vanilla, though." Paul noticed he had a tendency to tilt his head to one side or another as he spoke. The effect was self-effacing—and rather endearing. This was Julia's son, he reminded himself. He *would* be endearing. He could picture him even, as a young boy. How could a father leave a son like this? How could any father leave his child? But he knew as well as anyone that they did it all the time.

"Johannes, I really am very fond of your mother. Quite fond. But I'm not doing this so she feels she owes me anything. Or that you do. I just want to help."

Johannes eyed him. "She likes to think she can take care of herself." He sighed. "We all need help sometimes."

"It must have been hard. Growing up. After what happened."

"It was," Johannes admitted, staring intently at a chip on the table. "She tried to make it better, and she did. Her and Aunt Lena. I didn't want for anything really. Well, at least not anything physical."

"I'm sorry for what I said. About wanting to kill your father."

Johannes gave a little laugh. "I'm sure you're not the only one."

"Still, he is your father."

"I barely remember him."

"My father left, too, when I was young," Paul added. "It does leave a hole."

Johannes was quiet for a moment, taking this in. "Does it ever go away?" he asked finally.

"No," Paul said simply. "It never does. But it becomes easier to bear. Or at least, that's been my experience." It wasn't long before the food came.

"How long have you been seeing my mother?" Johannes

said, after taking a sip of the egg cream to wash down his first spoonful of ice cream.

"Only a few months. January. It feels as if time has stopped since then. I guess it has."

"There have been other men who were interested. When I was in second grade, the man who ran the fruit stand sent her flowers for some time. Aunt Lena always wondered why he didn't just send fruit; it was more practical. But Mama must have had a talk with him because eventually he stopped, although he was always polite to us after that. Mr. Winczyk at the butcher's used to give her extra cuts of meat and wink at her as he took her order. I think it embarrassed her—she sent me to the butcher's as soon as I was old enough. But she never went out on a single date after my father left. That I know of."

"I should be honored then."

"There's something about you. Something especially sincere. And kind," he added. "I'm sure the accent helps too."

Paul laughed. "Well, thank you. I'm glad to hear I make a good impression. I'm sure she'd be upset to find out all this has been going on behind her back. Right now it seems best though. I don't want her to feel any pressure. Like I said, I just want to help. It's not often the opportunity to make a terrible thing better, perhaps, just falls into your lap."

Johannes shrugged. "We can lay it all on Mrs. Sciorra if we have to. It was her idea anyway. Besides, Mama wouldn't hold anything against Mrs. Sciorra. At least not for long."

Paul raised his coffee cup. "To Mrs. Sciorra."

Johannes raised his glass. "To Mrs. Sciorra, and to making terrible things better. As many of them as possible."

"Indeed," Paul said. "That covers quite a bit."

"It has to."

"Good luck," Paul told him as he dropped Johannes off at the end of the street. "And keep on the straight and narrow. You've got a congressman looking over your shoulder now. You know where to find me if you need anything."

"I will," Johannes said, ducking out of the car. "And after all of this is over, I will find you. Whatever happens."

Paul watched him walk up the street, loping as if he still hadn't quite gained full control of his long legs, his chin tilted down ever so slightly, as he took the steps up to Julia's enclosed porch.

Whatever else happens, Father, he found himself thinking as Johannes disappeared behind the door, *I hope you can find it in yourself to at least bring that one back home.*

FRANKFURT, GERMANY

Late April 1945

Sometimes at night, when Johannes was restless and could not sleep for all the strangeness around him in this unfamiliar, demolished landscape, he would reach under the cot and grope through his duffel bag for the blue velvet sack that held the napkin ring. Holding it settled him, steadied him like holding a portal between the past and a possible future.

Here. I've been keeping this for you all this time.

The first time he saw the napkin ring he had been sitting on Aunt Lena's bed as she rifled through her bureau for her gloves. The royal blue velvet flashed a rich contrast to the plain white slips and underwear in her top drawer. He'd wondered about it but kept silent; she was in a hurry to get them to school and work and it never paid to ask Aunt Lena a question when she was in a hurry.

He watched her pin her stiff white nurse's cap to her hair, dark blonde waves cut to her chin. She turned to face him. "Are you ready? Do you have your satchel? Go get your coat."

Johannes nodded and climbed off the green chenille bedspread, wondering as he pulled his coat on in front of the hall rack: What could Aunt Lena be keeping in such a bag? How long had it been there? He had never seen it before.

He was quiet as they walked to school, thinking about how this must be a clue to the mystery of Aunt Lena's life, like the kinds of clues Sherlock Holmes puzzled over on the radio. All day in school he considered the bag's contents, staring out the window of his second-grade classroom at the playground, the hopscotch court, the basketball net, but seeing instead a sparkling diamond or sapphire the size of a walnut—perhaps his aunt was not really a nurse, perhaps that was just her cover.

Perhaps she was a gem smuggler…. Or perhaps the bag contained a code reader. Yes. A code reader. That was it. Aunt Lena was a spy for the U.S. government, translating code.

By the time his mother met him at the school's iron gates, Johannes had considered that Aunt Lena could be a top-secret scientist, with the antidote for polio or malaria nestled in a bottle in the blue bag. Or maybe she was one of the mysterious turbaned women at Coney Island, tapping her fortune-telling cards out of a velvet drawstring sack.

He'd tried to slip unnoticed into Aunt Lena's room while his mother cooked dinner, but it was almost impossible; her door was in direct view of the kitchen. Finally, after the meal, with his mother at the kitchen sink and his aunt settled on the sofa listening to *The Eddie Cantor Show*, he tiptoed down the hall as if to go to his own room and stopped instead at his aunt's, concentrating all his energy on turning the cut-glass doorknob without a sound.

Bringing her door as close to the latch as he could without risking the noise of shutting it, Johannes stretched one leg across the wood floor from the doorway to the black carpet that led to the dresser, then the other, and tiptoed soundlessly the rest of the way. He tried not to look at himself in the mirror as he pulled at the drawer; it was wrong to look through someone else's belongings. But he had to know what was in that sack.

He untied the drawstring. The velvet was thin and stiff, the outside of the bag marked, upon closer inspection, in gold: *Holcomb and Sons, Fine Jewelers*. Johannes reached inside and pulled out a heavy silver napkin ring just like his own, carved all around with curlicues and leaves and stamped with seashells.

He held it up to the pool of light from the milky white glass lamp on Aunt Lena's dresser. At the top of the ring, where his own bore a bear curved around his initial, this ring featured two figures sitting atop a branch—a tiny, perfectly carved cherub reaching out to enfold an even tinier, precisely rendered squirrel nibbling a nut beside him. Protected by the bag, the silver still gleamed.

"John! What do you think you're doing?"

Running his finger over the top of the cherub's curls, he hadn't heard any noise in the hallway. Instantly his hands, one still holding the napkin ring and knocking it against the edge of the dresser, went to his side.

"I just…I saw the bag this morning and I really wanted to know what was inside!" He prayed his mother couldn't hear them over the dishes; she'd be so disappointed. Nothing was worse than his mother's chin tilted toward her collarbone in disappointment. Not even Aunt Lena's wrath.

To his surprise, Aunt Lena put her finger to her mouth and closed the door. "Shh, I don't want your mother to hear." She sat down at the edge of the bed. "Why didn't you just ask?"

Johannes shrugged. He was afraid to, of course, but he would not tell her that.

"It's a napkin ring," she told him. "It was for Nicholas. I bought it for his christening, just like I bought you yours. But I never got to give it to him. I didn't want your mother to find out about it. It would just upset her." She sighed. "Many times I've thought about selling it but I've never been able to bring myself to do it."

"Maybe you're saving it," Johannes offered. "For when Nicholas comes back."

Aunt Lena shook her head. Her dark green eyes were sad but she would not look at him. "I wish your mother would not fill your head with such ideas."

"She doesn't. We don't talk about it. You said not to," he reminded her. "She hasn't spoken of Nicholas in a long time. But that doesn't mean we don't think about it. Don't you want us to find him?"

Johannes flinched with regret as soon as the words came out. It would not do to talk this way to a grown-up. No, it would not.

Aunt Lena sat on the edge of the bed and took his face in her soft hands. Johannes breathed in the scent of the rose hand cream she smoothed on every night as she listened to the radio.

If his aunt and his mother had anything in common, Johannes thought, it was their lovely, powder-soft hands.

"Johannes." She never called him Johannes. "You will be disappointed. So disappointed. I am just trying to protect you. What happened has happened. It's best now to just lead your life. Try to forget."

"But I can't," he protested.

"You must try."

Johannes was silent. He'd never even known he'd wanted a brother until he'd had one. Of course, everyone at school had brothers and sisters. And fathers. He was certain he was the only one who did not. And no one knew he'd once had both. No one could know. Aunt Lena did not seem to understand how desperately you could want something back, even if you'd only had it for a little while.

"It is very beautiful," he said. "Especially the squirrel."

"It came from the same shop as yours. They were together on the shelf, behind the glass. I picked out yours, with the bear, first of course. And then, after Nicholas came, I went back and this one was still there."

"They must be a set."

"I don't know," Aunt Lena said. She seemed about to say something else but she paused, closing her mouth for a moment. "I tell you what," she said finally. She reached out and took his hand. "I will let you have it if it can be our secret. If you promise never to tell your mother, never to let her find it."

He nodded and felt the ring's concentrated weight.

"Perhaps," she said aloud, as if to herself, "a small keepsake will help you get past it. But it must be our secret."

Johannes understood. It was just like the other secrets they kept between themselves, like the lollipop she always bought him from Merkens on the way home from the playground, even though she complained it was his mother who let him have too many sweets.

Johannes slid the napkin ring back into its sack and turned toward the door.

"What do you say?" Aunt Lena was right behind him.

"Thank you," he whispered, looking both ways to make sure the hallway was empty before turning toward his room.

The barracks were dark, but he was used to holding the napkin ring in the darkness, had memorized the tiny pointed tips of the leaves under his fingers, the smooth contours of the squirrel's tail. The bag still smelled faintly of the black licorice tin he'd kept it in under his bed at home. He'd kept his promise, kept it hidden from his mother all those years. Years of imagining holding it out to his brother, whose face he never could see but whose body he felt sure grew apace with his own.

He preferred it, actually, to his own, to the bear curled around the silver oval stamped with a J. A cherub—a little boy, really—sitting beside a docile squirrel was much more interesting. He named them: Nicholas, of course, for the boy and Frederick for the squirrel. When he was very young, he imagined that Frederick could talk and would tell him all about his adventures in Forest Park. Eventually the idea of Frederick faded as he grew older and understood, wistfully, that there could be no such things as talking squirrels. But little boys, little brothers were real.

"This is your little brother, Johannes," his mother had said to him once as he peered at the swaddled pink creature in her arms. "He will always need you to look out for him."

At that moment, he remembered, Nicholas had yawned and his mother had smiled down on him in such a way that his heart burned for a moment. Why did they need another baby? Didn't he make his mother happy enough? She'd never even asked him if he'd wanted someone to take care of.

"Even after Mama and Papa are gone, you will always have each other. Always."

After Nicholas was gone, he'd been so ashamed of that moment, of the one time he'd thought maybe he hadn't wanted a little brother after all. Grudgingly he'd grown used to the rhythms of life with this utterly helpless being, who seemed to require an enormous amount of attending to just to keep him fed and happy, as well as an enormous amount of quiet despite the constant baby noise he made, the snuffling and sometimes, the wailing. Then suddenly, strangely, it was all over and just when there was no need to keep silent, the world went quieter than ever.

As he passed the heavy silver ring back and forth in his hands, he remembered watching Nicholas kicking on his mother's bed, before Helene had had a chance to shoo him away. He remembered his brother's dark hair and eyes, his unblinking stare.

"See," his mother would say, "already he knows you are his big brother. Already he knows he should look up to you."

Growing up, his friend Joey had complained bitterly when his little brother, Andrew, wanted to follow them wherever they went. "You know," he'd tell Johannes, "we don't have to always let him tag along."

Sometimes Joey would try to hide, to knock Andrew off their trail, but Johannes would do something obvious, like pretending to sneeze or sticking his hand out from the side of the handball court they were hiding behind, to give them away.

"What're you guys doing?" Andrew would always say hopefully when he found them, as if they'd never been hiding, as if they'd been waiting there all along. "Can I play too?"

Three years younger, Andrew struggled to keep up; Joey made him watch when they played handball, claiming he wasn't good enough to play with them.

"But how will I be good enough," Andrew always muttered, tossing his own ball back and forth in his hands and pacing on the sidelines, "if you never let me play?"

It felt good, Johannes thought, when they let him in on one of their games, when Joey relented and let him play army with them in the park. Even though they were always the Generals and Andrew perpetually relegated to Private, he was always so grateful just to be included.

Nicholas would have been younger still.

Would Johannes have let him join them?

You must always look out for your brother.

Tomorrow they would process the new POWs, these men who had sent boys into fire, secure them somehow in an enormous one-story building with no furniture, a giant drafty space surrounded by mud and a freshly dug latrine. He would try not to look into their eyes, just as he had averted his gaze from the small band of men they had recently processed; men, who had been caught escaping from Dachau just after they'd set fire to a building with hundreds of Jewish prisoners still inside. The stories coming back from the camps were difficult to stomach, difficult to believe had he not seen the anguished faces of his fellow soldiers telling him about it—as they seemed to need to do, over and over again, after the Dachau POWs were secure in the barracks, describing what they'd seen as if only telling it could prevent it from being real.

Tomorrow night he might have to listen to someone waving his stein in the air, telling him about the little brothers sent out for slaughter. But tonight, as long as he held his talisman, felt its weight in his palm, Nicholas was alive somewhere, still.

QUEENS, NY
April 1945

Dear Johannes,

I hope you had a good crossing. I didn't want to tell you this before you left, but the open sea has never agreed with me. You probably don't remember, but when you were a toddler and we sailed home to visit Grandmother and Grandfather Kruse, I was so sick. I spent most of the voyage in the cabin, while your father walked you around and around the ship. And when he and I came to America the first time, it was the same. I would not wish that sickness on anyone, let alone you. It is such a miserable feeling and there is nothing to be done for it until you reach land.

I saw Mr. Merkens the other day. He says hello and to take care of yourself. Perhaps if you will not listen to me, you will listen to him. I hope, if you are where you said you would be, that you are not taking any undue risks. According to the news reports, victory is close, but that does not reassure me that you are out of danger. Nothing will assure me that you are out of danger until you are home again and I can put my arms around you and you can start living the life you were meant to live. The closer victory is, the more desperate the vanquished will become, or so they say. Every day I close the papers, full of their awful news, and tell myself I should stop reading them. But how can I when my son's fate, when both my sons' fates, hangs on the news? Johannes, you are all I have. I know it is selfish of me to burden you with this, but you already know.

Aunt Lena writes that she is very busy; the soldiers are pouring in from the Pacific theater with considerable wounds. Sometimes she works for weeks without a day off; she says she hardly knows what it's like outside anymore.

She is very impressed with the number of men that have been saved in this war. She says the field hospitals have improved by leaps and bounds from the Great War, and you know how difficult it is to impress Aunt Lena. But I imagine she writes with such news to you as well and I imagine she also reminds you to stay safe.

Mrs. Sciorra sends her love. We're still shorthanded at the bakery, but I am happy to pitch in. I am not so busy with the pastries, as you can imagine. I miss the sugar work but I am keeping my hand in. I practice, so when this is all over I will be able to pick it right back up. When you come home, Johannes, we will have a party and a big cake that will be so rich with sugar and butter and eggs, you will hardly be able to stand it. Finally put some more meat on those bones. You seem skinnier every time I see you. Aunt Lena would have been horrified this last time. We'll have to fatten you up before she sees you or she'll take General Eisenhower to task herself.

Johannes, you are such a good boy, you always have been. But I worry your desire to find Nicholas will cloud your judgment, send you to places where you should not be, put you in harm's way. Let the Red Cross do their job and you can do yours. I have been so spoiled with you serving at home these past years. Dreading the day they would send you over; praying that somehow it would never come. Johannes, you know I want to find Nicholas; I always have, but please understand how much I need you to come home safe.

I will write again soon. All my love,

Mama

Dear Judy,

How often I think of you these days, how long my thoughts of you have kept me going. Of you, and Papa. I think of the woman who taught me to read and write, who taught me English and history and science and mathematics, and I think about how that woman had already lost her husband and son when I met her. Back then, of course, it hardly mattered to the mind of a child except that those facts made you mysterious, romantic even. But later it would matter so much.

Ever since Robert left, ever since I lost Nicholas, I would close my eyes and see your face, your broad, beautiful face, your deep blue eyes ringed by smile lines, delicate half stars. Smile lines, Judy. How could you smile after what you had lost? But you did.

Perhaps we saved each other; perhaps I received the love that you could not give to your son, but I received it gladly and without a second thought. Who knew how much I would have to borrow your strength, too, after you were gone. If Mrs. Stephens could survive, then somehow so could I.

You will never know how many times your example got me out of bed. Mrs. Stephens could do it. Mrs. Stephens could do it and so must I.

But then I had a son at home. I had Johannes. Judy, I don't know what I will do if I lose him now too. Is this how it is meant to be for me? Because I don't think I can bear that. And so I must invoke your face again, although like Papa's it has faded, like a blurred photograph now, an incandescent ball of white light. I tell myself, Judy lost everything and still she lived on.

I only wish, now that I am a grown woman and no longer a child, I could ask you how. After your son left this world, after your husband. How did you grieve? Did you take to your bed? Did you pound your fists against your mattress in the night, did you stain your pillows down to the feathers with tears and then rise? Or did you swallow back your pain like a burning coal, swallow it over and over until the hot flame gave way to smoldering ash? Were you swallowing it still when you came to us in Stuttgart? I wish I knew.

Mrs. Sciorra sees it in my face, sees the dark predawn hours when I lie in bed, heart pounding, eyes wide and dry, wishing for the obliteration of sleep. "Julia, Julia," she says, taking my hand. "He is safe, as far as you know he is safe. You are making yourself crazy." And she tries to send me home early for some sleep.

She does not understand. I lost Nicholas out of the blue. I lost Nicholas because I was not paying attention. Now I cannot stop paying attention, as if somehow my galloping heart and sleepless nights are keeping Johannes alive.

And then, in the midst of this, innocent and bewildered, is Paul. Or was. So tempting; I felt it too, I felt it so much that I almost forgot how easy it was to lose so much. Johannes reminded me. Johannes came back and I remembered how much I had lost and how much I still had left to lose. Losing Paul was the only thing I could control.

Even though the phone rang and rang each night and I had to hold myself still, my nails digging half-moons into my arms through my sleeves, I did not answer it. I could not take on more to lose.

Johannes reminded me. I could not be happy even for a moment. I might stop paying attention. Bad things have always happened when I stopped paying attention, Judy. Papa. Nicholas. You know, yourself, it's true.

Johannes would never tell his mother this, he might not ever tell anyone this, but he felt comfortable in-country, in spite of the chaos. He fit somehow, among these people, these men, mostly POWs who seemed grateful to them, who seemed happy to be out of the fighting. The most resistant ones, he'd heard, committed suicide rather than be captured or lived in marauding packs—wolf packs, they called them—in the forests.

Sometimes, when he was on night watch, when he heard them murmuring in German amongst themselves, it reminded him of when he was young, listening to his parents talking to each other in the living room while he lay snug in his bed, drifting away to sleep. When it was just the three of them. Once Nicholas was born, there was little time for talking, with Mama recovering and Helene flitting over her and the baby. That was his strongest memory of Helene. Her restlessness. It made him nervous, the way she'd eyed him suspiciously whenever she'd brought Nicholas into their parents' bedroom while he sat with his mother.

"Why don't you go play?" Helene would suggest. "Somewhere you won't disturb the baby."

"He can stay," he remembered his mother telling her. "He'll be quiet. Won't you, Johannes?"

"If you insist," Helene replied.

He could still remember the day his mother came home from the hospital with Nicholas. It alarmed him at first; she had been in a wheelchair.

"It's okay," his mother had whispered when she saw the look on his face. "It won't be for long. I just need to rest." And then, "I'm still here. Still your mama."

He peered at the tiny red bundle in her arms. "So that's my

brother," he said. Nicholas didn't look like much of anything yet.

"That's your brother," she told him.

"When will he be old enough to play with my trains?"

"Someday," his mother told him. "Someday you'll be playing together and you'll hardly be able to remember when he was a helpless little baby, like this."

"He'll have to be careful with my trains."

"I'm sure he will. You'll show him how."

"That's enough." Helene took him by the shoulders and brought him back a few inches. "Not so close."

All there was for Johannes to do was watch and wait. They had built the kitchen and the guard's quarters but now the building was on hold until they received further instructions.

"Why?" they all wanted to know. "We're losing time. We're going to be overrun with prisoners. We already are." The British had just stopped taking them. They were full up, sending men home or over to the French zone or the American.

While he waited, Johannes sat in a room with a handful of other men from Camp Ritchie huddled around a phone, ready to serve as translators when the need arose, which it did often enough. On breaks he studied the lists of prisoners who had already been processed, with their names and dates of birth, hometowns and dates of capture, and where they had been sent. The surname Kruse had appeared on several of these lists, but never combined with the name Nicholas or even Robert.

He bunked in a room with two other translators from Camp Ritchie in a boarding house that had been commandeered for them. The boarding house was comfortable, clean, and whole, but the buildings on either side were just facades fronting piles of bricks and gray rubble. Everywhere in Frankfurt looked like that, although he had had been told that compared to some of the other cities, it had received far less damage. It was hard for Johannes to imagine much worse—all of Frankfurt looked as if a giant had thrown a temper tantrum, stomping to bits whatever was in his path and yet leaving some buildings completely untouched.

"Oh, there are plenty of places worse than this," Sergeant Strauss, one of his roommates, told him. "You'll see."

Most of their translating was done for the wounded and captured, in the field hospitals nearby or for German officers making an official surrender. It wasn't until his third week in Germany that Johannes was called to an interrogation over in Bonn, in the British territory, a high-ranking official who had once overseen the production of land mine maps in Berlin and who was believed to know where whole caches of them were located throughout the country.

In training, Johannes had received his lowest grade, an 81, in interrogation. His commanders always said he needed to be meaner, to be more tough, but no matter how much he tried, he didn't seem to have it in him.

"All right then," they told him. "You'll have to be the good guy."

So he was the one with the chocolate and cigarettes making small talk while his partner threatened to turn the prisoner over to the Russians or held a gun to his head.

He was usually partnered with Sergeant Reynolds, who had been a couple of classes behind him at Camp Ritchie but who'd been overseas longer. Everyone, it seemed to Johannes, had been overseas longer, thanks to his construction prowess.

This time it was the chocolate and cigarettes that worked in the end, though. Truthfully, the *unteroffizier*—a sergeant just like they were—seemed as though he just wanted to get it over with. He wasn't SS; he was just good at making maps.

The whole meeting took less than thirty minutes.

They weren't expected back until the end of the day, so they grabbed lunch at a mess tent and Reynolds said he'd take him up the road to show him Koln.

They were about halfway home when they started taking sniper fire. Reynolds, who was driving, picked up speed but one of the bullets must have hit a front tire because they were suddenly weaving all over the road and then the windshield was shattered by one that went right between them.

Reynolds pulled over. "Get behind! Dammit. It's flat."

They crouched behind the jeep. "What do we do now?" Johannes asked, his heart racing. He'd been under fake fire dozens of times in maneuvers, but this was completely different.

"Give me a second to think."

It was silent for several moments. A light, warm wind threshed a green field, with thick woods beyond it where the fire seemed to be coming from.

"It stopped," Johannes said.

"They're just waiting for us to try and change the tire," Reynolds hissed.

He crouched as still as he could while his legs shook so hard he had to hold on to the jeep to stay on his feet.

From the side of the jeep, Reynolds reached into the back and pulled out the bag of maps, which brought on another succession of bullets and then two louder shots. Then silence.

"Those last two sounded like a pistol," Johannes whispered. "Either it's the same guy or there's another one."

Reynolds smoothed out a map on the grass. "What was the last sign we passed?"

"Rosrath."

Reynolds frowned. "Shit."

"What?"

"We can't change the tire. We have to drive on the rim; I'm trying to figure out if we should go back or press on."

"But there's two of them now," Johannes said.

"You want to wait it out until one of them gets on the other side of us and there's nowhere to go? If we can step on the gas, we can get out of here—according to this, there's a French field hospital a couple of miles ahead. If we can make it that far, we can change the tire there. Or at least get out of here."

"No, I just—" Johannes had no intention of disagreeing. Reynolds outranked him and, besides, he obviously knew what he was doing. "I was just pointing it out."

"I'm going to get in from this side and then you're going to come right after me. On the count of three." Reynolds adjusted his helmet; his face was streaked with sweat and dirt.

"One. Two. Three."

By the time Johannes was in the seat the jeep was already started and they were peeling out.

"Hang on," Reynolds yelled. "Hang on!"

They sped forward, still weaving. Johannes's heart pounded in anticipation of the gunfire, but nothing came. Eventually Reynolds slowed down and was able to gain better control so they weren't all over the road.

They were at least a mile away before Johannes could speak. "What happened? It just stopped."

"Shit if I know. I don't care as long as we're out of there."

"Should we try to change it now?"

"Not unless we have to. I want to get to the hospital."

They drove the rest of the way in silence, Johannes waiting for the fist gripping his heart to let go. He'd know soon if it was possible to die of fright.

By the time they got to the hospital, located in an abandoned monastery just off the road, the rim was so bent they couldn't get the new tire on. They had to call headquarters and have them send another jeep.

"Was that your first sniper fire?" Reynolds asked. They sat on a stone bench in front of the hospital.

"Real fire, yes."

"You think the field training will prepare you for it but it never does, not entirely. Still, I haven't taken fire since February. I thought they had the route cleared out. I guess there's still pockets of resistance."

"You've taken fire while driving before?"

"A couple times," Reynolds allowed. "And I'm still here, although I did have a couple bullets ricochet off my helmet a few times. It's harder to hit a jeep; that's why you have to keep moving. Fortunately, it'll be dark by the time we leave. We shouldn't have anything to worry about the rest of the way."

Johannes was relieved but he thought better of saying so.

"Anyway, the most important thing is that we're coming back with these." He patted the bag with the maps on the bench between them. "If you ask me, we have a lot more to worry about with land mines than with snipers."

"I guess," Johannes tried to say casually as he felt his stomach drop into his pelvis.

"Oh yeah." Reynolds whistled. "Half this country is booby-trapped."

Johannes fell asleep instantly that night, only to wake to the sounds of a group of men out in the street singing a loud, drunken version of "Happy Birthday." He sat up and looked around, but none of the others were awake. He blinked out the window at the moonlight, watching the men slink away together, like a many-legged rodent, into the arched walkway that led into the building across the street. Then he remembered. He'd been dreaming of being shot, of lying at the edge of a large field alone, unable to move.

I haven't been shot, he told himself. *I haven't been shot.* He felt the sheets beneath his palms, touched the hard edge of the bedpost.

In his dream, there had been a large basket in the center of the field, swathed in a halo of barbed wire—a giant, jagged silver nest with cries coming from it.

A baby, crying.

All he could do was reach out his hand.

PART III

FRANKFURT, GERMANY

May 1945

There was plenty of translation to do at headquarters; it would have been easy to stay close to Frankfurt, but two days later there was another surrender scheduled at Stuttgart, an entire division, so a large group of them were needed. Johannes volunteered; it was best to get back on the road again. Also, Stuttgart was where his grandparents had lived. He could barely remember the time he had visited; he had been only a toddler, but he wanted to see it again.

The surrender took place at the outskirts of Stuttgart, in Kappelburg. The sun shone down on the roads, on their caravan, on the legions of displaced persons walking in the other direction, toward Frankfurt. Were his family among them? The family that had turned their backs on him and his mother. He watched the faces filing past them until they became one long unrecognizable throng.

The countryside was as green and gold still, among the ruins, as he had remembered it. So many different colors of green, he recalled, through the haze of memory, in such contrast to the variations of gray in the city where he lived. Standing on the patio overlooking his grandparents' garden was the first time he remembered being able to see so far in the distance. Aunt Marie Therese, who was so young and smiling, like his mother, had taken his hand. Had she really done this or had he just dreamed it? He did not know. Sometimes he went to the village where his grandparents had lived in his dreams.

They passed the train station in the center of the city on the way back to headquarters, the walls thickly papered with the words of people searching for family members, just like the station in Frankfurt.

The first time he'd seen such a wall, a wave of nausea washed over him and he'd had to reach for a lamppost to steady himself as the names shimmered in front of him like a mirage. The ocean of loss knocked him back at first, but he was beginning to grow used to it. In fact, he found a strange comfort in being among so many other families that had been torn apart. Everyone was looking for someone. Sometimes, in the cries, the reunions, the embraces in the street, they even found them.

Dear Mama,

Today begins my third week here. I remain well; you have nothing to worry about. In fact, there has been a pause in our work so I'm a little bored. Of course, I cannot reveal my location but I hope you take comfort in this. We are told it won't last long, that construction should pick up again but in the meantime I spend hours reading telephone directories and poring over lists of captured. If I don't need glasses now, I surely will by the time this is over. No real leads yet, though. In retrospect, this may not have been the best time to begin our search, but I did not have much control over that. We take what we can get. I hope you are sleeping better and that you are receiving these letters and they help you to feel some ease. That is my purpose, that and to send you my love.

Always,

Johannes

Orders came the next day that he would stay with the translation pool at Frankfurt, that he had been dismissed from building POW barracks. There were too many prisoners to build barracks—instead, they were going to try to contain them in field camps fortified by barbed wire. Erecting such fences was straightforward enough. His German skills were far more in demand.

Too many prisoners. Too many prisoners. He tried not to let this discourage him. Perhaps he could visit these camps. Surely they needed personnel who spoke German. He'd take it up with the CO the next time he saw him.

He and Reynolds were playing cards, waiting for their next assignment that morning when Colonel Newbern strode in. They stood at their chairs and saluted him.

"Sergeant Kruse," he began after he returned their salute. He looked puzzled.

"Yes, sir."

"You have a brother? In Germany. In the German army. CENTCOM has been looking for him?"

A bolt of ice spread from the base of Johannes's spine up his backbone. He gripped the back of the chair.

"Sit down, son," the colonel said. "Before you pass out. You're white as a ghost. Well, it seems they found him."

"They found him?" Johannes lowered himself into the chair.

"You knew about this brother?"

Johannes nodded. "I haven't seen him since he was a baby. Is he all right? How did they find him?"

"I don't know a lot of details. All I know is he was wounded and he came up on some list."

"Wounded. How bad? Where?" In this sea of men, Johannes had already begun to accept that he would only be able to find his brother if he was wounded. He took a deep breath. *Please, not too badly. Please, not too badly. Please.*

"It's pretty serious. He took a bullet under the rib. Shot by one of his own."

"One of his own. Why would they shoot him?"

"He was trying to surrender to an American convoy outside Koln. They don't take too kindly to solitary surrenders in the Wehrmacht. Anyway, that's the extent of what I know, besides that they want you at the hospital in Koblenz stat. I told them I'd get you there."

"Outside Koln? We were just there last week!"

"Well, you're going back. To Koblenz, anyway."

Reynolds stood up. "I'll drive him."

"We need you here," the colonel said. "I've got a driver from the jeep pool waiting out front."

"Let me just run to my room—I need to grab a few things."

"If you can be fast."

"I know exactly where they are. Five minutes."

Besides the napkin ring, he slipped a photograph of his mother and a photograph of Nicholas as a newborn in the hospital into his pocket. His mother had given it to him as he packed his bags before his last deployment. "It might be useful," she said, "if you find him."

"I've never seen this before." Nicholas's face was pinched in the photograph; he looked almost angry.

"He was just about to cry when they took it. He was hungry. But it might help him to see it. If he doesn't believe you."

He kept his hand over the photographs, keeping them safe as they drove over the winding roads to Koblenz. He wished Reynolds had been allowed to drive; he could have talked to him, gotten rid of some of his nervous energy. Reynolds knew a little about the situation. This driver was nice enough, but he was a stranger and he was all business.

"How long have you been in-country?" Johannes asked.

"Long enough," the driver answered. He didn't seem too happy to be making the trip either.

"Sorry to inconvenience you. Haven't been here quite a month myself."

"I make this trip all the time," he said. He was older than Johannes, or maybe he just looked older. He looked like he might have even been forty. "A replacement, huh?"

"Yes," Johannes told him. "I was building barracks in the States—I'm with the Engineer Corps. We were building them here. You know. Gotta have places to put people."

"Sure you do."

The sun was directly over the hills beyond them, glowing fiercely orange against a bright blue tent of sky. The forest, where they had taken sniper fire the week before, was now peaceful, a corridor of pines on either side. It was fine day. A fine day to be going to see his brother. Surely that was a good sign.

KOBLENZ, GERMANY

Allied Field Hospital

May 1945

"Breathe. Breathe. That's it. You've got to breathe." There was a nurse standing over him. Johannes gasped and gazed up at her as she came into focus, an auburn-haired woman with a dusting of freckles across her nose, smiling an ample smile now that he had apparently done his part. "You've just come out of anesthesia, Sergeant Kruse. You're at a hospital in Koblenz. You were in an accident. Your jeep hit a land mine. You've had surgery on your leg but they've managed to save it."

"What about the driver?"

"Corporal Mattox is still in surgery. His injuries were more extensive."

"My brother. I think my brother is also here in this hospital."

"I don't know about that, but I do know there are some officers waiting to talk to you here, when you're more awake. Perhaps they know more about it."

"My coat. The pocket."

"Your trousers had to be cut off, but we managed to save your coat. It's in a bag with your personal effects. It will be waiting for you at your bed, as soon as it's ready. I suppose you're in some discomfort, with the anesthesia wearing off. We've started you on a morphine drip so that should start to improve."

"Yes," he said. He had begun to notice a stabbing pain coming from his right side. "What happened?"

"You took a load of shrapnel just below your knee, but you're going to be all right. It could have been much worse."

Her face started to blur again; he couldn't tell if she was just stepping away but he could still hear her voice. "That's it. Rest now while we set about finding you a bed."

"Now that you're awake, why don't you try to sit up. The doctor is waiting to see you."

It was a different nurse this time; she spoke English with a French accent. She disappeared and then reappeared with a man with round glasses and short, wiry black hair. "Captain Addison." He reached for Johannes's hand, shook it, and pulled up a chair. "I operated on your leg. Let's see how the incision is coming along." He removed the bandages and inspected his work. "Lovely stitching if I do say so, though it was digging all the shrapnel out that was the chore. The femur was grazed but nothing you won't be able to overcome. You'll be up and around in a few days."

Johannes gave him a weak smile. It was good news, anyway. "I don't remember any of it. They say the driver is worse."

"He'll be okay. Captain Miller and Captain Birnbaum worked on him together; he had a lot of damage to the right side of his face and to his shoulder. He has a long road ahead of him, but he'll survive."

"That's good. Actually, we were on our way to this very hospital. If I'm in the one I think I am. I was coming to see my brother. Nicholas Kruse."

"I know. I operated on him too. As soon as I was finished, they told me that he was on a list of soldiers the army was looking for. I thought they wanted to arrest him at first but then they explained."

"How is he? They wouldn't tell me his condition, just that I needed to come here."

"Not as good, I'm afraid. He took a bullet that went through his spleen and clipped part of his upper abdomen. We couldn't save the spleen."

"Is he going to die?"

"The body can live without the spleen. It's possible but it's very difficult. It will depend on how he recovers. The first few hours after he wakes up will be very telling."

"When will he be awake?"

"He'll be sedated until tomorrow."

"Can I see him then?"

"We have a lot to discuss before that. There's another officer waiting to join me. Nurse Girard, please tell Major Riley he can come in now."

The nurse left and returned a moment later with a barrel-chested man with a continual squint, as if he was inclined to doubt everything he heard.

"Sergeant Kruse," Major Riley began, "I understand you've only been with us since early April. Shame this had to happen. From all accounts you were doing good work in Frankfurt."

"Yes, sir. But they had just taken me off construction detail. I was mostly working as a translator."

"Regardless. You were on your way here to see your brother, yes?"

"Nicholas Kruse, yes. I've been looking for him. I haven't actually seen him since he was a baby."

"Well, as you probably know, we were looking for him too. Or rather, he was on our master list. We didn't know any of the details until he turned up wounded and we started to investigate. Sergeant Kruse, it seems we have a situation on our hands. An American fighting for the Krauts who was wounded trying to surrender."

"And he is very seriously wounded," Captain Addison put in again. "Even when he wakes up, we need to be careful with him."

"He's barely eighteen," Johannes said. "I'm sure he was only just called up. In the Volksturm. It's not as if he was a career Nazi."

"We've done a little investigating, Sergeant Kruse," Major Riley said. "Your brother was in the Jungvolk, we know that. He was a leader, in fact. As a Ritchie boy, you must know all about the Jungvolk. So we have to find out a lot more about him, especially what he knows, before we figure out what to do with him."

"Every boy from ten to fourteen had to be in the Jungvolk; just as every male from fourteen to eighteen had to join in the

Hitlerjugend after that. They did not have a choice," Johannes said.

"Not every male had to be a *leader* in the Jungvolk," Major Riley said. "We'll figure all this out but we have to know who we're dealing with." He turned to Captain Addison. "When did you say he'd come to?"

"He's sedated until tomorrow. But we still have to be cautious. Perhaps you should let me speak to him with another translator first. A neutral party. Introduce him to this situation gradually." Johannes considered this. He wanted to see Nicholas as soon as possible, but it was probably best for Captain Addison to deliver the news first. After that, if he seems ready, Sergeant Kruse can see him. And then we'll contact you, Major Riley."

"Well, he'll have to talk to me eventually, whether he's ready or not."

Captain Addison nodded. "I recognize that. Just give us some time."

"Perhaps Sergeant Kruse can shed some light on a few things for us meanwhile," the major suggested.

"I will answer any questions you have, truthfully, to the best of my knowledge."

"As I understand it, you have always been aware of your brother, Nicholas Kruse, but he may not be aware of you, or of the fact that he was taken from his mother as an infant and brought here."

"That is true. I would be surprised if he was aware of that at all."

"And it was your father who took him and returned to his country of origin with him."

"Yes. He and the nurse. Helene. They ran away together and took him with them."

"And your father's name?"

"Robert. Robert Kruse."

"Robert Kruse. Well, we'll get a trace started on him immediately, but unless he's a prisoner or wounded, he may take some time to suss out. Do you have any idea where he might be living?"

"I don't know. We lost track of them immediately; my mother was never able to find him. But my grandparents lived in Stuttgart. They were quite a prominent family, actually. They owned a string of jewelry stores. My mother wrote to them for help soon after it happened, but they never responded."

"Stuttgart Kruses. Well, that will help. How did your brother manage to get on this list anyway?"

"I've always wanted to find him. My mother tried several times. I was connected with a congressman who knew about this list and said he could get him on it."

"Well, thank goodness for congressmen," Major Riley said. "Always willing to do their part and stick their noses where they don't belong."

QUEENS, NEW YORK

May 7, 1945

Julia looked up from the piecrust she was braiding. Mrs. Sciorra walked around the register to the front of the bakery. She was talking to someone. Julia's chest tightened. Paul.

She looked back down quickly. Probably he was just picking something up for Mrs. Bello. She would just keep her head down until he was gone.

"You have a visitor." Mrs. Sciorra stood in the doorway of the bakery workroom.

"Mrs. Sciorra, you can see I'm busy right now," Julia said evenly. She would not look up. "Tell him to call me."

"He says he has called you. You don't answer the phone."

What was he doing here? What did he want? "Mrs. Sciorra, please do not get involved in this. Besides, I'm in the middle of this lattice. I can't just drop it."

"I can finish the pie. Julia, trust me, you must talk to him. You must hear what he has to say. It's not what you think it is. He has news."

He had news? News was everywhere. Everyone had news.

Paul stood in the doorway of the workroom.

She tried not to look directly at him. That look in his eyes, always searching, would be her undoing.

"Come here to me." He held out her sweater. It was cold and windy for May. "Let's have a walk."

And his voice—so honeyed and smooth. Her arms, suddenly overcome with weakness, fell to her sides; if she had been carrying anything, she would have dropped it. She had been right not to look at him. His voice. She had missed his voice.

"Paul, I'm sorry." She stared at the floor. "I just—I can't."

"Julia, please. I have something I absolutely must tell you. It has nothing to do with us."

She hesitated. What could he possibly be talking about?

"It's about your son."

"Johannes?" She looked up. "What about Johannes?"

"It's about Nicholas. Please. Walk with me."

"Nicholas? What about Nicholas? How do you know about Nicholas?"

He lifted her sweater higher, an offering. She searched his face for disdain. Condescension. His cheeks were smooth and pink from the cool air and there was a gentle mournfulness in his eyes. Almost as if it were happening to someone else, as if she were a puppet on a string, Julia turned slightly and held out first one, then the other arm, and he adjusted her sweater over her shoulders. Her heart pounded. "Is he alive?"

"Yes. He's alive."

She let out a breath. "How do you know about Nicholas?"

"Mrs. Sciorra. We were both worried about you."

"What did she tell you?"

"Everything I didn't know. Julia, why didn't you tell me?"

"I meant to. But it just kept getting harder. I didn't want to ruin anything. And then Johannes came back. Regardless. What is it?"

He had taken her to a row of houses around the corner. They sat down on the first stoop.

"Mrs. Sciorra thought we should get Mr. Bello involved. That he might have friends who could help. And she was right. He does. Congressmen, even, who can do things a soldier can't, even a soldier right there on the ground."

"What do you mean?"

"Mr. Bello pulled some strings with Congressman Latham and got Nicholas on a list. A list of people the Allies were searching for. It went to all the POW camps, all the field hospitals. That was how they found him. And he is alive. But he's badly wounded. He's in a hospital in Germany."

"How badly? Will he live? What happened?"

"He was shot trying to surrender. The bullet destroyed his spleen and part of his stomach."

She sniffed. "He was trying to surrender?"

"Yes. Julia, there are people in the War Department who want to talk to you. They're coming up from Washington now. Mr. Bello wants me to bring you to his office first thing tomorrow morning."

"Am I in trouble? Is Nicholas in trouble? We did not do anything wrong."

"No, no. I imagine they will have more to tell us about his condition. And they have questions for you. This is all very complicated."

"He was surrendering," Julia said again.

"I know. A good sign, we can hope."

"What about Johannes? I must get word to Johannes. He can stop looking."

"Julia." Her hands, both hands, were shaking and he took them in his and then brought them slowly to his lips. "Julia, he knows. He's with Nicholas right now."

"He is? They are together?"

"Yes. As soon as they found him, they sent for Johannes."

"How did they know?"

"That was the plan. He was not far away; he was assigned to Frankfurt, and Nicholas was brought to a hospital in Koblenz."

"How do you know where he was? He couldn't even tell me in his letters."

"Mr. Bello has been keeping track of Johannes as well."

"That is good. Someone watching over Johannes too. Mr. Bello, I don't know how I will be able to thank him. But you knew all this? And I didn't? I'm his mother."

"We wanted to wait until we knew something, one way or another." He put his arms around her. "You're trembling."

"Of course I'm trembling." It was as if all the fear and worry that had been knitting her bones together all these years had suddenly been released and turned her into a shivering mass. "I'm grateful. But I still wish you hadn't kept this from me. All of you."

He took his coat off and draped it over her shoulders. "It's

a lot to take in." Julia nodded. Across the street a circle of children ignored them, bent over jacks. on the sidewalk. She felt
his arms around her, entwined her fingers in his own, and let
this settle her. "Julia, there's one more thing I have to tell you.
About Johannes."

She sat up. "What? What about Johannes? Say it, quickly!"

"I will. I will. Give me a chance. He's been wounded too,
Julia. It's not so bad. It's just his leg. But he's in the same hospital
as Nicholas. He was on his way to see him."

"His leg? What do you mean, his leg? How do you know it's
not so bad? How do I know you're telling me the truth?"

"All I know is what they're telling me, Julia. I would not lie
to you."

"People lie," Julia said. "Even white lies. Think of all you've
been keeping from me."

"You'll always hear the truth from me. From now on. You'll
hear the same thing from the War Department tomorrow. You
can ask them anything you want."

"I'm his mother. I should know these things before anyone."

"You'll probably get a telegram. Starting tomorrow, I imagine you'll be the first to know anything."

"I hope so." She rubbed her eyes. "Everything changes all
at once. In a single moment. Things I have been waiting for all
my life."

Paul sighed. "When things happen is not something people
like us ever seem destined to control."

"Paul, after everything. Why did you even do this?"

"Because Mrs. Sciorra asked me to. And because I wanted
to. Because I could. As soon as Mrs. Sciorra told me, as soon
as she said there was something I could do, I wanted to do it."

"No one has ever done anything like this for me."

"After Mrs. Sciorra told me, I couldn't stop thinking about
it. I couldn't imagine how someone could do that to anyone."

"You must think I'm a fool."

"No. He's bollocks, your ex, pardon me, but you were very
young. I wish you had trusted me enough to tell me the truth."

"Paul," she said gently. She didn't know how to make him understand. "It was hard enough to tell Mrs. Sciorra."

"Well, it's a good thing you told her, because otherwise none of this would be happening."

"So she knows—about all of this? The rest of it?"

He nodded. "She said to just take you home. And bring you in after we go to the Bellos' tomorrow."

"I can't believe it. You found him. Of all people. You."

"Well, Mr. Bello. And Congressman Latham. And the War Department. And Mrs. Sciorra."

"But also, you."

"Julia." Paul cleared his throat. "I want you to know that I did this because, well, I do love you, but really because I wanted you to have this piece of your life back, if it was possible. If I could have my daughter back, if there were any way I could do that, if I could have gone back in time, to when I was a young man, making foolish choices, I would have done it. But I can't. I made the choice not to insist, to walk away instead of standing up for myself. I wanted to make a different choice this time. To stand up for you. I wanted to do something, if I could." He paused before continuing. "But you don't owe me anything. If you still feel the same way, I'll just bow out after it's all settled."

"It was so hard the first time," she told him. "I don't know if I can give you up again."

KOBLENZ, GERMANY

May 1945

Captain Addison appeared at his bed with a wheelchair the next morning.

"How is he doing?" Johannes wanted to know.

"As well as can be expected, given his wounds. He's in a fragile state. You have to remember that."

Johannes nodded. "But you talked to him."

"I did."

"What did you tell him?"

The captain took a deep breath. "I told him where he was. What had happened to him. He remembered being shot. He remembered being carried off by the Americans. And then I told him about his family situation. His new family situation."

"And? Did he believe you? Does he believe you?"

"He's very confused. The drugs don't help. I showed him the orders from CENTCOM to find him."

"Did you tell him I was here?"

"I did."

"Does he want to see me?"

"*Want* might be a strong word at this juncture. He's agreed to speak with you."

Johannes slid the photos into his robe pocket for the journey. He would save the napkin ring for another time.

"I know this should be a private moment," Captain Addison said when they reached the room, "but I'd like to stay. Keep an eye on him, medically."

"Of course," Johannes said, his heart thrumming. He just wanted to get on the other side of that door.

"Herr Nicholas Kruse." Captain Addison pushed him ahead

in the wheelchair, through the door. "*Dein bruder. Unteroffizier Johannes Kruse.*"

They stared at one another. Johannes took in Nicholas's eyes, a rich chocolate brown, like Mama's. "*Ich sprech Deutsch. Ich erinnere mich an dich.*" *I speak German. I remember you.*

"*Ich haben einen bruder, sagen sie.*" Nicholas nodded slightly. "*Komm naher.*" *I have a brother, they say. Come closer.*

Johannes wheeled himself to the side of the bed. Nicholas did not seem able to lift his head. He regarded Johannes evenly.

"My mother is dead," Nicholas told him. "She has been dead for five years. Now they tell me I have another mother?"

"You were taken from her. She has been looking for you always. We both have."

"This makes no sense. Why would my papa do this? I do not understand." He looked away.

Johannes put the hospital photograph in his hands. "From when you were born."

Nicholas brought it to his face. He closed his eyes. "A baby. So. How do I know that is me?"

"Mama always told me that Papa said both of us would be too much for her to take care of alone. They took you, he said, because you would not remember. But it nearly killed her. Losing you." He gave Nicholas the other photograph. "That is Mama," he explained. "You look like her."

Nicholas stared. "So. My papa was very pale and blond. Like you. Does that mean you are his son? You look like half of the men in Germany."

"She is a kind woman. She was a wonderful mother."

"As was mine," Nicholas said, finally. "I miss her every day."

"Is Papa still alive?"

"I saw *my* papa not long ago. Our unit was near Bonn. I deserted them to see him. There were only three of us left anyway. I told him of my plan to surrender. Why wouldn't he tell me about all this then?"

"I don't know," Johannes said. "I don't know. Our grandparents? Are they still alive?"

Nicholas shook his head. "My grandparents died years ago. Before Mama. I don't know what or who you are talking about."

"I visited them once. Before you were born."

Nicholas made a face. "How do I know you are not making all this up? Or perhaps you have me confused with someone else."

"How did your mother die?"

"Breast cancer," Nicholas replied.

"I'm sorry," Johannes said.

Nicholas frowned and looked away. "My papa was a teacher. A physical science teacher at the gymnasium, until they closed the schools. He was strict. A very strict teacher and father." He paused. "But he took care of me and, most important," he glanced sidewise at Captain Addison, "he was not a Nazi. Not in his heart. None of us were. Yes, he saluted Herr Hitler every day, it was part of his job, but he did not believe in the cause. Neither did Mama. They never thought Hitler would last as long as he did. We did what we had to do to stay alive. Why are you all here asking these questions, making these insinuations about us? About my family?"

"I believe you did what you had to," Johannes said. "Nicholas, I remember Aunt Marie Therese. Do you remember her?"

Nicholas paused. Johannes thought he saw a flicker of recognition in his eyes. A tiny flicker; he was not sure. "Please go away. Just go away. I do not know who you are talking about. Stop trying to make me confess something I have not done, that my family has not done."

Captain Addison stepped forward. "Perhaps you need some rest now."

"Yes, rest," Nicholas said, "rest from this nightmare you have visited upon me."

QUEENS, NEW YORK

May 1945

They stood in the hallway after a silent ride to Julia's house. "If Nicholas had stayed with me," Julia observed, "he wouldn't even have been drafted. He's too young. He shouldn't have been in the middle of all this. He'd still be with me."

Paul nodded. "Do you want me to leave now? I can come by in the morning to fetch you."

"I'm sure Mrs. Bello needs you back with the car."

"Actually, she gave me the rest of the afternoon off."

"You can stay?"

"If you want me to."

"Yes." She went into the living room and switched on the radio.

Hours ago, the German general, Alfred Jodl, signed the formal documents of Germany's unconditional surrender to the Allies in Reims, France.

"To those people, Nicholas was a soldier." Julia sank into the sofa. Paul lowered himself into the armchair beside her. "A grown man. Not to me."

"Do you think there's a chance he knew about you?"

"I hope not. Robert would have to go to great lengths to explain that. What would he tell him? That he was unwanted? That I was an unfit mother?"

"But still you wanted to find him."

"And when I did, *I* would tell him."

"That he had two mothers."

"Yes," she said. "Later, that is what I would have told him. The first time, I simply planned to take him back. Lena was against it," she continued. "I got the better deal, she always said. She wasn't much for babies. She would rather have a house."

"Mrs. Sciorra told me."

Julia got up, went to her bedroom, and returned with the passbook. She handed it to Paul. "When I found him, I would give him this."

He glanced at the balance. "That would have gotten you pretty far."

"Me, yes." She fitted herself back into the corner of the sofa. "But then Johannes wanted to go. After what had happened, I was afraid to leave him for too long. Worried that he would think I wasn't coming back. I kept saving. Banks were failing all around us, but I kept my money in. The president of the bank himself promised it would not fail. And then, one day, it was all gone."

"Mrs. Sciorra told me that too. She still feels bad about it."

"She lost money too. Did she tell you that? Quite a bit. More than I did." He nodded. "Johannes would have been just fine, you know. Lena would have taken perfectly good care of him. I had enough money for myself. I even went down one day, that August, to withdraw it all. I got as far as the lobby of the bank before I turned around. I couldn't do it. I couldn't leave without Johannes."

"Did he know about the money? Johannes?"

"He knew I was saving. He didn't know I'd lost it all until he was older. And then one thing led to the next. The war. There was no safe passage."

She leaned, like a child, against the arm of the sofa, her hands under her cheek. "I'm so tired."

"Perhaps you can sleep for a bit. It's all over. They're both safe now."

"Wounded, but safe." Julia closed her eyes. "Robert said I wouldn't be able to choose, so he decided for me. I just wanted to have them both."

"Of course you did."

After her eyes had been closed for several minutes, Paul saw tears running down her cheeks, as if she had been holding them back. She slept deeply and did not stir. Paul got up and lowered the volume on the radio.

American forces had just liberated the Channel Islands.

KOBLENZ, GERMANY

May 1945

The next day Johannes held the blue velvet sack in his pocket as he and Captain Addison made their way to his brother's bedside, readying himself to present it, but when they arrived there, they found Nicholas weeping.

"What is it? Has Major Riley been here? Has he said something to you?"

Nicholas shook his head, lips pursed. He held up a copy of *Stars and Stripes* with photographs from the liberation of Buchenwald on the front page. Carts stacked with skeletal bodies. Rows of incinerators, their doors open to reveal half-burned corpses.

They've been liberating camps since January, Johannes thought. How could he not have known until now?

Nicholas pointed to the caption. "Buchenwald," he said.

"Yes," Johannes told him. "And there are others. Many others."

"Many others?"

"Camps. Many other camps," Johannes explained. "Auschwitz. Dachau. Bergen-Belsen."

"But these are work camps. Not death camps," Nicholas said.

Johannes regarded him evenly. "And a work camp is a suitable place for hundreds of thousands of men and women? Children?"

"Communists. Criminals, Papa said."

"You did not know about Kristallnacht?" Johannes said quietly. "You did not know about the plan to eliminate the Jews?"

"Papa said there was a plan to keep Germany for the Germans. To force those who were not racially pure to leave. He thought they were extreme, dangerous—the Nuremberg laws. He was worried—but he did not know what to do."

"He could have left. He could have come back to America. It would have been easier for you, as non-Jews, to leave."

"Mama used to beg him to leave, before she got sick. They fought about it. He said he had already started over once. I had no idea what he meant."

"Did you ask him?"

"I asked Mama. I would never ask my papa such a thing. If you knew him, you would understand."

Johannes looked at him. "I did know him." He paused. "What did she tell you?"

"That it was best to not ask questions. That if we did not leave, we would only survive by not asking questions."

"Were there other times she told you that? Other times you were suspicious of anything at home?"

"No," he insisted. "There was nothing."

QUEENS, NEW YORK

May 1945

It was dark when Julia woke several hours later. She heard Paul moving about the kitchen and inhaled the warm, close odor of onions mellowing.

She blinked, reminding herself it was all still true. Nicholas had been found. It wasn't a dream.

Paul stood with his back to her, stirring a pot at the stove. She watched him for a few moments while he was unaware.

"Paul," she said softly from the doorway finally. He startled. He startled easily. "What are you doing?"

"Potato soup." He turned toward her, shrugging, his eyebrows coming together almost sheepishly. He had tucked one of her dish towels into his slacks, and for some reason the vision of him like this made her laugh out loud. It felt good. Laughing.

"I hope you don't mind. You had the potatoes. I didn't know how long you were going to sleep, but I thought you'd be hungry. And I am, rather. Hungry."

"No," she said, slipping her arms around his waist. "I don't mind." She stood on her toes and kissed the back of his neck.

"Don't get too excited. This and scrambled eggs and toast are the only things I know how to make. Though I am fierce with a can opener."

"It smells good."

"Straight from Mam's kitchen. I just added the milk. It'll need to simmer for a bit." He laid the wooden spoon across the top of the pot and took her in his arms. "Julia."

They danced silently around the kitchen, gliding softly past the table, through the living room and down the hallway, both of them in their stocking feet.

In the doorway of the bedroom she tugged the dishcloth loose from his waistband and let it drop to the floor.

KOBLENZ, GERMANY
May 1945

When Captain Addison brought Johannes back the next day, he found Major Riley pacing at the foot of Nicholas's bed and another interpreter in the chair beside it. Nicholas was sitting up.

Major Riley pounced as they came in. "Sergeant Kruse, your brother here tells me he knows nothing of the facts you're telling me. That his parents managed to hide all of this from him."

The interpreter translated this.

"That is probably true," Johannes said in German. And then in English, "My father was capable of great deception."

"They were my parents," Nicholas said, when the interpreter finished.

"It says here that you're a leader of the Jungvolk," Major Riley asked. "Is that true? I thought you said you weren't a Nazi."

"We all had to join the Jungvolk. My mother encouraged me to become a leader before she died. She had heard that the leaders of the Jungvolk would be called up last. And she was right. I have only been in the fighting since August."

"How did she die?" the major asked.

The interpreter hesitated and then put the question to Nicholas.

Nicholas frowned. "Nothing suspicious, I assure you," he said bitterly. "She had breast cancer. She was very sick."

"And you're sure of this?" Major Riley said. The interpreter hesitated again. "Go on," the major said. "Ask him."

The interpreter sighed and did as he was told.

Nicholas rose up from his pillows. "Why else would she have come home from the hospital with only one breast?" he hissed in German. Johannes could see that he was near tears.

"Major Riley," Captain Addison intervened. "Please. He has just had major surgery."

"I just want all the information. Man kidnaps his newborn from his wife. You never know what he'll do."

The interpreter paused. "*Wichtige Riley will einfach alle infomationen, die er braucht haben.*" *Major Riley just wants to have all the information.*

"All the same," Major Riley continued, "I will need to speak to him further at some point. Especially if he is going to be sent to the States to recuperate. They have to know what they are getting. Who they are getting." He turned to Johannes. "I was just telling your brother that Captain Addison thinks he should spend his recovery in the U.S."

"He has a long recovery ahead of him," the captain explained. "Without a spleen, he is highly susceptible to infection. A country like this, in ruins, is no place for him."

"What does Nicholas think of this?" Johannes asked.

"It's not really up to him." Major Riley stood. "Captain Addison, Herr Kruse, I think I have what we need for today. We'll be back tomorrow."

"I don't trust that man," Nicholas said after they left.

"He's just doing his job," Johannes said. "But I know what you mean."

"They want me to go to America now," Nicholas said.

"This is the first I've heard of it," Johannes said. He turned to Captain Addison. "When would he have to leave?"

"There's a hospital ship setting sail next week. I can get him a bed on it. He's a serious case, Sergeant Kruse. He can't stay here."

"The doctor thinks you should go," he told Nicholas in German. "He only wants the best for you."

"Tell him you can go back with him," Captain Addison said. "If that will make it any easier."

Johannes looked at Captain Addison. "I thought I was to recover here so I could get back to my duties."

"This is a complicated case, Sergeant Kruse. I think your brother will need his own interpreter. Someone who cares about him. I can put in another transfer."

"Mir wurde gesagt ich kann dich nach Amerika begleiten. Wenn das helfen wurde. Als ein dolmetscher und ein Freund." I am told I can accompany you to America. If that would help. As an interpreter. And a friend.

Nicholas turned to face him but said nothing. Johannes recognized that same unblinking stare.

QUEENS, NEW YORK
May 1945

Julia liked to walk and so this was how they filled the days while they waited for the hospital ship to return; it took the edge off a new kind of nervous energy that had begun to unsettle her. What would Nicholas think when he arrived here? Would he even want to see her again?

"You know, we have a car at our disposal," Paul protested amiably. "We don't have to walk everywhere."

"Walking is good for you," Julia told him. "You might as well get used to it. Germans love to walk."

The first time they returned to Luna Park they discovered the Couney Incubator Exhibition empty, the windows covered in brown paper and a note explaining that with units opening at hospitals across the city, the exhibition was no longer needed.

"Oh." Julia was a little deflated. "I was hoping to see them."

"It was time, I suppose," Paul said. "He made his point. He never gave up."

She nodded and they continued down the boardwalk, holding hands in companionable silence, stepping aside at one point to let two old men shuffle past, one in a brown sweater and tan trousers, the other wearing a bright-red plaid shirt with electric-blue trousers and a matching bow tie.

"Promise me," Paul said, when the men were out of earshot. "Promise me you will never let me out of the house like that when we are old."

When we are old. When we are old. When we are old.

"Julia?"

She shook her head, clearing it. "I promise," she told him. "But you would never wear such an outfit."

They had stopped in front of the stairway to the beach and so they took off their shoes and walked to the edge of the shore, the wet sand massaging her feet, hugging her toes. The waves were empty but for a few intrepid swimmers; it was still too cold. "I used to think I hated the sea," she said. "But it wasn't the sea. It was the boats." She watched the icy water brush her toes, following the foamy edge out to the horizon, where it would return to lap the ruined shores of Europe and the ship that was returning her sons to her. "I always got so seasick. But I would have boarded one again. I would have done it, to find him."

"Yes," Paul said.

Suddenly he turned and took a few steps backward and sat down in the sand where it was drier. They were still facing the ocean, murky and roiling. Julia sank down beside him, pressing against his chest, warm in the icy breeze.

"Such incredible things," he said, "come in on these dark waves."

"What do you mean?"

"They brought you here, didn't they? Here to me, after all. Because of a war, I found you."

It seemed she had already waited so long—to find Nicholas; for the war to be done and Johannes to be done with it. Her life had been so preoccupied with waiting that Julia realized she'd given no thought to what would happen afterwards. She felt she had already lived a lifetime. Many lifetimes. There couldn't possibly be more. *When we are old. When we are old.* And yet there it was. Right beside her.

Two seagulls alighted in front of them, great gray wings flapping, and then strutted, bumping into each other and picking at the sand. She wanted to tell Paul: *I am doing this for you; for you, I am leaping off a cliff.*

But it wasn't just for him. It was also for her. She had been stepping off cliffs her whole life. That was what everyone did, didn't they? Whether they knew it or not, every single day, Paul, Johannes, Nicholas, Judy, Lena—well, perhaps not Lena— stepped off cliffs. The only difference this time was that she did know. She knew exactly what she was doing.

He took her hand and squeezed it, brought it to his lips, those exquisitely soft lips, and kissed it, and she breathed in the heady scent of motor oil now mixed with the salty wet air.

When we are old.

There was no need to tell him anything. He already knew.

When Captain Addison did not arrive to take him to Nicholas the next morning, Johannes decided to go himself. It was twice as far as he'd practiced with crutches—but he'd be out of the hospital and onto the ship in a few days; he needed to get used to them.

When he pushed open the door to his brother's room, however, he found another man at his bedside, where Captain Addison usually sat.

Johannes froze in the doorway. Robert turned around.

"Johannes." His father stood. He was bent and gaunt, almost skeletal, and his hair, once white-blond, was now a dull, yellowed gray. Johannes could not speak. "Look at you. You are a man."

Johannes nodded and swallowed. If Robert had straightened, they would have seen eye to eye. He waited, agonizingly, for his father to reach out in some way, but Robert did not move toward him.

"So. You have found each other," his father said, uselessly.

He nodded again, his hope fading. All the years he had imagined finding Nicholas, he had never, for whatever reason, imagined also finding his father. He did not want to. But even if he had, he would not have imagined it would be like this. Like talking to a distant uncle or even a stranger.

"And your mama? Is she well?"

At first he did not want to say anything. What did this man deserve to know about his mother? But he did not want to imply that she was anything but thriving. So he answered finally, haltingly, "She's fine."

Captain Addison entered not long behind him. "Johannes.

I'm sorry. I was going to tell you when I came to get you this morning. He had to be brought in for questioning. And to help your brother understand."

"Papa," Nicholas said darkly, "has made me into a liar. Just like him."

"They tell me they want Nicholas to go to the U.S. to recover, that this is best for him?" Robert said.

"Yes," Johannes said. "That is what they recommend."

"And you will go with him. That puts some of my worries to rest. You were always a good boy. You will take care of him."

"I will," Johannes told him. "After all, that must be why I'm here. To put your fears to rest."

"Johannes. Please understand."

Johannes put his hand up. "Enough. I will take care of my brother. You just take care of yourself. That is what you are best at. Although"— he looked his father up and down—"it seems as if you are struggling now."

"But look at you," his father continued. "So tall and strong. Your mama did a good job. And you're here building, Nicholas says. And translating."

"Mama did very well, given the circumstances. And, yes, I am with the Engineer Corps."

"Like your mother's father—you are good with your hands."

Captain Addison turned to Johannes. "Herr Kruse has brought some documents. An American birth certificate."

"Papa has brought your American birth certificate?" Johannes translated for Nicholas.

"So he says," Nicholas said bitterly. "Which he hid from me all this time."

"I had just gotten it out. I was going to tell you before you left, the last time you came home, that one night. I was going to give it to you in the morning. And then you were gone, without saying goodbye."

Nicholas sat up on his elbows. "That was just a week ago. You've had eighteen years!"

"We thought about telling you. First, you were too young.

Mama thought you wouldn't understand, that you would think your real mother might come and steal you away."

"Like you and Mama did?"

Johannes looked at his brother with surprise.

"Nevertheless," Robert said wearily, as if he was burdened with some special knowledge that his sons could never have. "She didn't want to upset you. After she died, I knew that I should tell you. As the war went on. But there was never a good time."

"The time is never right for telling such things," Nicholas said, his eyes flashing. "For telling me my life has been a lie."

"Your life," Robert began, his voice rising, "was never a lie. We loved you. We gave you everything we could."

"Except my mother. And my brother."

"Nicholas." Robert sighed. "I don't know how to make you understand."

"I don't think that is possible," Nicholas said. "I loved my mother, the woman I thought to be my mother. This is true. But I cannot believe that she raised me to think that what you've done is somehow right."

"There are some things," Robert continued, "that you are simply too young to comprehend. Both of you."

At this Nicholas looked up at Johannes and an electric arc of frustration passed through the air, linking them together, while their father stood haplessly outside of it.

"Like the difference between a work camp and a death camp? Like staying in a country driven by a madman rather than facing what you had done? Like telling me my aunt was a lunatic rather than telling me the truth?"

"What?" Johannes said.

"I did know Aunt Marie Therese. I did not want to admit it to you. I was still hoping this was all some kind of mistake. But just after the Volksturm, she told me that I was an American and that if I was wounded or caught I needed to tell them that. When I asked her what she could possibly mean, she told me to talk to Papa. And when I asked him, instead of telling the truth, he told me she was a crazy person, talking madness out of fear for my life."

"I was going to tell you the truth before you left the house," Robert repeated. "I was about to."

"Were you?" Nicholas said. "Do you even know how?"

"Nicholas," Captain Addison interrupted. "This agitation is not good for someone in your state. It was Major Riley who wanted your father brought to him for questioning. I'll bring him there now." He reached for Robert's elbow and guided him to the door.

"I'm still glad to see you," Robert added over his shoulder. "Glad to see you're all right."

Nicholas frowned. He waited until the door closed and they were alone. "I am ready to leave this place now," he said. "This is not my country, my family. Anywhere is better than this."

Johannes telegraphed again to say they were on their way, that he would call after the ship docked and the patients had been transferred, and then he would be home to tell her everything.

She smiled as she read the telegram and then handed it to Paul. "He said he's no longer a patient. He'll come and stay here while Nicholas is in the hospital and they're sorting everything out."

"Do you think I should stay here? I mean, while he's here?"

"I don't know. I can ask him. What do you think he'll say? After all, you were conspiring without me. It's not as if you're strangers."

"Blame it on Mrs. Sciorra. Not me. That's what your son said to do. Although we didn't want you to get your hopes up at first, that's true."

"Since when are you taking directions from Johannes?"

"In my experience, he's very wise. Especially in the ways of his mother. And, I reckon, after he's had a good meal," Paul said, "he'll agree to anything."

"I've already planned all that. I've been saving ration coupons since he left."

Paul laughed. "I see how it is."

"He is a growing boy," Julia said. "Besides, it's not as if you're starving."

"Indeed," Paul said. "Feeding people is one of your many talents. It's a good thing we do so much walking." He grew serious. "Actually, I prayed for him to come home safe. I'm no Holy Joe; I haven't gone to church in a long time. But I did pray for that."

"Well, as long as you're having such good luck with God," Julia said, "then perhaps you can pray for me to know the right thing to say to Nicholas when I see him. If I'm able to see him."

"I'm sure you'll be able to see him."

"What if he doesn't want to see me? He has to be so upset about all this. Confused. He hasn't been preparing for seventeen years. And who knows what the last few months have been like for him."

"You'll know what to say. You're his mother."

"I'm getting anxious, the closer the day comes."

"I'm aware," Paul said. "My feet are aware."

"Anxious in a new way. Not anxious to know if he's alive, if he's safe. I much prefer this kind of anxiety, if I'm allowed to choose."

"Of course."

"And he's a young man now. Like Johannes. Now I wonder, what is he like? What was he like as a boy? All I remember is what he was like as a baby. He liked to be held. More than Johannes, even, he wanted to be held, all the time. As long as I was holding him, or Helene was holding him, he was content. He was always happiest in someone's arms…" She shook her head, frowning. "Better not to dwell on that. Someone was holding him, even if it wasn't me. That is what matters. He is coming back now. That is what matters. To love him now. To love him for the rest of his life. If he'll let me."

USHS *WISTERIA*

Late May 1945

The USHS *Wisteria* had only recently been converted to a hospital ship, but from a construction standpoint, it seemed to be in good repair. It was at full capacity, so Johannes was assigned to a civilian bunk, although he had to report to physical therapy every morning. Nicholas, on the other hand, was quarantined with a handful of other patients, at the other end of the ship, tended by two doctors and five nurses. Johannes was allowed to visit, but he had to scrub in each time, under the supervision of one of the nurses.

Most of the other quarantined patients seemed sicker than Nicholas; he was the only one who was able to sit up most of the time. They passed the afternoons playing cards; Nicholas was surprised that Johannes already knew how to play Schnapsen, that his older brother was actually quite good at it.

"Aunt Lena taught me how to play," Johannes explained. "She also taught me Pinochle. Aunt Lena loves to play cards and she likes to win, which she usually does. But I was starting to beat her once in a while, before I left for basic. How did you learn? Papa?"

He shook his head. "Papa did not have a lot of patience for games. I learned from the Ruhle boys next door. Wilhelm and Max. Max was older. Wilhelm was my age. You and Aunt Lena must have played a lot," Nicholas said, watching his brother gather the cards after winning another game.

"Yes," Johannes said. "But I also played at Camp Ritchie and with some of the POWs."

"There were German soldiers at Camp Ritchie?"

"Camp Ritchie was full of German soldiers—German-Americans, like me, and POWs."

"There was a whole U.S. camp just for Germans?"

"Yes. It was top secret."

"And this is how you found me?"

"Not exactly, no. I had a lot of help. And you were wounded. I don't know if we would have found you otherwise."

"Help?"

"Friends who had access to government officials."

"I had already planned to surrender. I told Papa I was going to surrender to the first Allies I saw. What was left of my unit had already split up. I was looking for someone to surrender to. I spent the night in a barn with another part of a unit who insisted I join them. When I tried to surrender the next time"— he touched his bandages—"one of them did this."

"I have never been in battle," Johannes said. "Not a real battle, anyway—plenty of battles in training. But I have been shot at. And blown up."

"Close enough. You don't need to experience battle. No one does. There's nothing to be gained from it. Just death and guts flying and more death. I was called up in August with three of my village friends. They are all dead now. They died in ways I will never forget."

"Was Wilhelm one of them?"

"No," Nicholas said. "I don't know what became of him. They moved to Berlin some years ago. His father was a leader in the Party. He got a promotion. He is probably dead now too. Or captured."

"His father? Or Wilhelm?"

"Both," Nicholas said. "And his older brother, most likely. Either in the war or through bombing. There's not much left of Berlin."

Nicholas was silent for a few moments. It was his turn to discard. "Our neighbors on the other side, the Gottliebs, the father, he was older, but he taught with Papa. Geography. One day he refused to salute the Fuhrer. The next day he and his wife were both arrested. The new teacher they hired lives there now. Or did until they closed the school and called up the rest of us.

"Papa probably did not want to salute the Fuhrer either.

Teachers are not stupid. They knew he was leading us to ruin. But they did not know what else to do. If Papa had been arrested, what would have become of me and Mama?"

"You could have left."

"Yes. That is true. And Mama did want him to. But after she died, he didn't really care what happened or how bad it got. He still doesn't, really."

"He doesn't look well," Johannes observed. "He doesn't seem to be taking care of himself."

"He's doing the best he can," Nicholas said. "He'll survive if he wants to."

"You're not worried about leaving him?"

"Mama was our family," Nicholas said. "After she died, it all fell apart. And then when the school closed—if he regretted not leaving, it was probably then. There was nothing left. Maybe when they finally reopen, he will get better. But I need to get away from all of it. Nothing but pain and lies. Whatever wasn't painful was a lie. And it all started with Mama dying." He paused. "He even lied to me then." Johannes was surprised that, after all the talk of battle and death, his brother's eyes were now filling with tears. "The last time she came home from the hospital, he told me she was coming home to get better. But she quickly got worse. I could see she was getting worse. But he would never admit she was dying. One day, I went to school and when I came back, she was gone. If I had known, I never would have gone that day. If I had known, I could have said goodbye."

Johannes wanted badly to remind him that he did have a mother, his real mother, who was waiting for him, who had been searching for him. But it did not seem to be the right time to say this. Instead, he laid his cards down and reached into his coat pocket. Finally, he laid the velvet sack in his brother's lap.

"What is this?"

"Put down your cards and open it and I'll tell you."

Nicholas untied the drawstring and drew out the napkin ring. "A napkin ring?" He was puzzled.

Johannes nodded. "Your napkin ring. I found it years ago

among Aunt Lena's things. She bought it for you as a christening gift, but she never had a chance to give it to you."

Nicholas laughed, wincing, and held it up in front of him. "A squirrel and a little boy?"

"Aunt Lena said it was a cherub," Johannes said. "She gave me the same gift for my christening, from the same store, only mine is a bear. A bear cub, actually, I think."

"It's awfully heavy," Nicholas said. "For such a small thing."

"It's sterling," Johannes told him. "I have been keeping it for you all these years."

"We changed napkins at every meal," Nicholas said. "Mama said that was sanitary. She was a nurse, after all. But the Ruhles—there were five of them, and each of them had their own napkin ring. I spent so much time over there that eventually Mrs. Ruhle made me one. I think she crocheted it, a red cotton flower with a green ring, like leaves. But when they moved, they must have taken it with them."

"Now you have your own," Johannes told him. "The one you were meant to have. Also..." He showed his hand. "I have just won again." Nicholas frowned. "I'm older," Johannes said. "I've had more practice."

"I don't like to lose," Nicholas said.

"I lost to Aunt Lena all the time," Johannes told him. It was time for him to return to his bunk anyway. "I'm used to it. It's just a game."

"She never let you win?" Nicholas said.

"Aunt Lena?" Johannes said. "Never!"

"Ah, this Aunt Lena. So when I meet her I should challenge her to a game?"

"If you dare," Johannes said. "But you won't meet her yet. She's still in California, as far as I know."

"I'm just meeting my mother, then?" Nicholas said.

"Just Mama," Johannes said.

"Good. Just Mama. That will be more than enough for now."

"Who knows," Johannes said, "maybe you should challenge her to a game. She probably *would* let you win."

QUEENS, NEW YORK

May 1945

"He's well. He's sitting up, talking, eating; although he tires easily," Johannes said, between mouthfuls of the egg noodles Julia had heaped on his plate. "The last few days they had him get up and walk around his quarters, but he still has to stay in quarantine. They're still worried about infection. The highest risk is right after the surgery."

"What kind of infection?"

"Any kind, I guess. They said something about pneumonia. I think he looks like you, Mama. You'll see."

"Do you think I'll be able to see him soon? Does he want to see me?"

"He does. He is curious, anyway. He didn't know anything about us."

"I'm not surprised," Julia said.

"Apparently Aunt Marie Therese tried to tell him after he was called up, to keep him safe. But Papa said she was out of her mind."

"Dear Marie Therese," Julia said. "If anyone would try to help, it would be her."

"I told you that his mother"—Johannes paused to correct himself—"that Helene is dead. Five years ago. Breast cancer."

"Well," Julia said, resigned. "She was the only mother he knew. It must have been awful for him."

"He said it tore them apart. That Papa was never the same. Mama, I met him. The day before we left. I met Papa."

Paul put his hand over hers. She felt herself starting to tremble. She straightened. She must stay composed for Johannes.

"It was... I don't know how to describe it. It was very difficult." Johannes swallowed hard. For a moment Julia thought he might cry. She had not seen him cry in years.

"I'm sure," Paul said gently.

"Liebchen." Julia leaned toward him, her chest beginning to ache, a dull oppression spreading out just below her collarbone.

"I don't know what I thought would happen. I suppose I thought he would be happier to see me, but he didn't really seem to care that much."

"Oh, Johannes. Are you sure?" She had ached with missing Nicholas. Hadn't Robert felt the same about Johannes?

"I couldn't be more sure." His voice caught as he said the words. "It's not your fault, Mama. He said he was glad I would be looking after Nicholas now. He asked about you. He said you had done a good job with me."

"Oh, Johannes," Julia soothed. "He is such a fool. More a fool than I ever thought possible." If she could have gathered him up in her arms right then and brought his sadness into her own body she would have.

"A fool. Yes," Paul said. "I'd say that's the least of it."

"Never mind Papa," Julia said. "Let's not waste any more words on Papa. Tell me about Nicholas."

"We've been together every day since I found him," Johannes said. "He's upset and confused—about a lot of things—but he's trying."

"Are you getting along, then? Are you becoming friends?"

"Of course we get along." Johannes smiled broadly, as if this were a ridiculous question. "We're more than friends, Mama."

Julia smiled and looked at her son. Johannes. One moment crushed by disappointment in his father and the next so full of the pure, innocent hope, that finding Nicholas would conquer everything. That youthful confidence was so like Robert's when they first came to America—but there the similarity ended. Johannes had been wounded deeply, irrevocably in a way his father never had. Johannes knew all the ways love and family could go wrong, and none of them had turned him back. She was lucky to have him here, with her now. She had always been so lucky to have him.

Dear Judy,

There have been times, in the last few weeks, when I have almost sat down to write but stopped, out of the fear that describing everything that has happened will somehow tempt fate, that in putting words to the page, the real events themselves will disappear as if they never happened. Will I always be afraid that what is good will disappear? Of course. How could it be any other way?

Tomorrow I will see my son for the first time in seventeen years. It is difficult to imagine. All I know is that somehow, all the aching, all the yearning, will be over. The corridor that has followed me all this time will not be empty. It will take every ounce of self-control I have not to gather him in my arms and hold him there, never letting go. But how will he see me? He is my son, but he has never known any other mother than Helene. Will he never be able to know another? Will I lose him again?

And so now I am discovering what happens just before the end of longing. You have to decide to risk everything, all over again.

STATEN ISLAND, NEW YORK

Late May 1945

"You're sure he's ready to see me?"

They had left Paul in the lobby with a magazine.

"Yes, Mama. He's ready. I told you, he's expecting you."

Johannes knocked gently and opened the door, first just a sliver and then all the way. Nicholas was sitting up with the *Staats*, the German daily, spread out on the bed before him.

"Nicholas. I come with a visitor today."

Nicholas smiled, a wistfully sweet expression she recognized instantly, the one he had just begun giving her before Robert took him away. A shy, gentle smile that lit up his whole face.

Yes. This was her Nicholas. As if she had ever doubted it.

"Nicholas," Julia said. Her eyes brimmed with tears but she was determined not to cry first thing.

"Hello," he said, gazing at her almost curiously.

"Has the doctor been in to see you yet today?" Johannes asked in German.

"Not yet," Nicholas told him.

"Ah," Johannes said. "Perhaps he'll come while we're here." He pulled out a chair for his mother beside the bed and took another one in the corner by the window.

Julia looked at Johannes. She had not heard him speak such perfect, rapid-fire German since he was small, before he went to school.

Johannes grinned proudly. "I did go to training for this," he reminded her.

Dazed, she took the chair. Now she was less than a foot away from him.

"Nicholas knows a little English," Johannes explained, "but we mostly speak in German. And I translate for him."

"They tell me you are my mother," Nicholas said, his English halting.

If she closed her eyes, he sounded just like Johannes.

"*Ich bin. Und ich habe nach dir gesucht. Immer,*" Julia said softly. *I am. And have been searching for you. Always.*

"I have another mother," he returned, in German. "She's in heaven now."

"Johannes told me. I'm sorry." She was, she thought. She was sorry that Nicholas had lost her too. "I understand," she said. She took in his curly dark hair and dark eyes. The dimple on his left cheek that had delighted her when she had seen him for the first time, after he was born. Her own papa had had such a dimple.

"Johannes said you would," Nicholas told her. "He has said many wonderful things about you."

Johannes gazed shyly at the ceiling.

"I don't know what to say for my father. Or for her," Nicholas said.

Julia leaned forward and put her hand on his. She let it rest there for a moment and then drew it back gently. "You don't have to say anything. You were a baby."

"Still. They never told me."

"I know," Julia said.

"They lied to me," Nicholas said, his own eyes becoming glassy now.

"They had to," Julia found herself saying.

"And now my life is a lie."

"Your life is not a lie. They took good care of you, yes? They loved you, yes?"

"Yes," he said. "Perhaps it would be easier if they hadn't."

"No," Julia said. "Nicholas, no." She leaned forward again, venturing closer this time and brushing a lock of his soft, dark hair from his forehead. "I wanted you to be happy. Besides having you back, it's all I ever wanted. For you to be safe. And loved."

"But now what? How am I to go on knowing this? It changes

everything. Darkens all my memories. Even happy memories."

"Nicholas," Julia insisted gently. "Your memories are yours. They can't be taken from you."

"Oh, but they can," Nicholas cried, and Julia realized she was getting her first glimpse of the child he must have been. Dramatic. Determined. "If you learn that the people in them were not who you thought they were."

"They were still the people who loved you," she heard herself telling him. "So much they could not leave you behind. That has not changed."

He nodded, grudgingly. "But they did a terrible thing. And I have lived, for so many years, in a place where more and more terrible things happened all around me. And still, we stayed."

"I know," she said. "But you are here now. And that is also because you were loved. Because we were here, loving you, Johannes and I, all this time, and you didn't even know it. I know you have been through frightening times, Nicholas. We all have. But there also is so much love. Right here. Right now."

"Perhaps," Nicholas said. "But if all of this is true, then it was also love that took me away from you." Julia bit her lip. "I don't say these things to upset you," Nicholas continued. "I'm just trying to make sense of it all."

"Love is perfect," Julia said. "People are not perfect. They are far from it."

"I suppose," he said. And then, as if he was testing her, "but I am not a little baby anymore. Not so lovable."

"That doesn't matter," she said. "To have you in front of me, right now. This is what matters. Getting you well, this is what matters. Getting you well."

"And then what?" Nicholas said.

"I don't know," Julia said. "That will be up to you. It's your life. I'm not going anywhere."

"Thank you," Nicholas said. "I have a lot to think about."

"We'll leave you here to think about it then." Julia started to rise. "And to get some rest."

"I didn't mean that you had to leave," Nicholas said quickly.

"Visiting hours are over soon enough. I'll have plenty of time to think then. I just meant, thank you for understanding."

Julia looked at Johannes and when he nodded, she sat back down.

"I want to know about the family I came from," Nicholas said.

Julia folded her hands in her lap. Her sons both stared at her expectantly. They were men now, she knew, young men, but when she looked upon them she would always see in them the shadows of the children they had been. Even Nicholas.

"Well, your grandpapa," Julia began, "was the head chef at one of the grandest hotels in all of Munich...."

Johannes stood when the hall lights flickered. "That means the end of visiting hours," he explained. "I have to stop at the men's room. I'll meet you and Paul in the lobby."

"Paul?" Nicholas said. "Who is Paul?"

"Paul," Johannes said, "is a story for another time."

"He's not another brother, is he?" Nicholas asked urgently. "You would have told me that."

"No, no, nothing like that," Johannes said, leaning over his brother conspiratorially. "Paul," he continued in a stage whisper, "is Mama's boyfriend."

"Mama's boyfriend?" Nicholas whispered back. "Do we like him?"

Johannes paused, for effect. "Yes," he said, finally. "We like him very much."

The next morning, on their way to see Nicholas again, a nurse flagged them down as they passed the nurse's station.

"The doctor needs to talk to you first," she said. Her face was grave.

Julia looked at Johannes. Her heart rolled over in her chest.

"It's probably nothing," Johannes said. "We didn't get an update yesterday. He probably just wants to give us an update. We are his family."

"He's on his way," the nurse said.

"Dr. Francis, this is my mother. Nicholas's mother, Julia Kruse."

"This is what we were afraid of," the doctor said as he shook her hand. "He spiked a fever during the night. We're waiting for test results, but going by the chest scan, he seems to have contracted pneumonia."

"Pneumonia?" Julia said. "Overnight? How could this happen? Everything is so clean here."

"It can come on very quickly. And we do our best, but we can't eradicate every germ. His body is so susceptible."

"What will you do?" Johannes said. "Is there something? Some medicine?"

"We've already started him on sulfonamide. We'll know soon if it's working."

"How will you know?"

"If it stops progressing. Pneumonia moves so fast with patients like this."

"Aren't they using penicillin now?" Johannes said. "They say it can knock out anything."

"It might help," the doctor said. "But penicillin is only approved for our soldiers. They don't have a large enough supply for civilians. If that is what you want to call your brother. They are still trying to determine who he is, exactly. A civilian or an enemy combatant."

"Can we see him?" Julia wanted to know.

"I don't think that would be a good idea right now. We're treating him with everything we can. But you can stay here, and we'll keep you updated."

"Please," Julia begged. "Please just let me see him for a moment."

"Mrs. Kruse, we're doing all we can."

"Is there a phone we can use?" Johannes asked.

"At the nurse's station, yes," the doctor said as he turned to leave. "Tell them I said you could use it."

Julia looked at Johannes. "Who do you want to call?"

"Mr. Bello. If he can get him found and ship him all the way home from Germany, surely he can get him some penicillin."

They were the only two people in the waiting room, pacing the perimeter. Neither of them could sit.

"It would help if I could just see him."

"I know," Johannes said. "I know. But we have to trust the doctors."

The elevator opened; Paul stepped out.

"Mr. Bello told me. How is he doing?"

"I don't know," Julia said. She frowned, hugging herself. "They won't let us see him."

"All right then." He rubbed her shoulders. "I'll be back. Right back."

"Where are you going? You just got here!"

"To the water closet. I was in such a rush to get here. Then I can wait with you."

Paul was gone longer than she expected. Julia paced in front of a window that looked over the back of the hospital grounds, watching rain clouds roll in over a stand of pines that seemed to guard the parking lot.

"You can see him," Paul announced when he returned.

"What?" Julia said.

"Come along," he told her. "I had a talk with one of the nurses. You can go in one at a time, for a few minutes." He held his hand at the small of her back and she felt herself relax against it.

"How did you manage that?"

"A mother needs to see her boy if he's sick. That's all there is to it."

"I hope you didn't make a fuss."

"I did not make a fuss. Not at all," Paul said, smiling. "But you know yourself, I can be very convincing. When circumstances warrant."

Nicholas was sleeping when she went in, so Julia moved quietly
to the chair beside him. He had an oxygen mask over his mouth
and nose, but still his breathing was rapid and shallow.

She reached over and lightly brushed back the insistent lock
of hair that seemed to always fall across his forehead. He did
not waken, so she risked letting her fingers gently stroke the top
of his head. His forehead was so warm.

Asleep like this, he looked not unlike he had when he was a
baby—eyelids smooth, lips pursed. He was so beautiful; both
her boys had been such beautiful babies, with long dark lashes
and porcelain skin.

"At least he's resting," she told Johannes when he stepped
into the room.

They stayed the night, all three of them—Julia sleeping on the
sofa when she could, Paul and Johannes dozing on the chairs
on either side of her. In the morning, they let her in again and
she sat with Nicholas for as long as they allowed her. He was
awake this time, although his breathing was still labored.

"We're working to get you approved for penicillin," she told
him. "The same man who helped us find you is working on it.
As soon as you can get penicillin, you'll feel better. Until then,
just rest."

Nicholas smiled at her, that shy, gentle smile, and closed his
eyes.

Mrs. Sciorra joined them that afternoon to take her turn, sitting
and pacing. At one point she took out her black rosary beads
and began murmuring. Paul sat beside her, his eyes closed, listening at first and then joining in, in the softest whisper. There
was nothing else to do.

As evening came on, Dr. Francis returned to tell them that
Nicholas seemed to be fighting, that although he wasn't getting
better, he also wasn't getting worse. "It's good news," he told
them. "His body is holding the line."

Julia and Johannes were allowed in for a few minutes every

hour during visiting hours but after that the hall grew dark and quiet and all they could do was pace and try to sleep.

At some point during the night she was awakened by a nurse gently touching her shoulder.

Julia sat up. Johannes slept curled in an oversized ball in the armchair on one side; Paul snored faintly on the other.

"Your son," the nurse whispered. "He's asking for you."

"His fever is up again. 104. And he's complaining of pain." She led her to his room.

"Is there something you can give him for it? For the pain?"

"I have a call in to the doctor."

"It's okay as long as I don't move," Nicholas whispered.

Julia sat beside him. His eyes were wet and rheumy and his teeth chattered. "Then don't move," she said, arranging his blanket around him. She remembered when Johannes used to run fevers, how sometimes the shaking and the teeth chattering came just before they broke.

"It's so lonely here at night." Nicholas winced as he spoke. "After visiting hours."

"Shh, don't talk," she told him. "I'm here now. I'm not going anywhere."

"But I need to tell someone."

"What, liebchen?" His voice was raspy and light. She moved closer so he wouldn't have to work as hard to be heard. "What is it?"

"I'm never going back to Germany."

"Well, first you need to get well, then we can talk about—" she began.

"No, I mean I can't go back. I have done something terrible. Unforgivable."

"It can't be as bad as you think."

"But it is." He closed his eyes, gathering strength. "I killed another soldier. A German soldier. On purpose. It wasn't even an accident."

She stroked his head; he was becoming agitated.

"I had left Papa's and I was walking in the woods, along one of the roads between Koln and Bonn. I was planning to surrender when I saw a jeep coming over the hill. It was an American jeep. I started to run toward it. But someone else was shooting at them. The jeep got a flat and they pulled off the road and ran behind it. I stopped. The shooter was about fifty yards in front of me, behind a tree. In the shooting, he didn't even hear me." He stopped. "I knew that if I wanted to surrender, I had to kill him first."

He took another breath. "It is treason, what I have done. High treason. Punishable by death."

"How will anyone know?" Julia said.

"I will always know. I will always worry someone will find out. Here I can be free, somewhat. I can begin again."

"But it was brave, what you did," Julia pointed out. "You saved American lives."

"It wasn't brave," Nicholas said. "It was cowardly. I just wanted to live and get out of the war. I am guilty too. So guilty. Just like all the rest."

"Shh. Don't worry," Julia told him. "You're here now. Far away from it. Everything will be all right. I'm here. I'll stay here."

Perhaps he did know, she thought, as she watched him breathe, watched his eyelids flutter and then relax into sleep. Perhaps something deep, deep inside of him had always wanted to make its way back to her.

Julia stayed beside him, watching him sleep, until she felt herself starting to doze. She was awakened near dawn by Nicholas's sudden crying out. "*Nein, nein. Es tut mir leid. Es tut mir leid.*" *I'm sorry. I'm sorry.*

"Shh," Julia told him. "Be still. Moving makes it worse, you said so yourself."

He let out a long moan then and seemed to look right through her.

"What's going on?" A new nurse appeared.

"I don't know," Julia said. "He just started crying out. Can't you do something?"

"Let me find the doctor," the nurse told her. "He should be in the building by now."

Julia held Nicholas's hand, his face contorted in such pain it was frightening.

Suddenly Dr. Francis appeared in the doorway. "Mrs. Kruse, I'm going to have to ask you to leave for a few moments. You can come back, but I have to examine him and have some blood drawn."

Julia began to step away. Nicholas grabbed her hand. "No. Stay with me, please. Don't go."

She looked pleadingly at the doctor.

"It will only be a few moments," he told Nicholas. A nurse appeared, adding something to his IV bag. "She will be right back. I promise."

Julia stood in the doorway for a moment. The doctor was listening to his heart. Nicholas relaxed and closed his eyes again.

"There. The medication is taking effect. I promise, Mrs. Kruse. You can come right back as soon as I'm done."

Julia went to the waiting room, where Paul and Johannes sat nursing paper cups of coffee.

"Well," Johannes said.

"He's in a great deal of pain now," Julia said. "They've increased his medication and they're having blood drawn. Dr. Francis is examining him."

"Pain," Johannes said. "Where?"

"In his stomach, he says," Julia said. "His side."

Paul slapped his knees and stood. "I'm going to call Mr. Bello again and see what's going on with the penicillin."

The doctor met with them after the results of the blood test came in. "I'm sorry," he told them. "It's as I feared. He's going into sepsis. Is there any word on the approval for the penicillin?"

"Sepsis?" Julia said. "What is sepsis?"

"It's an advanced stage of pneumonia. Blood poisoning.

He's very prone to it, in his condition. It causes the organs to shut down. It's affecting his kidneys right now. That's where the pain is coming from."

"Congressman Latham is working with the War Department to get them to telegraph approval this afternoon," Paul explained. "Can't you just give it to him now and tell them you're sorry later?"

"I wish I could," the doctor said. "But I can't risk even the slightest chance they might not approve. Giving penicillin to a German POW is a court-martialable offense. Not just for me but for the chief of staff and all the attending nurses."

Julia rose. "Can I go back in?"

The doctor nodded. "Yes. He's in and out of consciousness, though. The pain has subsided. I'm going to tell them at the nurse's station that the minute we get word from the War Department, they are to find me immediately.

By the middle of the morning, Nicholas had lost consciousness completely.

"Even in a coma," the nurse who came to check his vitals told her, "he can still hear you."

"You want to know about your family." Julia stood beside him. "I will tell you."

She told him the story of his birth, of how hard it had been, of Johannes's birth, of being young and falling in love with his father. Johannes told him he had to get better so he could take him to Ebbets Field to watch the Dodgers play.

"I always wanted to watch a Dodgers game with my brother," Johannes said.

Julia watched as Johannes went on, murmuring about Leo Durocher and Ed Stanky, pantomiming plays, but she knew. She knew he wasn't going to get better. Somehow, she just knew.

Eventually, the doctor took her aside and described the process of organ failure. "It is not a pleasant sight," he told her. "Sometimes, for lack of oxygen in the blood, the limbs turn black."

"I'm staying with him," Julia said.

"Of course," the doctor said. "I just want you to be prepared."

But his limbs did not turn black. As his breathing became more and more labored, Julia put her arms around him.

"It's all right, my liebchen. You know your mama is waiting for you. She will be there. You will not be alone." And then over and over, murmuring. *"Ich liebe dich. Ich liebe dich. Wir alle lieben dich geliebt."* I love you. I love you. We all loved you.

She knew when the life left him. She felt it but she did not tell anyone at first. Paul and Johannes were out in the hallway. She held his hand, gazing into his face, as smooth as putty but for a shadow of stubble along his chin. When she had stared as long as she could, longer into his face than she had ever dreamed but long enough to know that he was no longer there in his body, she let go of his hand and went to tell the others.

Julia was up before anyone else. She drew a bath and sat in the great claw-footed tub in the early quiet, replaying every moment of the last several weeks like a movie in her mind, until the water began to cool. Then she dressed and put the coffee on and started breakfast. Eventually Johannes stumbled into the kitchen and then Paul. There were phone calls to be made, telegrams to be sent. And yet the three of them sat, leaden and silent, weighted to their chairs by what had happened and by the magnitude of what must be set into motion.

"Nicholas told me something yesterday," Julia said, gazing over her coffee at the kitchen wall, at an ironwork clock that read quarter after nine and a wooden plaque with a Pennsylvania Dutch couple on it that said "Welcome Friends." Johannes had given it to her for Christmas long ago. "He was so upset. He said he'd committed treason. High treason. He said if he were found out, he could be put to death."

"He was on a lot of pain medicine," Paul pointed out.

"No," Julia said. "He was in his right mind at that moment."

And then she told them the story, Nicholas's story, about shooting the German sniper to protect the Americans he wanted to surrender to. "Then they turned around and drove away anyway," she said.

Johannes looked at his mother steadily. "Yes," he said. "The windshield was shattered. We had to get out of there. We drove on the rim for several miles and had to send for another jeep from Frankfurt."

"What?" Julia stared at him. "I don't understand."

Johannes continued. "I told the driver I thought I heard a pistol coming from somewhere else. And then the shots stopped. We were on a stretch of road outside Koln. We'd driven up to translate at a surrender, and we took sniper fire on the way back."

"Johannes," Paul said, "are you sure?"

"That was exactly how it happened," Johannes said. "In a jeep with a flat tire outside of Koln. Mama, that was me."

"Jesus, Mary, and Joseph." Paul whistled.

"You mean to say, Johannes," Julia said slowly, incredulously, "that your brother saved your life?"

"I think he might have." Johannes shook his head, his blue eyes wide in disbelief. "I think maybe he did."

QUEENS, NEW YORK

July 27, 1945

Dear Judy,

So much has happened. Lena was here to see Nicholas buried. Just before she left, Paul and I went to City Hall and got married, with her and Johannes and Paul's brother and his wife as witnesses. Lena thought it was too fast, of course, much too fast, and she had no reservations in telling me this, more than once. But I could see that she liked Paul well enough. I told her I wanted her to be there when I got married this time and I didn't want to wait for her next leave. Who knows when the war in the Pacific will be over?

Johannes, too, is returning to Europe in a few days. Amsterdam now, to help with the reconstruction, maybe London after that. He tells me I can't imagine the devastation he has seen there, that the photographs don't do it justice. It will be good for him to do something again with his hands, to be building again. I worry, still, I will always worry about him, of course, but at least the fighting there is over.

After Nicholas died, Johannes gave me a photograph taken of him and Nicholas on the ship. Nicholas in bed and Johannes beside him with a card game spread out on the blanket, both of them looking at the camera, grinning for all the world. Paul says they look like they're up to something.

He also says Nicholas has my smile, the smile, he says that he fell in love with. He put it in a frame and it sits on the sideboard in the dining room along with our wedding photograph.

Each day the radio and the newspapers bring more bad

news, even though the war in Europe is over. Starvation in my homeland, soaring casualties in the Philippines. Burma. China. Japan. So many other women's children, lost. And yet it was this war that brought me to the front of Sciorra's. It was through the loss of one son that another was saved. I do not know what to make of this. I probably never will.

Sometimes, still, I wake in the middle of the night and stare out the window into the lamplight and think about this world, such as it is, the world Johannes will come home to, make a life in, that his children will inherit, and I would be lying if I said that I did not despair. You left us just as the Great War was bearing down, Judy. The war that was supposed to end them all. You must have felt it too.

Then Paul turns and reaches for me in clumsy sleep, his warm breath at the back of my neck reminding me that all we can do is mend ourselves. Mend ourselves by reaching out for one another, even when it's hard. When it's frightening. Honor the dead by living. By telling their stories and inhabiting our own.

ACKNOWLEDGMENTS

Deep thanks to the people who helped this novel grow:

For Anne Bohner at *Pen and Ink Literary*, otherwise known as the Manuscript Whisperer, without whose effort, support, and wisdom *The Lost Son* would not exist.

For Jaynie Royal, Publisher at Regal House Publishing, who brought this manuscript to the world and Pam Van Dyk, whose editorial guidance made all the difference.

For the Dairy Hollow Writing Colony in Eureka Springs, AR, whose sublime residencies supported several intense revisions of this book. The Culinary Suite is magic.

For those who championed *The Lost Son* from its earliest incarnations: Maureen Pettei, Patricia Vanderslice, Hannah Treitel Cosdon, and Chris Motto.

For my writing companions over many years: Anna Leahy, Adrian Lurssen, Bill Lychack, Chris Motto, Donna Wake, and Jeff Whittingham.

For those whose friendship has been a life raft: Michelle Barnes, Hannah Treitel Cosdon, Sarah Monsma Billings, Caren Fishman, Elisabeth Lavin-Peter, Kelly Magoulick, Chris Motto and Dawn Stahlberg.

For all writers who struggle to bring their stories to a world that does not always know what to do with them but who have also come to know that the work *is* the gift.

Finally, for my sons, Jackson Vanderslice and Wilson Vanderslice, whose stories I am privileged to watch unfold.